Final Notice

A Damaged Goods Mystery

Jennifer L. Hart

D1384395

Table of Contents

She's serving up mayhem in the Magic City....

FINAL STRAW

Dishing out bad news is Jackie Parker's job. So when her boss grabs her assets one time too many, she serves him her notice and hopes he chokes on it. There must be a better way for a certified process server to make a living in Miami than working for a lousy lecherous lawyer. Whatever Jackie decides, her number one priority is to spend time with her husband, Luke, preferably without his brother Logan—AKA the Dark Prince.

FINAL WARNING

Despite Logan's objections, Luke asks her to join forces in their own property management team, Damaged Goods. Drawing the line between professional and personal lives proves challenging, especially when Logan serves her an ultimatum—tell Luke the truth about what really happened the night they first met, or he will. Sexual harassment is looking better and better.

FINAL NOTICE

Fester Gomez is three months behind on the rent for his pricey South Beach condo and Damaged Goods is on the job. Either they convince the tenant to pay up or he'll face eviction. The simple task turns deadly when the team discovers Gomez missing and a Jane Doe slowly decomposing in his bathtub. Serving a killer up to justice, wrestling family secrets—it's just another day on the job for Damaged Goods.

Final Notice

A Damaged Goods Mystery

Jennifer L. Hart

Chapter One

That creep had grabbed my ass for the last time.

I raised the clipboard I'd been holding up over my head—ready to smash it down on the booty grabber's cranium—when Marcy Regan snuck up behind me and snatched my makeshift weapon out of my hands.

"Don't, Jackie. He'll file an assault charge."

"Then I'll file the sexual harassment charge." I seethed.

"Think of the paperwork," Marcy hissed. "And the lawyers."

It was not an idle observation. Marcy worked for the Miami-Dade County Clerk's office and she spent her days up to her eyeballs in paperwork. And I was currently employed by Stan Cunningham, the ass grabbing lawyer. Neither of us wanted to bring the job home with us.

Ugh. She was right, I knew it but as I glowered at my still smirking boss seated behind his ostentatious mahogany desk, I wanted him to suffer. Boils and sores were too good for this hump. "Dude, what part of 'I'm married so keep your paws to yourself,' *don't* you understand?"

His face went blank "I didn't do anything."

As I stared into his doughy face, one thing became clear. No job was worth such crap, especially not the peanuts I'd been paid.

"Give me the clipboard, Marcy." My voice remained steady.

"What are you going to do with it?" Her tone was wary, but she handed it over.

I flipped over the case we'd been going over, scrawled *I quit, you big tool*, and dropped it on his desk. Terminating my employment on a notice of termination—how appropriate. "Cough up what you owe me or I'll send my husband for it. With his entire marine platoon." Their version of collecting was of the turn your head and cough variety. I doubted the pervert liked them apples.

The smarmy grin slid right off Stan the Shyster's face. "Take it out of petty cash."

"Gladly." After backing away slowly, I pivoted on my heel and made for the front office, cleared out the petty cash and moved to the glass door.

I gestured to Marcy. "Let's go, lunch is on me."

We headed down to our favorite little Panini cafe where I ordered a Piña Colada the size of a fishbowl—a reward for my restraint. Though I offered one to Marcy as well, she declined.

"Some of us have to go back to work," she groused.

"I'll make it up to you this weekend." I owed her, big time. If I had hit Stan the Stain and he took me to court, I could've lost my process serving certificate. Then I'd really be out of luck.

I slid my oversized sunglasses up and took in the scenery. A cloudless blue sky, palm trees swaying hither and yon. Pedestrians in micro dresses, short-shorts and swimsuits strolled by. Oh, to be able to loll around and enjoy the sea breeze.

"So, what are you going to do now?" Marcy took a delicate bite of her mozzarella and tomato Panini.

"Tell Luke I quit. After I throw him a bang, of course." My husband was always so much more agreeable while basking in post-coital bliss.

"Did he find a job yet?"

"He's doing security with his brother."

Marcy's big blue eyes got even bigger. "Logan's back? Why didn't you tell me?" She fanned herself. Apparently the wind off the water wasn't enough to contend with her heated thoughts of my brother-in-law.

"Sorry, I didn't think you cared." The lie scalded my throat. Truth was, I'd done my best *not* to think about Logan Parker for the six years Luke and I had been married.

"He's the hottest guy on the face of the planet." Marcy fluffed her blonde hair as though just mentioning the Devil's name would draw his notice. "Is he seeing anybody?"

"A therapist, I hope." I drained my drink. "I should get home. Do a little feminine maintenance before I break the big news."

Marcy grinned. "Or you could look for another job."

"Oh you and your zany ideas." The thought of going to work for another sleazy lawyer made my skin crawl. We had some money saved up and I could afford to take a little while to consider my options.

9

I left Marcy outside the county clerk's office and hailed a cab. Last thing I needed was a DUI. Luke was gonna be upset already.

Not with me though, never with me. My husband didn't think the sun rose until I got out of bed in the morning. No, the censure would be totally focused inward. On himself for being unable to land a permanent job post-military. Luke was old-fashioned—he wanted to support me, not the other way around.

Stubborn Parker men. My brain shied away from thoughts of Logan, hoping to God that Luke wouldn't drag him home for a beer after work. Not only did I *not* want to see him, I didn't want to compound Luke's humiliation by fessing up about the grabby attorney in front of his brother's hawk-like stare.

To my surprise, Luke's big black truck was parked in front of our little bungalow in the neighborhood known as Coral Gate on the west end of the city. The house was 1920's era that had been remodeled hideously in the 1950's and again in Technicolor in the 70's. We were slowly upgrading it with a more modern color scheme while restoring the historic appeal, an arduous and costly proposition. After paying the cab driver, I made my way up the cracked concrete walkway and followed the sound of hammering around the side of the house.

Luke stood there with his shirt off, golden sweat-slicked muscles gleaming in the sun. His dark hair was damp, pushed back away from his face, having grown out since his last tour of duty ended. My heart sped at the sight of him and I wrapped my arms around him from behind, pressing my body into his. "Hey there, sexy."

10

Instead of hugging me back he stiffened instantly, muscles freezing into granite. He looked over his shoulder. Piercing blue eyes, not the expected melty chocolate I loved, stared down at me. "Jacqueline."

Logan. "Holy Mary and a bag of chips, sorry! Sorry!" I let him go instantly, but the damage was already done. Stupid, delicious rum based drink had impaired my judgment. Crap on a cracker, could this day get any worse? "I thought you were Luke."

"Obviously." His gaze dipped from my face down to my chest. "That's a nice look."

Huh? Glancing down my body I saw that the cream-colored shell top was now plastered to my chest thanks to his manly sweat saturating the fabric. I plucked it away from my skin, flustered beyond belief. "Friggin hell, I want a do-over for today."

"If only I had that power." There was censure in Logan's deep tone. Censure and regret.

My gaze flew to his, my heart pounding like it wanted out of my ribcage. Oh no, he was *not* going there, not when I was half drunk and fully freaked out.

"Hey babe, thought I heard you." Luke moved out onto the verandah. He was also shirtless and sweating, a reprieve for my reeling senses. My safe harbor.

From the front he and Logan were similar in both height and build, but Luke was rangier, designed for speed more than heavy lifting. His smile was the most welcoming sight.

Brushing past Logan, I moved up the steps to press myself against my man and he pulled me into the safety of his arms.

"You smell like rum." He laughed and kissed the top of my head. "And did I see a cab drop you off? Something wrong with your car?"

"I quit my job." Frick, there went my awesome seduction to help break the news plan. I cast Logan a dark look. It was his fault for throwing me off balance.

Luke rubbed my back in a soothing motion. "And the rum?"

Since I'd already spilled the beans.... "I got blitzed on a giant Piña colada after I cleared out the petty cash. Seemed like a good idea at the time." Before I knew I was destined to humiliate myself in front of Logan.

Again. Why did I always end up running into him when I had a snoot-full?

"Looks like you've got stuff to deal with, man. I'm gonna take off," the Dark Prince intoned.

I sagged, but my relief was premature because Luke said, "Hang on a second. This could be a good thing."

As far as I could tell, the only good thing had been the booze and that was long gone. I pulled back to study his face. "What do you mean?"

He grinned, that boyishly charming grin that had snagged my heart at first sight. "Come inside and we'll hash it out. It's hot out here. Logan, you want a beer?"

"No." Logan's tone was emphatic and I got the feeling he wasn't talking about the beer.

"Man, she's qualified and she knows everyone. Where are we going to find—?"

"I said no." A muscle jumped in Logan's jaw.

I glanced between the brothers and worried my lower lip. "What are we talking about here?"

Luke looked down at me. "Logan and I were thinking of going into business for ourselves."

"Like your own property management company?" The work Luke had been doing was of the odd jobs, thankless part-time variety and I knew it didn't make him happy. He wanted to make a difference and do something he felt was important.

"Right. We'd try to strike a deal with the tenants without legal intervention. It's less expensive for all parties involved."

Which meant less work for guys like Shyster Stan. "Sounds like a good idea to me."

"But we need a certified process server on board, someone who knows the county laws and could make sure we stay on the right side of them. A person who can serve the papers on behalf of the owner and, if necessary, can legally write notices for eviction. We were going to look for somebody else, but since you're free...." He tossed me a wink.

"Wow." I blinked from more than just the harsh sunlight. "I don't know what to say." Maybe it was the rum talking, but it sounded like a stellar idea. With Luke in the military, I'd barely seen him. If we went down this road, we would work side by side on something that mattered to us both.

Plus there was no shortage of work. With the housing market hit hard in Florida, properties stood empty and owners were constantly searching for property management teams to take care of messy situations. Ousting squatters, collecting past due rent, stopping unlawful activity and, when necessary, streamlining Florida's complicated eviction process to rerent the property to decent tenants as soon as legally possible. It was hard, often thankless work, but it paid well. I knew how to make sure that all the i's

13

were dotted, the t's were crossed so anyone who hired us wouldn't end up with a giant lawsuit on their hands.

"Luke," Logan's tone held a warning. "It isn't safe. Are you really willing to put her in harm's way?"

I turned to face my brother-in-law. The living, breathing downside to this seemingly awesome plan. If working with Luke was a dream then working with Logan was a nightmare. Were his objections really about my safety or did he just want to nix the idea before it took root? "I've served in that capacity before, at the sheriff's office. Luke's right, no one knows the eviction process in this county better than me, at least not in the private sector."

"We could take on Aaron's job. Go there tonight and see what's what. He owns near half the damn county and if he likes our work, he'll recommend us." Luke was like a little kid in a toy store, his enthusiasm contagious, at least for me.

I hadn't heard him so hopeful for the future in a long time. Turning toward Logan, I made up my mind then and there that I would do everything in my power to help him make this dream a reality.

Logan and I would just have to deal with each other. Be professionally courteous. We were adults, we could handle it and we would if I had anything to say about it.

If not he could take a long walk off a short pier.

"I'm in." I said. Luke squeezed me and Logan looked like he'd chewed on a fresh turd.

For better or worse, I had a new job.
****

Aaron Tanner was a marine who'd gone through boot camp with Luke. After serving out one

14

tour, he'd inherited his father's condo complex in South Beach and left the military to be a full time landlord. According to the file Luke had given me, Aaron's tenant, a Mr. Fester Gomez, was three months behind in his rent.

The eviction process is complex in any state, but Florida had its own special quirks. The laws were written to protect tenant rights before those of the property owner. Knowing what I do about the eviction process, I'd rather stick a hot poker in my eye or spend ten minutes locked in a closet with Logan, than ever choose to be a landlord.

As Luke drove over the MacArthur Causeway, I read the file out loud. "Fester Gomez, Latino, age sixty three, widower. Lived here for ten years, never had a late payment before. Aaron wants us to talk with him, inspect the property for damages if he'll let us and find out why he's not paying his rent."

"And if he doesn't let us?" Luke asked.

"I'll post a twenty four hour inspection notice and we'll go in tomorrow."

"You'll stay in the car." Logan didn't phrase it as a request and I didn't appreciate his tone.

"I'm going in. Mr. Gomez has no criminal record, he's not a threat. Besides, if you two scary guys knock on his door and give him a heart attack, Aaron might get sued. Then we're SOL."

"Jackie's right, Logan. We're just going to talk this out. Aaron doesn't want to go through the trouble of eviction if there are any other options."

From my position in the back I saw Logan shift, so I was prepared when he pivoted to glare at me. "Don't do anything stupid."

"Broke that habit years ago." The passive-aggression was so dense you could eat it with a spork.

15

I saw the instant the barb struck home. His eyes narrowed to blue slits. I raised an eyebrow, daring him to take it further.

"Knock it off you two. We're almost there." That from Luke, the peacemaker of our little trio, who multitasked brilliantly as he turned the truck onto Ocean Drive.

He stopped the vehicle near a pristine white stucco apartment complex. I whistled low as my feet met asphalt. "Hot damn, you think Aaron would rent to us while we finish the house? I always wanted to live near the beach."

"We couldn't afford it." Luke said, sending me a rueful smile. "Maybe in a few years, if this business works out."

Logan remained quiet, assessing our surroundings with watchful eyes.

We trooped across the street and into the breezeway, stopping at the door to 1C. I held my clipboard with the 3-Day notice all filled out, should Mr. Gomez not provide an adequate reason why he'd been skipping his rent. Luke and I exchanged a glance, he nodded, and I knocked on the door, going over the spiel I'd prepped.

A spiel, I didn't need because the unlatched door creaked open ominously. "Uh oh."

"Get back," Logan snarled, shoving me behind him and several steps to the side. I didn't protest the rough treatment because my nose had picked up the same stench that had put him on high alert. Something that reeked like death.

"I'm going in," Logan said.

"Don't be an idiot." Luke grabbed for his brother's shoulder but Logan shrugged him off.

16

"If whatever's in there is still alive, it needs help. Get her back to the car." Logan barreled forward like a freight train.

"Idiot." Luke growled. "Jackie, go back to the car. Call 911. Tell them what's going on."

Luke shoved his cell phone at me and I fumbled it. "You don't know what's in there."

"Logan's in there," he said simply and disappeared into the place.

The Parker brothers might be big, tough heroes but I sure as hell didn't want to see what was making that smell. Week-old garbage rotting in a Dumpster was more appetizing. I couldn't just go lock myself in the car though. What if they needed help?

I dialed the phone and gave the 911 operator the address. "Probable DOA. My husband and his brother have gone in to check on the resident."

"Do you require an ambulance?"

Considering Mr. Gomez's rent was three month's late, I seriously doubted it. Still, I called out, "Luke? Is there anyone alive in there?"

It was Logan who appeared, his T-shirt pulled up to cover his mouth and nose. "Whoever did this is long gone."

I was craning past him, looking for Luke. "Did what?"

Sirens blared in the distance, announcing help was on the way.

"Luke, get out here!" Logan called, shoving me back into the breezeway. "Put your hands up so the cops can see them."

"Ma'am? Are you there?" The 911 operator's voice crackled over the line.

Luke slipped through the door, face ghostly pale as his eyes met mine. He'd seen his share of dead

17

bodies and I doubt discovering Mr. Gomez had passed peacefully in his sleep would have brought on that kind of reaction.

"What's wrong?"

Logan and Luke exchanged a look and I knew Logan didn't want to tell me, the jerk, while Luke couldn't see any way to avoid it.

"It's not Gomez."

Chapter Two

It was dark by the time the truck pulled up in front of our little work-in-progress bungalow. Between the police and Aaron, I felt like I'd answered a zillion questions. I was hungry, tired and more than ready to crawl between the sheets with my husband and a bowl of mac and cheese. I needed comfort on every level.

If only Logan would bugger off.

We all sat in the truck and I waited for my brother-in-law to slither back into the tall grass from whence he came.

Instead Luke turned to me. "I'll be in in a sec, babe."

"Sure." Knowing a dismissal when I heard one, I exited the truck and trudged up the walkway, unlocked the door and stumbled inside, directly to the refrigerator. The contents left much to be desired. No mac and cheese ready for nuking, no cold pizza or leftover Chinese food. Where was a girl supposed to go for comfort when the carbgasm proved elusive?

"To the freezer, of course," I mumbled. Opening the other door, I sent up a silent prayer and lo' and behold a carton of chocolate fudge swirl ice cream appeared. Unopened, score.

"We really need to go to the store." I told Luke when he came in from his private discussion with the Dark Prince. "This place is like a two bit hostel in a third world country."

"Do people even use bits as currency anymore?" Luke moved past me and reached into the fridge. Of course there was beer. Luke had his priorities in order.

"Not a clue." The bedroom was too far away so I took my ice cream and flopped on the couch.

"No bowl?" Lifting my feet, he slid underneath me and plopped my stems on his lap.

"Bowls are for quitters. And this was at least a one pint day. Possibly two."

For a time there was only the ticking of the cheap clock on the wall and the sound of my spoon scraping the carton. He didn't turn on the television, his expression a bit dazed. I didn't ask what he'd discussed with Logan. It was between the two of them and if Luke wanted me to know, he'd tell me in his own time.

"Ugh." I said, tossing the empty carton onto the coffee table. "Why'd you let me eat all that?"

I waited for him to give me that *like I could stop you* look, but he was staring off into space. "Hey? You okay?"

He turned to face me. "I messed this all up."

"How is the mysterious dead girl in Gomez's apartment your fault?"

"No, not that. I put you and Logan into this situation."

Though it was an effort with my new ice cream bump, I struggled until I made it upright. Then,

20

swinging one leg around to straddle his lap, I did what I did best and got in his face. "Hey, I'm all for the own your own shit way of life, but you, sir, take on *way* too much."

"She was so young. I knew the second I saw her that it wasn't Gomez. Even before I saw the purple nail polish...." He closed his eyes and sagged into the couch. "If we'd been there sooner maybe we could have saved her."

"Luke, stop. You have a nasty habit of taking responsibility for things that aren't your fault. There was nothing you could have done for her. You heard what the M.E. said, she'd been dead for at least three days. You and Logan hadn't even fully committed to this venture then. Hell, you hadn't even told me about it before this afternoon."

His lids lifted and I saw the chagrin there. "I was working up to it. I didn't want to try it without you but Logan was dead set against having you on the team."

Though I tried to hide how much that hurt me, Luke knew me too well. "Hey, it's nothing personal. He doesn't know how strong you are, he doesn't know that you've been taking care of yourself since you were a kid."

Instead of answering, I kissed my way down the side of his neck. "I really don't want to talk about Logan right now."

"Me either." Luke groaned as I pressed myself against him, his hands tightening on my hips. Nothing like death to make one appreciate the finer points of living.

In the next instant he'd stood up so fast he knocked the coffee table on its side and carried me

21

into the bedroom where we didn't talk for the rest of the night.

****

My eyes popped open and I stared at the alarm clock. 5:45. Luke had one arm slung across my waist and he snored, a big manly rumble that I'd adjusted to in the months since he'd been home.

Though we'd been married for more than half a decade, his military service relocated him quite a bit. We'd both decided that instead of me packing up and moving around with him, it'd be better if I stayed in our hometown of Miami and focus on my career. He came home on leave and when he was stationed in nicer places for more than a few weeks I would visit, but otherwise we'd lived separate lives. It'd made sense. Now that I knew what it was like to be with him full time, it was a decision I resented with every fiber of my being. We were like newlyweds, having our honeymoon phase six years after the fact.

Unwilling to start my day, I snuggled into his warmth and let my mind wander. For no particular reason it stumbled over the missing Fester Gomez. Where was the tenant and why had he gone AWOL? Was the dead girl in his place a relative, like a niece or a granddaughter? Or maybe she was there for a less reputable reason. With a name like Fester Gomez, maybe paid company was his standard. Though I doubted her violent death by multiple stab wounds was par for the course.

The gruesome possibility haunted me, but some things didn't add up. Gomez hadn't paid his rent in three months but the M.E. said she'd only been dead for a few days. So it was possible the girl had never even met Gomez. Where could he have gone and, more importantly, when had he left?

Mind churning, I climbed out of bed and searched for my bathrobe. The floor was littered with boxer-briefs, socks, a few telltale scarves from some earlier adult play, plus a slew of shoes but no robe. Last thing I wanted to do was turn the light on and wake Luke. He'd had a rough day and needed his sleep. I was only after a drink of water and sulfur smelling tap from the bathroom wasn't gonna cut it.

Had we drawn the shades in the other room? Eh, it was still dark, if any of the neighbors sat out on their lawn chairs all night, waiting to catch a glimpse of me in the raw, I wasn't about to deny them the cheap thrill.

I'd bought our outdated three bedroom bungalow for a song while Luke was still overseas. While the bones were sound, everything from the electrical system to the plumbing, to the roof needed a great deal of TLC. Luke had been tackling it slowly whenever he was home, a sink here, a window there, but it was a humongous project. I'm sorry to say that other than picking out fixtures and paint colors, I was no help.

Currently the half bath was nothing but a closet with some holes in the floor, and most of the boards on the verandah were missing. Though I was tempted to hire someone to finish the place, my stubborn husband insisted it was a matter of pride. Besides, my recent career overhaul meant money was tight. I had every confidence the job would be done well. Eventually.

I padded to the kitchen, retrieved a glass and filled it from the filtered fridge hook-up. We had three bedrooms, but currently were only using the master. The others would someday be our children's spaces, whenever we were ready for that step. More accurately, whenever I stopped breaking out in a cold sweat at the thought of spawning. Luke said he was ready whenever I was, but there were two things common for people with kids. Their asses got bigger and they were forced to bend over a lot more so the whole world noticed. My ass was already big enough, thanks to my best frenemies, Ben & Jerry. Call me selfish, but I wanted to have some time with my man before we added a tiny, demanding infant to the mix.

I drained one glass and filled a second then headed down the hall. The second bedroom held Luke's tools, so I bypassed it and moved on to the third. It would work for our home office. All that was in there now was a ragtag pullout couch. We'd need filing cabinets, a desk, maybe a new computer, but shopping was something I could contribute to the building of our business.

I was so lost in thought that I didn't notice the pullout had been unfolded until I tripped over one of the legs and landed on the solid body sprawled on top. A very male body.

Stunned, I struggled to get up, dropping my glass in the process.

A slew of curse words followed—none of them mine—when I dumped water on the squatter's lap.

Strong hands gripped my arms and the air seethed with barely leashed violence. I shrieked, it was pure instinct.

More cussing, and a lamp clicked on, blinding me. I threw an arm up to shield my eyes when a familiar voice said, "Jackie, it's me."

"Logan?" I blinked against the harsh light, recovering enough sight to witness his gaze dropping steadily downward.

"That's an even better look." His deep voice rumbled.

I gasped, remembering my nudity and yanked the sheet off of him to cover myself. Of course that didn't solve the problem because the linen was soaked through from my upended glass and he was also naked.

And that's when Luke arrived.

"What the hell's going on here?" he bellowed.

"Your wife threw herself on me," Logan grunted.

I smacked him on the shoulder. "I didn't even know you were here! What the hell are you doing in our house in the middle of the night?"

"Sleeping, until some naked chick dumped water on me." No remorse, or even a word of apology.

"You're lucky I don't shoot you in your stupid head, Logan Parker." Scrambling off the bed I heard him groan as a knee connected with something sensitive. *Good.*

I dropped the sheet and bolted for our bedroom, Luke hot on my heels.

He could stay there, the dog. Crossing the bedroom swiftly, I locked myself in the bathroom, my heart pounding wildly.

"Jackie. Are you all right?"

"Go away." Cripes, he'd turned me into one of *those* women, the neurotic messes that locked themselves in the bathroom. I now understood why they did. To avoid the pinhead men who drove them insane.

"Babe, open the door."

"What the hell is he doing here, Luke?" Logan might be a world class jerkoff, but no way would he have broken in to our house and taken up residence

25

sans invitation. And since I didn't give him permission, that meant Luke had.

Without bothering to tell me.

"His place is being fumigated for bugs. He needed somewhere to crash, what's the big deal?"

My blood pressure skyrocketed and I yanked open the door with enough force that it thudded against the wall. "The big deal is that you didn't *tell* me. Hell, you were actively hiding him from me, pretending he was going home last night. This whole scene could have been prevented if you'd just let me know he was here!"

I saw it there, the remorse that his brother lacked flashing across his handsome face. "Babe, I'm sorry. Believe me when I say he had nowhere else to go."

Tears of pure frustration welled because this hard-headed man was so missing the point. "Why didn't you say something?"

He looked away. "You two rub each other the wrong way and I figured you'd say no."

My heart clenched up. "Luke, Logan and I might not get along, but that's beside the point. This is your home, too. I know it doesn't feel that way sometimes because I've been here on my own for so long, but you don't need to ask my permission for anything you want to do or anyone you want to invite to stay with us. He's your family. I'd endure him—and worse—for you."

He pulled me into his arms. "I'm sorry, babe. I really am. I shouldn't have tried to keep it a secret from you."

Guilt hit me full-force and I felt dizzy. I'd kept a mac daddy whopper of a secret from Luke since the day we met.

His shoulders started shaking and I realized he was laughing.

"Stop it." I punched his shoulder the same way I had his brother. He laughed harder.

"It's not freaking funny!" Maybe in a million years and with a few hundred Piña Coladas under my belt I could laugh about my butt-in-the-moonlight stroll that ended up in a water-logged swan dive onto my unsuspecting houseguest.

Luke struggled and I gave him credit for reigning in his laughter. "Okay, since we're all up, we should talk shop."

I pushed him to the door. "Go make coffee. I'll be out after I shower."

He kissed me on the lips. "Yes, Ma'am."

The smile slid off my face the second the bedroom door closed behind him. I should have told Luke the truth years ago, back when we first met. Fact was, this morning wasn't the first time Logan and I had seen each other naked.

Time hadn't made the reality any less complicated. The only thing that had helped was when Logan would disappear for months on end. His presence was a thorn in my side and a reminder of the mistakes I'd made and of screwed up kid I'd once been.

As the hot water poured down on me, and I lathered a loofa with shower gel, I scrubbed my skin clean, wishing I could cleanse my tarnished soul as easily.

Chapter Three

Fully dressed, we congregated around the shaker table in the eat-in kitchen. Though I could feel Logan's hot gaze on me, I ignored him as I filled my coffee cup. Luke had the Gomez folder spread out before him. "We've got two choices. Either we wait for the police to track down Mr. Gomez, or we do it ourselves."

I frowned at the picture of the missing tenant. "Why would we do that?"

"Because Aaron can't reclaim the condo as long as it's part of an ongoing crime investigation," Luke answered. "The sooner Gomez is found, the sooner our client gets his property back."

"If he doesn't get paid, neither do we." Logan added.

"So, what do we do?" I had no idea where we should even begin to look for the missing man.

"You've got contacts with the police and the sheriff's offices. First thing we need to find out is if they've I.D.ed the dead girl." Luke gestured to the folder. "While you do that, Logan and I will go question some of the neighbors, ask if they've seen Gomez."

"We ought to officially get this business up and running." I said. "The reason I went to the third bedroom earlier is because I was thinking of turning it into an office. We need a place to keep paperwork and to do research." I tried not to let agitation creep into my words, my pride still stung from the scene.

"I'll clear out the second bedroom." Luke offered "Since the third is occupied."

"Make a list of the supplies." Logan set his coffee mug down. "I'll pick up whatever we need to start."

"Just make sure to save the receipts for tax purposes." I told him. "We can write it all off."

He nodded once.

"We need a name, too, like a company name."

"Why?" Logan asked.

I rolled my eyes, finding it difficult to believe I was in business with a man who didn't know the first thing about running a business, yet challenged every word out of my mouth. "Because, real businesses have names, phone numbers, ways for people to contact and maybe even hire them."

A grunt of acknowledgment, but no suggestions.

"Luke? This was your idea, do you have any names picked out?"

"Parker Security?"

I made a face. "It's so—"

"Sensible." Logan muttered.

"Boring."

His turn to do the eye roll.

Luke picked up my hand and kissed it. "Then you pick something, babe. Whatever makes you happy." Sneaky man just didn't want to be bothered with the practical matters.

"Fine, I'll do some research—try to come up with something that is both catchy and to the point. We'll also need business cards to hand out, to give us a more official presence and a way for clients to get in touch with us later if they think of anything else. Nothing fancy. Plain white cardstock with bold, black print. Oh, and a website for an online presence. Social networking, <u>Facebook</u> and <u>twitter</u> to help spread the word. I should write this down." Pushing back from the table, I went hunting for a legal pad.

By the time I came up for a second cup of coffee I had three lists. A to-do list of stuff that needed handling, a contacts list of folks to call regarding the murder or Mr. Gomez's whereabouts, plus a shopping list that was an all-inclusive home office starter kit.

While I'd been organizing, the guys had cleared Luke's tools out of the second bedroom and set them out onto the back patio.

"I was thinking about getting one of those climate controlled storage sheds anyway." Luke said as they reentered the kitchen. "More room to work and the noise won't bother you if you're doing home office stuff."

Logan shut off the shop vac and gestured. "Does this work for you?" His tone implied he didn't give a fig one way or the other.

"Perfect." I smiled at the now empty space. "I think Marcy has a desk she was going to get rid of that would work great in here." Mentally, I tagged her name on to the to-call list.

"Swell," Logan's tone was dry. "Do you have that shopping list ready?"

Luke went out back to fuss with his saw. I turned to my brother-in-law and shoved the mental image of him naked out of my head. That way laid the dark path and it would not dominate my destiny. "Look, we're doing this for him. I'm willing to let bygones be bygones if you are. Forgive and forget and all that jazz. What do you say, truce?" I met his gaze and stuck out my hand.

Logan looked from my proffered hand and then back to my face. His warm palm engulfed mine, but it was more a caress than a professional handshake. "Did you tell him? About us?"

"There is no us, never was, never will be." Snatching my hand back, I marched over to the legal pad, ripped the shopping list free and shoved the mangled piece of paper in his general direction.

"There could have been if you hadn't run away like a scared little rabbit." Logan insisted on twisting the knife and dragging me back down to the place I'd fought so hard to escape. "I won't call a truce until you start being honest. With me and with my brother, but mostly with yourself."

Scooping up Luke's keys, he sauntered out the front door, letting the screen slap shut with a nerve-jangling bang. I heard the sound of the big black truck's engine roaring to life and then watched it motor down the street.

"That could have gone better." I sighed and dialed Simone, my gossipy friend who worked for the Miami-Dade County Sheriff.

"Hey girlfriend, what's shaking? I heard you quit on the lawyer. Is that true?"

Good news traveled fast. "He's a smarmy little troll and it was past time. Actually, I'm going into business with my husband, doing property management. We were on scene in South Beach last night—"

"Oh, the teenage girl, right? That was you? Hot damn babe, you get around."

"Any leads on her identity?" Even though Simone worked for the sheriff and not the police, she was plugged in to every crime scene, a true font of information. I had no idea where she got some of her intel but it was usually dead-on-balls accurate.

"No, she wasn't in the system. I'd wager she was illegal. There's been a rash of break-ins to empty residences, especially with the snow birds."

Snow birds were a nickname for people, mostly from the Northeast, who migrated to Florida during the cold winter months. "Gomez is a full time resident." Or had been until he disappeared. Stumped, I switched gears. "So, what do you think would be a good name for our company?"

"Two hot guys and Jackie."

"Doesn't exactly instill boatloads of confidence in our property management abilities."

"Yeah, but you'll get *a ton* of calls. Let's meet up for a drink, soon."

"Sounds good." I hung up with Simone and moved on down my list. Mr. Gomez wasn't in the hospital, the morgue or anywhere else in the greater Miami-Dade county area. Maybe he'd been abducted by aliens. I put a Google alert notification on his name because honestly, how many Fester Gomez's could be running around out there?

The phone rang, breaking me out of my thoughts. "Jackie Parker."

"Hiya, baby girl." Celeste Drummond's voice was soft, coated in honey—quintessential Southern Belle.

Eep. "Kinda busy here, Mom. Can I call you back?" At quarter to never.

Celeste sighed. "I want you to meet Mr. Stevens."

I blew hair out of my eyes. "I've met him. I pay him your rent every month." My mother lived in Richard Steven's mobile home park. Though she owned her double wide, I rented her spot in the retirement community.

"You know what I mean. You, me, Dick and Luke, like a couple's thing. He's become important to me."

I put my head in my hands. "Are you sleeping with him?" What an awful question for a daughter to ask her mother. But Celeste and I didn't have the typical mother-daughter relationship. Out of the two of us, I always had to be the grown up.

Silence on her end.

"Mom, I'm begging you, don't get involved with the landlord. If it goes south, I'll have to find somewhere else for you to live."

"Oh Jackie, you worry too much." In my mind I could see her waving me off, press-on nails clicking like white trash Morse code.

"Just, be safe, okay?" I looked at the clock, wondering if it was too early for a drink.

An hour later gravel crunched beneath the wheels of the big black truck. Through the window I watched Luke and Logan unload the preassembled tool shed and mulled over what exactly we should call our motley little crew. I supposed we could have been boring and gone with Parker Property Management, but I was not a plain Jane kinda girl. I needed pizzazz and maybe something that would make Logan twitch every time he heard it.

Lightning struck and I jotted it down before I had a chance to think better of it.

****

"Sorry coach, I struck out," I said as I handed Luke a glass of the Lemon Zinger ice tea I'd just whipped up. Unfortunately ice tea and frozen Margaritas were the extent of my cooking abilities. I was kitchen cursed. It actually ran in the family, all the way back to my great grandmother Lynette who'd stuffed her wedding dress in her oven after catching her lying, cheating no good husband in bed with her sister and burned the house down. When I was three my mother had cooked her hairless Chihuahua, Mr. Snookums, who I was still convinced committed doggie suicide to escape the pink sweater she'd knitted for him. How he'd gotten into the oven remained a mystery.

Needless to say it was better for everyone that I didn't cook.

"Nothing on Gomez or the girl?" Luke took a big swallow, draining the glass.

"Nada. Though there is a rumor that she might've been illegal and squatting in the unoccupied place that she thought belonged to a snowbird."

"There's been a lot of that lately. People case a home to make sure it's unoccupied, break in and set up residence and suddenly, they're the new tenants with the law on their side. But I never heard of that happening at a condo complex before. Usually it's a private home." Logan looked to the glass in my other hand but didn't say a word.

Though I was tempted to just drink the damn thing down and let him sweat like a pig in labor, I handed the glass over with a tight smile. He was careful not to touch me as he took the glass with what I can only imagine in Logan land was a grunt of thanks.

"Okay, so where do we go from here?" The Dark Prince asked.

"Gomez's rental application form has a Rosie Harris listed as his next of kin. We should go see her, find out if she knows where he is." I pulled my hair off my sweaty neck. "And any plan that involves AC is a good one."

We locked the house and piled into the big black truck, again with the Parker boys in the front seat. I leaned forward to catch their reactions. "By the by, your mom called to remind us about the vow renewal."

Matching theatrical winces. Marge Parker was an awesome—if sometimes overbearing—maternal figure. She'd survived breast cancer, having both of her sons join the military and almost forty years of marriage to the same man. She drank like a fish, cussed like a sailor and loved her family with a rabid ferocity. I wanted to be like her when I grew up.

"Oh, come on, it won't be that bad." I chirped. "Free food and drinks, what's not to love about that?"

Luke hesitated. "Mom gets...emotional at big family gatherings. All the booze and the kids running around. And the next thing you know she's asking when she can expect grandchildren."

"We've come to an understanding about that." I'd threatened to move to Nova Scotia if she so much as mentioned the word baby to me again. It was an

35

ugly business, but in my experience, so was extended family.

"I hate getting dressed up in a suit." Logan grumbled. "She wants us to walk her down the aisle. *Again*. And for what? It's not like we're giving her to him, he already has her. *Nothing's* changing. They'll be married before and after the ceremony, so what's the point?"

"The *point*," I hit the word hard, "Is that they love each other and want to bask in that feeling in front of their friends and family, you big dummy. The least you can do is support them."

"The least I can do is nothing," Logan fired back.

"Mom'll be crushed if you don't show." Luke said. "You have to go."

"Can we focus on work and save the family stuff for later?" Logan intoned.

"Okay, work stuff." I had the file out on Gomez, supplied by Aaron Tanner's assistant. "Looks like Rosie Harris is Fester's sister-in-law. He married her sister, Cheryl, who died during child birth in 1979. She never married and Fester never remarried so they are each other's ICE contact."

"ICE?" Luke asked.

"In case of emergency. You're supposed to have someone programmed into your cell phone under ICE so whoever finds your phone knows who to call if something happens to you." Logan said.

My mouth dropped open. "This from the man who didn't understand why we ought to name our business?"

"I get email forwards, too," he said simply.

I wondered who Logan's ICE person was. Probably Luke. But what about when Luke had been away in the military? Maybe his parents, but they lived kind of far away.

I didn't have much time to dwell on it because Luke turned the truck onto Rosie Harris's street.

"What number again?" Logan asked.

I checked the rental agreement. "It says four twenty."

We all looked at the pistachio green ranch modular. "Curtains are drawn. No lights on behind them," Luke said.

"Almost like she's trying to hide something. Or someone." I whispered, a little thrilled at the prospect.

Logan opened his door, paused and turned to me. "Stay in the car, Jackie."

"Like hell." Thank God for 4 door trucks because my feet were the first ones to hit the pavement.

Chapter Four

Rosie Harris was a creepy doll lady.

I sat sandwiched between Luke and Logan on her plastic-covered couch in her dank little house and tried to ignore the dozens of lifeless eyes staring at me. The place smelled of mildew, as though it hadn't been aired out in a while. A thick layer of dust coated every surface. But those rows and rows of dolls were the kicker, baring silent witness to all that went on here.

Okay, no more late night horror flicks for me.

Rosie's blue tinted gray hair had been recently set in a fresh permanent—the turned egg smell was unmistakable. She had the classic aged sunbather complexion and more wrinkles than a basset hound. She wore a flamingo pink tracksuit on her gaunt frame, which was at odds with both her orange nails and her dismal abode.

"I don't know what I can tell you, I haven't seen Fester in months." Her aged whisky voice was creaky, as though she didn't talk much.

"When, exactly?" I shifted a little closer to Luke. The couch was a tight fit for the three of us. "It would be a help."

One drawn on eyebrow went up as she eyed me suspiciously. "About three months ago. Who did you say you were again?"

"Damaged Goods Property Management."

Logan made a choking sound and though I didn't look, I knew he and Luke exchanged a glance over my head. Served them right for not taking an interest in the details. "We represent Fester's landlord. He's three months past due with his rent and there was someone else living in his apartment. Someone who wasn't on the lease. Do you have any idea who that might be?"

Rosie lit a cigarette. "You mean that dead girl the police asked me about?"

"Do you know who she was?" Luke asked. "Or why she'd be staying at your brother-in-law's place?"

"Fester's a pervert." A stream of smoke swirled around the porcelain faces of the dolls perched on the shelf behind Rosie's shaking head. They looked like the damned staring out from the gates of hell. "I told Cheryl that, but she married him anyway. And look what happened to her. Had an aneurism and died in childbirth." Her tone implied her sister had somehow gotten what she deserved.

"What happened to the baby?" I don't know why I felt the need to ask—it had nothing to do with our case—but it seemed like a logical follow-up question.

"Fester gave her up for adoption. If you ask me it was the best thing that could have happened to her, what with her mama dead and all."

"Did he stay in touch with the adoptive family?" Luke asked.

"I doubt it. Fester had his own interests and playing daddy wasn't one of them. Pervert." She spat the last word through thin lips.

"Did Fester say anything to you the last time you saw him?" This from Logan, who'd been silent up until then. "Anything that led you to believe he intended to disappear?"

"No. He called, asked to borrow my car but I told him to kiss off. God alone knows what he would do in it and with whom. Then he asked if I'd give him a ride to the doctor's office. Said it was an emergency. Probably had a case of the crotch crickets." She laughed and the dolls stared.

It was too much to hope that she'd driven him, her opinion of her ICE person was obvious. "Do you know which doctor?" Not that it would help us all that much what with doctor patient confidentiality and all, but if he was going to see a specialist for ongoing treatment, it might be a way to find him.

"Dr. Feinstein. Same one I go to." Rosie lit another cigarette and Luke turned green.

I stood up and dug a gum wrapper and a pen out of my purse, scribbled my cell number down and handed it to Rosie. "Call me if you hear from Fester or think of anything else that could help us locate him."

She took it and stuffed it in her sweat suit pocket. Fester would be an idiot to trust her, because she would love nothing better than to fink on him to us, to the cops or anyone else who wanted a piece of him.

We moved out onto the street and sucked great lungfuls of oxygen.

40

"Well, that didn't help." Luke shook his head. "She was our only lead, too."

"She gave us the doctor." I pointed out.

"Yeah, a GP." Logan shook his head. "Although a shrink would be too much to hope for. I swear those dolls were watching us."

We piled into the truck. "Hey, can we swing by Cunnigham's office? I have to pick up my car."

On the way there, I dialed Marcy. "Hey you, you still have that desk you were going to sell?"

"Do you have a buyer?"

"Yeah, me." Briefly I summarized our business venture.

"Tell you what, I'll give it to you if you do me a favor and take Gertie to the hospital for me tomorrow. She's scheduled for a colonoscopy and I just found out I have to be in court until one. I don't want to reschedule, she's already taking the cleansing gunk."

I bit back a groan. Gertie was Marcy's shut-in older sister. She didn't collect dolls but I'd had enough dysfunctional asses this week. "I'll have to check my schedule."

"Come on, Jackie, you said you owed me. I'll be there to take her home and care for her. All you have to do is give her a ride and sit in the waiting room until I get out of court."

Damn it all. "Fine, what time?"

I hung up the phone and laid my head back against the seat. "I just turned a trip ferrying an antisocial woman to the hospital to have her colon checked into a free desk. The hand is faster than the eye, boys."

Luke snorted and Logan gave me a weird look in the review mirror. "I don't think you got the better end of that bargain."

41

"You're just jealous you can't make furniture appear out of nowhere."

"It didn't come from nowhere, it's coming out of some woman's a—"

"Alright," Luke snapped. "Enough already, I'm getting a headache listening to you two bicker. Back to the matter at hand. Fester Gomez. Ideas what we tell Aaron?"

"If Rosie was his next of kin, he really didn't have anyone else to turn to," Logan muttered.

"Best bet, as soon as the cops release the crime scene, we start the eviction process. He had someone living there who wasn't on the lease, a clear violation of the rental agreement." I said. "I'll post a notice of termination on the door on my way home."

Logan swung into the lot behind Shyster Stan's office. "I thought you said you left your car here."

I looked out the windshield. No beat-up Barbie blue Civic with the disco ball and Mardi Gras beads hanging from the rearview mirror. "Son of a motherless goat!" I slithered onto the gravel lot and scanned the nearby street. Nada.

"I should have caved his stupid head in when I had the chance." I marched across the lot and around to the side door into Stan's office. I flung it open so hard it crashed against the stucco wall with a bang. "Alright, you steaming piece of refuse, where is it?"

The outer room was empty. A woman wearing white pants and a lime green blouse with matching heels and a purse containing a Lhasa Apso sat in front of Stan's desk. She turned, wide-eyed at my dramatic entrance.

"Jacqueline," The slimy excuse for a human being steepled his fingers together and leaned back, looking the part of the evil overlord. "Something wrong?"

"My car, douchenozzle. Where is it?"

"Why, I have no idea." He was playing the innocent card just to piss me off.

Luke gripped my arm when I would have gone for Stan's throat. "Simmer down, Jackie."

"My car—" I protested. I loved that car, the one I'd been driving since high school and dubbed Bessie Mae.

"Trust me." Luke said. "We'll handle this."

As though they'd choreographed it, Luke and Logan circled Stan's desk, one on each side, boxing the little weasel in. As one, they each folded their arms across their chests and planted their feet, eyes glued to the shyster's every move. They didn't speak, just let their looming presence unnerve their prey.

A normal man would have been intimidated by the display. Stan practically wet himself as he looked back and forth between the brothers. "What are you doing?"

"Waiting for answers," Logan said.

"For however long it takes." Luke added.

"You can't do this." Stan whined. "You can't threaten and harass me, I'll take you to court."

Spoken like a true weenie.

"We're not doing anything to him, are we, Miss?" Logan winked at the blonde.

"No," she giggled, shifting her purse—dog and all—aside to give him a better view down her low cut blouse. The dog whined in protest. Sorry, precious, you have to do without your standard 24/7 hours of nonstop attention. Mommy's on the prowl.

"See? We have a witness who'll testify that all we did was stand here." Luke's tone was deceptively calm and patient.

I leaned both hands on the desk and got in Stan's face. If he wanted to get away from us he'd have to slither out the window. "Dude, where's my car?"

Stan's head whipped back and forth like he was watching a Mach 1 tennis match. He shifted, but with us penning him in there was no way he could see all three of us at once.

I snapped my fingers in front of his face to get his attention. "Here, don't worry about them, talk to me. What did you do with my car?"

He swallowed. "I had it impounded."

Frick. Had I expected anything less?

Stan puffed himself up like a toad. "I was well within my rights. That lot is for employees and customers only. It's clearly posted."

I didn't want to hear it. His passive-aggressive maneuver was going to cost me a pretty penny. "Yeah, yeah, whatever helps you sleep at night. Come on guys, time to go visit the city impound."

****

"I'm gonna take it out of his swindling hide," I muttered as I counted out the cash to spring my ride. Poor Bessie Mae had a new dent on her passenger's side quarter panel but otherwise looked intact.

Luke rubbed my back. "It's fine, babe. We'll get the business off the ground and make it back in no time."

"You're right." At least I hoped he was. Failure was not an option.

He sighed. "It would be better if Aaron didn't have to go to court to evict Gomez."

44

I patted his arm. "Can't be helped, under the circumstances. The law is on his side though. We'll streamline the process for him, handle all the paperwork so it's less of a headache. You riding with me?"

"No, Logan and I are going to head home and see if we can finish with the verandah, maybe pick up dinner on the way. Any requests?"

"Sandwiches. And some fresh baked chocolate chip cookies." I'd totally earned them for not going postal on Stan. "I'm going to hit the grocery store, too. Old Mother Hubbard is better stocked than us."

"Grab some more beer." Luke dropped a kiss on my cheek and sauntered off.

The car was hot as hell and Bessie Mae's AC didn't work very well. After turning the engine over, I rolled down all the windows and headed back out to South Beach.

The crime scene tape was still in place and a few cops milled about out front. The CSU van was parked in the lot, too, probably collecting evidence with their special tools. I'd love to see that. Notice of termination in one hand and I.D. in the other, I walked toward the apartment door. "Hi, I work for the owner. Is it okay if I put this on the door in case the tenant comes back?" Having never served at a crime scene, I didn't know what the procedure was.

The two uniforms looked at one another and shrugged. "Fine by us, as long as you don't go inside."

After taping the intent to evict and twenty-four hour inspection notice to the door. I offered the nearest uniform my hand. "Thanks. I'm Jackie by the way. My property management team found the body." I believe in making friends where and whenever possible, especially with law enforcement officials.

Sometimes I got funny looks, but usually my straight-forward approach paid off. Taking chances, rolling the dice, that's what it's all about because honey, you can't win if you don't play.

"James O'Reilly." The taller of the two officers took my hand. "I've seen you before haven't I?"

"I used to work for the Sherriff's office, so probably." I smiled. "Any idea how long the girl had been staying here or who she was?"

"Come on, you know I can't tell you any of that." My new friend James looked pained.

"Is there anything hinky about the apartment? You know, broken lock or whatever that I should note so my client knows to fix it."

"Jim, don't say anything. She's sneaky." The shorter guy warned.

A lesser woman would have quit while she was ahead. A smarter one would have flaunted her charms and flirted the info out of him. I was neither. "Hypothetically speaking, of course. I'm just trying to stay on top of the to-do list. I don't get paid until the property owner is making money on this place. Can't you cut a girl a break?"

Jim shot me an understanding smile "Okay, hypothetically speaking, your client ought to invest in some spackle and sheetrock. That's on top of the professional grade cleaning the place is going to need."

Jim's partner cast him a dark look.

"Holes in the wall?" I asked. Considering the scene we'd stumbled across, I wasn't surprised Luke and Logan both missed it. "What could have possibly caused that?"

"Not the walls." Jim said, his eyes rolling heavenward.

46

"The ceiling?" Curiouser and curiouser.

"You didn't hear it from me." Jim put a finger to the side of his nose. His partner just shook his head.

"Hear what?" I winked and sauntered back to Bessie Mae.

What the hell had Fester Gomez been doing in that apartment?

Chapter Five

"Think you're wearing enough clothes?" Logan smirked at me over his morning coffee.

"I was cold." I lied, hoping the beads of perspiration on my upper lip wouldn't give me away.

"It's eighty degrees out and the sun's barely up."

I looked down at my ensemble. Marine wife sweats over bike shorts, tank top and socks. I'd slept in this get up, or hardly slept because the last thing I wanted was to sleepwalk into Logan's room and have him accuse me of throwing myself at him again. The clothes were just extra insurance because skin to skin contact was a horrible idea.

A solution was forthcoming. As punishment for hiding his brother from me, I told Luke no sex until Logan moved back into his own place. Yes, it was a classic female passive-aggressive maneuver and no marriage facilitator worth her salt would condone me using my body as a weapon, but it sure was effective. Besides, I had needs too, and there was no way I could concentrate enough knowing the Dark Prince lurked down the hall. Was possibly listening while we....

Nope, not gonna happen. I hid my smile. Logan would be relocated by lunch.

"So, my day's set." I leaned against the counter and crossed my sock-covered ankles. "What are you guys going to do?"

"Find Gomez." Logan looked at me as if I were a few bricks shy of a load.

"Riiiiggghhhtttt." Snagging a leftover chocolate chip cookie from the bakery box, I dunked it in my coffee so I wouldn't chip a tooth. We'd gone over this the night before. Gomez was a dead end. The man had nothing in the way of credit history, he'd lived at the same address for ten years, had no income we could track and had paid cash for everything. Rosie Harris didn't know anything and the adoption had been sealed so we had no way of finding his daughter. "With your superhero locator ring?"

Logan pushed back away from the table and rose to his full, imposing height. Odd how Luke was the same size but I never felt like he towered over me the way Logan did. Probably because he didn't skulk around like he was up to no good. "The old-fashioned way. We're going to look with our eyes, not with a million gadgets and internet searches. Knock on some doors and ask a few questions."

I tried not to roll my eyes and failed. "Good luck with that."

Luke moved into the room, bussed my cheek with a soft kiss before turning to his brother. "You good to go?"

"Whenever you are."

Luke poured his coffee in a travel mug and gave me a molten look. "See you later, hot stuff."

"No breakfast?" I asked.

"We'll get something on the road."

"No burritos, I have plans for later." I sent him a saucy wink and struck a pose. The effect was somewhat diminished by my choice of wardrobe.

"Save me from married flirting," Logan groaned.

"Noted." Luke practically rushed Logan out the door. Oh yeah, the Dark Prince better pack his bag of evil tricks.

After showering and dressing in taupe linen pants and a paisley print top, I picked up my shoulder bag and headed to the printers.

An hour later I had five hundred business cards each for myself, Luke and Logan with Damaged Goods Property Management printed in a classic black font. I'd paid out the nose for those babies, but they were worth it. I wish the guys had waited for me to get them before they headed out for the day. It was so much more professional to actually hand someone a real business card than to scribble your number on a napkin or gum wrapper.

I checked the time on my phone. Maybe they were nearby and could meet up with me. After shooting Luke a quick text, I tossed my bag into Bessie Mae, careful not to lean on her dirt encrusted door and smear my clothes with impound lot grime. No reply text, so much for that plan. I rolled down the windows to let some of the heat out and decided to wait just a few more minutes. Truthfully, I was stalling because I was in no hurry to pick up Marcy's weird sister for her colonoscopy.

"Jackie? I thought that was you."

I looked up and smiled when I saw the broad golden boy grin of Aaron Tanner. "Hey there, Aaron. Or should I call you boss-man?"

"You better not." Aaron shook his head and his charming smile turned rueful. I'd only met him once, but the man seemed very sweet for a retired marine. He wasn't as tall as Luke or Logan, but was broad at the shoulders and packed full of muscle, easily concealed under tailored clothing. I couldn't tell if his sun streaked hair was from a high end salon or the Florida sunshine but it was a good look for him.

"What are you doing here?" he raised an eyebrow.

"Getting our business cards made up." Reaching through the window, I plucked one of mine out of the box and handed it to him. It read, Jackie Parker, Certified Process Server for Damaged Goods. "Congrats, you're the first person to receive one. Only right, since you're our first client."

Aaron pulled out his wallet and placed my card inside. "I'm glad this is working out for you guys. Luke and Logan were made for this kind of work. They're imposing, but honest. Some of the teams I've hired in the past go too far, and wind up causing more problems than they solve."

Exactly what Logan would do if he didn't have Luke's level head to temper him. "I don't know if the guys told you, but I posted the notice of termination on the apartment door to start the eviction process. They are out right now hunting for Mr. Gomez, but until he surfaces, the best course of action is to move forward once the police give us the all clear. Get your apartment back and in shape to rent out again."

Aaron made a face. "It might be difficult to find a tenant after there was a murder there."

51

I shook my head. "It's right on the beach. It could be radioactive and you'd still have people scrambling for it."

"I hope you're right. I spoke to the police this morning."

"Have they I.D.ed the girl yet?" If we knew who she was, maybe we'd have someplace to look.

"If they did, no one told me. I can't believe some of the questions the cops asked me, almost as if they thought she'd been sexually involved with Gomez."

The notion had crossed my mind, too. "Out of curiosity, how did Gomez pay you for the rent?"

"No idea. I have a realtor who handles the rentals. Mara Young. She screens any potential tenants prior to leasing and collects the rent. I only get involved if there's a problem."

I nodded, getting a clearer picture of how far removed Aaron was from his business. "Like when a tenant stops paying. Did anyone else go there and try to collect before you contacted Luke?" Maybe someone had seen the girl at the apartment. Knowing how long she'd been there would help us unearth her identity.

But Aaron shook his head. "No, and I feel awful about that. Like maybe if someone had gone over there we could have prevented what happened." Sadness lined his face.

"Don't blame yourself. You owned the place but you had no control over what went on inside. That's what a rental agreement is for but some tenants are really sneaky about breaking them. Believe me, I know."

His expression turned to gratitude for my understanding. "Thanks, Jackie."

Not wanting to add to his guilt, I bit back the questions I had concerning Gomez's ceiling breaking activities. Poor Aaron had enough to deal with without my random speculation. My phone buzzed with a schedule alert. "Shoot, I gotta jet." One crazy ass to deliver for inspection. Maybe I should have put that on the business card. That desk better be in prime shape.

"Me too, I'm late for a meeting. Good seeing you, Jackie."

Settling down into Bessie Mae, I turned the engine over and merged with the mid-morning traffic.

****

Gertie Regan lived in a small rundown suburban neighborhood, in the house she'd inherited from her parents. Marcy had been the late life surprise for the Regans, who were in their mid-forties and already had a twenty year old daughter to their credit when Marcy arrived on the scene. When first her mother then her father passed on a few years back, Marcy had taken over caring for her older sister, who had severe agoraphobia and liked to cover the windows with tinfoil so "they" couldn't spy on her. The first time Marcy had dragged me along for a Gertie-check in, she'd stared at me the entire time, hardly blinking. From what Marcy said, that meant Gertie approved of me and I was now part of her inner circle. Lucky me.

"Gertie?" I called through the door before rapping lightly, in case she was in her closet again. "Gertie, it's Jackie Parker. May I come in?"

Marcy had assured me that her sister was back on her anti-anxiety meds and that everything would go smoothly. I had my doubts which were only

53

reinforced when Gertie came to the door covered in neon Post-it notes.

I softened my voice, like I was talking to a scared kid, instead of a woman with two decades of life on me. "Hey, sweetie. You remember me, right? I'm your sister's friend. We're going on a little trip today."

To me it sounded condescending as hell, but Marcy insisted that speaking slowly and repeating information was the best way to deal with Gertie.

"A trip to the hospital. Yes, I think I'm ready." She looked around, searching for God alone knew what. Maybe she'd written it on a Post-it.

I shifted, unable to stop staring at the florescent orange and green and pink notes stuck in her curly dark hair and to her tropical print tank dress. "Um, do you want to maybe leave your notes at home?"

Gertie shot me a pitying look, as though I was too stupid to understand just how foolish my suggestion was. "I don't want to forget anything important."

Yeah. I wasn't going to argue with her, but it would be a long, hot drive to the hospital because no way was I going to risk one of her important notes blowing out Bessie Mae's open window.

She handed me her keys, and I locked her house before escorting her to the waiting car. She sat down, fastened her seatbelt and waited patiently as I circled the car and climbed inside. So far, so good. I felt like I was carrying a bomb.

"Do you like music?" I asked, reaching for the radio knob.

"No!" She shouted and I froze. Okay, one hot and uncomfortably silent ride coming up.

54

"No music, got it." I turned at the end of the street and beseeched the traffic overlords to go easy on me. "So, Gertie, what do you do for fun?"

"I like dragons." Her gaze was fixed out the window,

"Dragons are cool," I murmured, making a left.

Again with the derisive look, like she'd caught me eating paste. "Dragons are hot actually. They can breathe fire."

Okay, the slang was causing miscommunication. Crap, could I even talk without it? "I meant, cool as in cold-blooded. They're giant lizards, right?"

"Dragons aren't real." Gertie stared at me with a duh expression.

I should have just paid cash for the stupid desk.

Ahead of us the light turned yellow and the blue hair in her antique Oldsmobile I'd been following slammed on her brakes, forcing me to do the same so I didn't rear end her. Gertie and I bucked forward, then back again, her Post-its making little clickity sounds as they resettled.

"Sorry about that. You okay?"

No response but I could hear her breathing through her mouth, so we proceeded on toward the hospital.

Of course the parking area was about six blocks away from the outpatient entrance, but no way was I going to drop my walking Post-it advertisement unsupervised while I trekked in from the outer reaches. After situating Bessie Mae between two huge SUVs, I held Gertie's door for her. "Here we are." My singsong voice could have made a diabetic's sugar levels spike.

She didn't budge.

"Gertie?" Had she lost a Post-it or something?

"I don't want to go in."

My eyes cut to the hospital, the destination of this agonizing voyage. So close, yet so far away. "Um, well, why?"

Slowly she turned her head to look up at me. "Do you know what they are going to do to me in there?"

"A test to make sure—"

"They are going to put a *tube* up my *ass*." She landed hard on the nouns, just to underscore her point. "And a *camera*."

"Katie Couric does it." I replied weakly. "It's good for you."

She gave me that scathing look again, like I was too stupid to draw breath. Maybe I was.

Time for a lifeline. I typed an SOS text to Marcy. Then one to Luke for good measure. He and Logan could carry little Ms. Sticky Note into the hospital if necessary. We watched traffic rush by, her in the car, me looming over her not knowing what the hell else to do.

My phone rang. "Help," I said without checking the caller I.D.

"Jackie? You okay, dear?"

Crap, it was my mother-in-law, not Marcy or Luke. "Um, now's not really a good time, Marge."

"Sorry, I didn't mean to disturb you at work. I just wanted to make sure you were on board for the bridal shower and bachelorette party."

The fact that my mother-in-law hadn't been a bachelorette in four decades was beside the point. Prior to the vow renewal, she partied like it was 1989, this year literally as the ladies were meeting at some eighties themed club downtown.

Watching a bunch of middle aged women get jiggy with it was not my designer handbag of choice but as Marge liked to remind me, you ought to stretch yourself for family. "Wild dragons couldn't keep me away," I said with a sidelong glance at Gertie.

"Tell the boys they'll need to take their father and go get fitted for their tuxes." Marge continued, just as my other line beeped.

"Sure will. I have another call, so I'll see you then." I clicked over before she could protest.

"What's wrong?" It was Marcy.

"We're in the parking lot in front of the hospital but Gertie says she doesn't want to go in."

"Put me on speaker." Marcy commanded.

Switching to speakerphone, I set the device on the dashboard and said, "Done."

"Gertie, it's Marcy. We talked about this. What happened to Daddy?" Marcy was rocking her official County Clerk's tone, brooking no nonsense. I felt suitably chastised, though I had no idea why.

"He died," Gertie's tone was soft.

"From what?" Marcy pushed.

"Colon cancer." She sounded sulky.

"And what did the doctor tell you this test helps us detect?"

"Colon cancer."

"I know it's unpleasant to think about but you'll be asleep, right? And when you wake up, I'll be there and we'll go home. So go with Jackie now and I'll see you in a bit."

Gertie nodded and then rose. I switched the phone back to privacy. "Thank you."

57

"I gotta run." Marcy hung up before I could ask her how to solve the Post-it debacle.

We entered the lobby and a stern face nurse pointed us to the diagnostic center. We collected many strange glances at Gertie's paper-coated ensamble. My phone buzzed, but I ignored it, intent on getting my companion squared away as soon as possible.

There was a small waiting room outside the imaging area and a nurse's station. I stopped at the desk. "Hi. My friend here has an appointment. Gertrude Regan."

She did a double take at Gertie's paper adornments. "Right, her sister filled out the paperwork yesterday." Good old Girl Scout Marcy, always on the ball.

I turned to Gertie. "Um, would you like me to hold on to your notes? I'll give them to Marcy so you can have them as soon as you wake up."

"Yes, thank you." Gertie said, surprising the hell out of me. She tugged the papers one at time free from her hair and dress then stacked them neatly. "Keep them safe."

I double checked but she'd gotten them all. "Will do. Just try to relax." I winced when I realized how stupid that sounded.

But Gertie seemed at ease as she followed the nurse down the hall, no more snotty looks questioning my intelligence. Or lack thereof.

Another nurse handed me a large octagonal device, the kind that lights up when your table is ready at a restaurant. "This works throughout the hospital, if you want to go to the cafeteria. It'll let you know when she's ready."

58

"Great." I smiled and turned toward the waiting room, then stopped as something occurred to me. "By the way, do you know how I can find Dr. Feinstein?"

"Never heard of him. Maybe he's out of a different hospital What's his specialty?"

"Not a clue."

She gave me an odd look and I felt the need to explain. "He was treating someone who has disappeared. I'm not after medial information, I just really need to find his patient."

"Try the internet." The nurse turned away, dismissing me.

I ducked into the waiting room. Sagging into the chair, I focused on the relief coursing through me. Poor Marcy, I didn't know how she dealt with the crazy all the time. I felt like I'd been dodging bullets all morning.

My phone buzzed again but the nurse shot me a deliberate headshake. "No calls in here."

Clutching my phone and the alert gismo, I headed toward the cafeteria. I needed something with lots of sugar to reward myself. I settled down with a bottle of juice and a frosted brownie the size of my fist and checked my messages.

The first was from Luke. "Call me."

The other was a text from my mother-in-law with another reminder for "her boys" to come to their father's bachelor party, sports themed, how original. Her snark, not mine.

I dialed Luke. "You won't believe the morning I've had." I told him with a mouth full of chocolaty goodness.

"Same here. We got back into Gomez's apartment."

"And?" my brownie bliss was forgotten in my excitement. Maybe they had a lead.

"And we need you to call Aaron and come vouch for us. The cops didn't believe we worked for him."

A male nurse wearing blue scrubs entered the cafeteria and looked around, a huge grin on his face. He headed right towards me. "Excuse me,"

Too much going on at once and not nearly enough sugar. "Luke, hold on a second." I covered the phone and looked up, praying I didn't have chocolate on my teeth. "Yes?"

"You came in with Gertrude Regan, right?"

I nodded and he handed me a pink Post-it. "We found this on her, um backside, after we put her under."

I read the note. "Caution: You are about to enter virgin territory." Jeeze, Louise.

He grinned. "The doctor almost collapsed, he was laughing so hard. We thought you'd want to put it with the others."

What I wanted was to boil my hands.

"Jackie," Luke's tone was impatient. In the background I could hear lots of noise, not road sounds like he was driving but people talking and phones ringing.

I blinked. "Where are you guys?"

Luke sighed. "The police station."

Chapter Six

At least the guys weren't under arrest. If they had been, I might have let them stay there for a spell. The detaining officer was my old pal, James O'Reilly. I saw him standing over the Parker brothers where they sat side by side on a large wooden bench.

I moved into his peripheral vision and ignored them while I addressed him. "Hi Jim."

His head turned and entire demeanor changed as he smiled, obviously pleased to see me. "Jackie, what are you doing here?"

"You know him?" Logan's tone was filled with disbelief.

"She knows everyone." Luke hissed. "Now shut up and let her fix it."

While I appreciated his faith in me, I needed to know exactly what they'd done wrong before I could begin to set things right. After fishing one of my new business cards out of my purse, I handed it to James. "They are the rest of my team, from Damaged Goods."

"*Your* team?" Logan again.

I ignored him and turned my smile up another notch. Damn, I needed more caffeine or sugar or something to clog my arteries to contend with this job. "What exactly were they doing wrong?"

"We found them in the Gomez apartment. The tape was down and they were going through the place. When I questioned them, they said they worked for the owner, but since I knew you did and they had no way to verify it—" he gestured and raised his eyebrows.

"You thought their story sounded suspicious." I summed up. "Well, I'm here to tell you they really do work with me and we were hired by Aaron Tanner, the owner. This is my husband Luke and his brother, Logan." I was actually proud of myself for recognizing this was neither the time nor the place to snark on the Dark Prince. We needed to present a united front to the outside world if we wanted to succeed.

I'd get him later, though.

O'Reilly's face fell a little bit when I mentioned that Luke was my husband, but he squared his shoulders and nodded—the consummate professional.

"We told you, we saw the door open and the tape down. We thought Gomez was inside," Logan insisted.

"Thanks so much for understanding." I gushed a little, going overboard as I gestured for the Parker brothers to get up and leave before Logan plopped them back in hot water. James eyed the three of us as we waited for the elevator and I gave him a little finger wave. Nothing to see here, officer.

The second we hit the parking lot I whirled on them. "What the hell were you thinking? You have no authority to apprehend Gomez. And until the

62

apartment is cleared from crime scene status, the cops hold dominion over that, too."

I focused my ire on Logan, since I was pretty sure it was all his fault. Luke would have followed his thick-headed brother into the fires of hell, never mind an apartment in South Beach.

"Dominion?"

My hands went to my hips. "Really? You want to play word games? You know what I mean."

"What were we supposed to do, ignore it?" Logan seethed.

"Hey," Luke tried to break in between us but both Logan and I were spoiling for this showdown.

"Call 911 or grab the nearest uniform to investigate for you. It was an illegal entry because it hasn't been twenty four hours since I posted the inspection notice. He could have arrested you for B&E. How would that look for our company's reputation?"

"Guys," Luke tried again, but Logan ignored him as he got in my face.

"Now it's our company? A second ago we were your team. And what the hell is with the name, Damaged Goods? It makes it sound like we're broken."

"It's a pun, dumbass. You know, a play on words? It's supposed to be catchy and easy to remember."

"Since when did you get to pick the name of our team? This was our idea, our company and you're taking it over!" He waved his hand between himself and Luke, intentionally excluding me.

I'd had enough. "Since Luke said I could! Since you two thought you had better things to do than the basics before you charged ahead at full speed. If you want me to stop, say the word and I'm out."

"Fine," Logan spat.

"Fine." I lifted my chin and narrowed my eyes. "I'm out."

"No," Luke shouted and all the cops in the parking lot turned to look at us. "Logan, knock it off. We screwed up, got into a jam and we couldn't get out of it on our own. We need her."

"To do what? Flirt with every cop we run across like some prostitute? You might be okay with your wife running around town like the whore of Babylon but I don't want to see it."

Time slowed to a crawl as we all processed what he just said. Even the Dark Prince appeared stunned, as though he'd been speaking in tongues.

"Jackie—" he tried.

Luke charged him but I was faster, throwing my full weight into my husband, ignoring the sting from Logan's words. "Don't Luke, don't do it. Not here." No way could I talk them out of a cell if they brawled in the parking lot.

I kept talking, totally ignoring the Dark Prince and focusing on my irate husband who wanted to beat his idiot brother into a bloody pulp. His body was stiff and I could feel his heart pounding beneath my hand.

"Is everything all right?" One of the police officers asked.

"Just a little family drama." I called out. "We're going."

I reached into Luke's pockets and dug out the keys for his truck. Without looking, I tossed them to a stunned Logan. "You, go get the truck. We're going home."

"Jackie, I'm sorry."

64

I made the mistake of looking at him over my shoulder. He really was the picture of remorse, but he'd cut me deeply and worse, he'd cut Luke. "Get it together, Logan or this will never work."

Luke moved on his own toward Bessie Mae. "Gimme the keys."

"You sure you are okay to drive?"

"Give. Me. The. Damn. *Keys*," he grated.

It was hot, I'd had a disaster-filled morning and the cops were still watching us. I handed him the keys and waited for him to climb in, turn the engine over and unlock my door.

I sat and kicked at the bag with the Damaged Goods business cards and tried not to wonder if we'd ever actually use them. The whore of Babylon. Really? He made my friendly nature out to be a bad thing, made it sound like I ran around behind Luke's back. Which I'd never *ever* do. But did Luke know that?

I turned to face him. A muscle jumped in his jaw and the knuckles gripping my steering wheel had turned white. "Luke—"

His eyes closed. "Just, give me a minute."

"I'll give you the entire ride home if you put it in gear and drive before those cops haul us back inside for questioning." I fastened my seatbelt and folded my hands over my lap like a good little passenger.

He let out a breath and then secured his own seatbelt before backing out of the space and turning into the flow of traffic.

I studied him while we drove. It was rare that Luke's temper got the better of him. Logan had pushed him too far, the way only a spouse or sibling could. Nature had made him a sweet, fun-loving guy, the polar opposite of his disgruntled, moody brother. If the Parker boys were eighties songs, Luke would be

65

Hall & Oates *You Make My Dreams Come True* while Logan was the Scorpion's *Rock You like a Hurricane*.

Ask any Florida resident which one they'd choose to spend their life dealing with.

****

"Damn, I needed that." I curled into Luke's side. We were sweaty and naked in our bed and I was feeling a million times better than when we'd walked through the door a half an hour ago.

"Me too," he smiled at me, that warm sunny grin back in place.

As much as I wanted to bask in the moment we needed to hash some things out. "You know I'd never cheat on you, right? Not ever."

"I know that." But he looked away.

My stomach flipped over that he'd experienced even a second's doubt. "Luke, I'm just being friendly. It's how I make connections. Sometimes men take it the wrong way, but I always wear my ring and set them straight. If they persist, I remove myself from the situation." Like I had with my scumbag ex-boss.

He pulled me tighter against him. "Ssshh, babe, it's okay. Believe me, I know some guys just see what they want to see. Logan was out of line saying those things."

"You can't let what Logan thinks about me bug you. I'm trying, Luke, I'm really trying to get along with him. His opinion of me is getting in the way. Maybe it'd be better if you guys did find someone else." Despite my rash proclamation in the parking lot, I didn't want it to come to that. I'd been pumped about being my own boss and working with the man I love even if it meant 220 lbs of seething brother-in-law glaring at me.

He ran a hand through my hair. "I want this, Jackie, I want to do this with you. Let me handle Logan, all right?"

"Only if you promise to do it with words and not your fists. You guys aren't kids anymore and you were about to get in a physical altercation in a police parking lot." I pushed my hair over one shoulder so I could nestle more snugly against him. "I don't want to keep coming in between you guys."

As if on cue, a heavy door slammed out in front of the house. Logan was back with the truck.

"And that marks the end of our reprieve," I grumbled.

"Keep trying, Jackie. He'll come around."

I seriously doubted it, but what choice did I have? "Promise me you'll tell me if you need me to step aside."

He kissed my forehead, then climbed out of bed and reached for his pants. "It won't come to that. You coming?"

"After I shower. I'm kind of a mess."

"Just the way I like you." Luke stole another kiss, tugged on his shirt and exited our bedroom.

I listened to the low murmur of masculine voices. The fact that they weren't shouting loudly enough for me to hear every word was a good sign. Also no thumps or crashes. Logan must have cooled off, too.

With the Parker brothers mending fences, I indulged in a long, hot shower. Logan calling me a whore had cut me deeply and the fact that Luke might have doubts about my commitment to him scared the hell out of me. Tangling a professional relationship into the mix seemed foolhardy, at best.

But Luke wanted this and so did I. That left Logan as the obstacle we needed to overcome. Something had to give.

After tugging on a pair of black capri pants and a sea foam green top with a Mandarin collar, I twisted my hair up on top of my head and secured it with a clip. Assessing my reflection with a critical eye, I nodded, satisfied that I was sending the right message. One hundred percent cool professional, and not in the skin trade kinda way.

Barefoot, I padded out into the kitchen, where the Parker brothers were seated. Luke's back was to me, but his posture looked relaxed. Logan had been saying something, but he cut off mid-sentence. "Jackie, I'm so damn sorry."

I had to give the jerk credit, opening with an apology was smart. Unfortunately for him, I was not so easily appeased. "What for, calling me a whore or getting your dumb asses hauled to the police station."

"Way to keep trying," Luke murmured.

"Both," Logan said, surprising us all, even himself by his expression. "I was so focused on finding Gomez that I didn't think about the legal side of things."

"Until Gomez has been forcibly evicted and/ or arrested for murder, that place is his home. If he doesn't invite you in, you can't enter. If it helps, pretend you're a vampire."

His expression turned skeptical. "A vampire?"

"Not the sparkly emo kind, the cool ones that can't enter without an invitation. That's you. No invite, no dice."

"This is why we need her," Luke said.

Logan opened his mouth but Luke cut him off. "No, man, not just a certified process server. We need

68

Jackie because no one else will be as invested in our success as she will."

It was his mother's *you do for family* speech. I saw Logan's expression change as he recognized it, too.

"If it helps, I've come up with a solution of sorts." I took the chair between them and folded my hands on the table.

"What's that?" Luke asked.

"If we're going to succeed, we need to separate the job from the family connection. When we're on the job, we are coworkers, not brothers, not husband and wife and not family. Just people with a job to do."

"This isn't exactly a nine to five operation," Logan pointed out. "So how do you define on the job?"

He was right. I leaned back in my chair, drumming my fingers on the table. "The office, or what will be the office in the second bedroom. The truck or anytime we are out on a job."

"So, you're saying we can bring work home with us, but not bring home to work?" Luke clarified.

"If we can manage it," I nodded. "We should start right now, this instant."

"There's nothing in the office," Logan said. He wasn't being snotty or belligerent, just stating a fact.

"Good point. Let's move the table in there until we get some real furniture. We never sit here to eat anyway."

I carried the chairs while Luke and Logan hefted the table through the living room and down the hall. The office was a little tight this way, and the bags of supplies Logan had left propped in one corner didn't exactly scream professional business, but it was a start. Once we were resettled around the table I withdrew the business cards I'd been so stoked over and slid each box to the appropriate Parker. "Now when you go door to door, you have something to hand out that makes you look legit. And gives people a way to contact you."

Logan withdrew one of his and stared down at it, his expression unreadable.

My anxiety spiked. "Do you really hate it? The name I mean."

Slowly, he raised his eyes to mine. "It's a good name. Like you said, memorable."

"Luke?"

"I said you could pick the name and I stand by that."

Consensus. It was a small but crucial step in the right direction. "Okay, so do you want to fill me in on what you found out before the police intervened?"

"Most everyone at that condo complex was gone at that time of day. The few we spoke to didn't know Gomez personally. From what I can tell he didn't get out much. No dog to walk. They'd seen other young women coming and going out of that apartment but no guess as to who our Jane Doe with the purple nail polish might be." Luke said.

"His sister-in-law made it sound like he didn't have his own car and we checked the DMV records," Logan added. "No vehicle registered to a Fester Gomez."

"So, no family other than his creepy doll collecting sister-in-law, no car, his neighbors don't know him and he doesn't have a job."

"Oh, he has a job, all right." Logan smirked. It wasn't his, *I'm being an ass* smirk, instead it was an *I know something you won't believe* smirk.

"You guys holding out on me?"

"Go get your laptop," Luke instructed.

70

I eyed him for a moment and then retrieved my computer. Luke took it from me and there was some clickity clacking of the keys.

When he spun the screen back to face me, my jaw dropped. My eyes were glued to the unbelievable website he'd pulled up and my gaze flew to the url.

"GomezKinkyGirlz.com."

"Look in the far left." Luke pointed.

I sucked in a sharp breath as I saw the flash of purple nail polish. "It's her. The murder victim."

Chapter Seven

"Didn't we just get back from the police station?" Logan asked as we headed out to the big black truck. "It didn't exactly go too well the last time."

"We don't have a choice." I climbed into the backseat. "If we don't reveal what we know to the police we could be charged with withholding evidence." Besides, I wanted to see the look on their faces when they found out that we cracked their case. Professional respect goes a long way with law enforcement.

Luke put the truck into reverse, but then slammed on the brakes so hard we all rocked forward. "That was close."

I rubbed my bruised sternum and craned my neck to see out the back. "What happened?"

"Mr. Murphy." He pointed down at the neighboring drive. "That boat of his is blocking us in. I swear it wasn't there a second ago."

"Someone's behind the wheel," Logan pointed.

"Crap." Mr. Murphy was the former postal worker who lived next door. Retirement wasn't treating him too well and he'd taken to roaming the streets in his maroon Oldsmobile long after his daughter should have snagged his license. "He can't handle city traffic."

"He's blocking us in." Logan said.

"Honk the horn, make sure he's awake." And alive.

Luke honked. We waited and then, like some urban mating call, an answering honk pierced the quiet afternoon.

"Looks like a draw," Luke said.

"Let me handle this." I slithered down from the backseat, sashayed over to the burgundy beacon and tapped on the driver's window. "Mr. Murphy?"

My neighbor jumped, obviously startled by my sudden approach. His thinning salt and pepper hair stuck up every which way and he wore stripped pajamas and soft soled moccasins on his feet.

He rolled down the window. "No thanks honey, I don't have money for a lap dance."

Masculine laughter erupted behind me. Crap, the Parker brothers would never let me hear the end of that. In my most conservative outfit, too. When a girl's hoisting double Ds, she could wear sackcloth and still look ready to party.

Ignoring the slight, I asked, "Are you all right? You're not exactly dressed to go out."

"No time for hanky-panky, I gotta pick Francine up at the station." He tried to roll the window back up but I wedged my shoulder bag in there.

"Francine?" Luke asked.

73

"His late wife." This wasn't good. Mr. Murphy was clearly having some sort of senior moment and we couldn't just leave him to terrorize the streets in search of his deceased wife. Florida's driving reputation was bad enough already.

I looked at the guys but they were no help. My motto is ,when in doubt, pull it out of your ass. "Mr. Murphy, your daughter called me. She said she'd take care of everything and that you should wait at home."

For a second I thought he'd call my bluff, ask why his daughter was calling me and not him, but eventually he nodded. "Okay then."

I saw his intention a second before his foot slammed down on the accelerator "Wait!"

The Olds lurched forward and ripped my bag right out of my hands. Without my support it flopped over in defeat and vomited up its contents in a trail as the car zipped forward. My wallet, tampons, breath mints, keys, Gertie's sticky notes, several pens and my cell phone plus about a thousand business cards scattered across the lawn.

Luke and Logan tried to stifle their laughter and failed.

"Fricking hell." No good deed goes unpunished.

Luke, still grinning, dutifully started to collect the spilled innards of my bag but I waved him off. "I got this. You guys go talk to the police. I'll stay with him until his daughter shows up then I'll follow you over in Bessie Mae."

"You sure?"

No, but I didn't want them sticking around for any more *octogenarian vs. Jackie* because I was already two points down. "See you later."

Because we were supposed to be in work mode, there was no goodbye kiss but I did eye hump my man pretty hard as he walked away. Logan noticed, but for once didn't glower at me when our eyes met. I guess even the Dark Prince's mood can be lightened with a dose of slapstick.

Mr. Murphy was still sitting in his car by the time I collected my things. "Ready?"

He continued to stare blankly ahead as though we hadn't just been talking. Uh oh. I needed to get him out of that car, pronto, before he changed his mind and decided to go for a spin. "Mr. Murphy, may I use your bathroom?"

I was banking on the fact that he wouldn't recall that my own bathroom was right next door.

Southern gentleman won over confused old man. "Of course."

I helped him from the car and snagged his keys under the guise of unlocking his front door for him. What I really wanted was to take his keys into the bathroom while I called Rebecca Murphy and clued her in to this situation so he couldn't continue his fruitless quest for his dead spouse.

Mr. Murphy's house was a nicer version of my bungalow. Eat in kitchen to the left of the front door, with the living room on the right. A hallway leading back to what I could only guess was three bedrooms plus a bonus room on top, facing the street. Instead of a verandah in front, the architect had installed a glassed in Florida room overlooking the small yard out back. The color scheme was a rich chocolate brown with navy accents, very masculine but still tasteful.

While the layout was almost the same as our digs, his place was in much better condition. Quartz countertops, hardwood floors, and snazzy lighting fixtures as opposed to our off the truck special hodgepodge mess. I knew his daughter paid for a cleaning service to come in once a week and a lawn maintenance company came over biweekly. Rebecca Murphy had tried to make her father's life as simple as possible, but he was still out of his depth.

"Bathroom's first on your left," he said.

I'd almost forgotten my fib because I was so entranced with the final product of the cozy house. "I'll be quick."

He nodded and shuffled off. I scooted into the bathroom and dialed Rebecca's number, praying my cellphone hadn't been damaged in the spill. Thankfully it worked and she picked up on the first ring. I identified myself and related our encounter as succinctly as possible.

"Damn," she said. "I knew this was coming, but I had no idea he was so bad. Thought I'd have a few more months to make arrangements. I'll be there as soon as I can. Thanks, Jackie."

I didn't envy her. Blood would probably paint the walls of my mother's trailer the day I had to take her keys away.

Worried that Mr. Murphy would try to cook something and accidentally burn the beautiful house down around us, I exited the bathroom and went in search of him. I found him in the master bedroom, this one done in a soothing deep blue with white accents. The shades were closed tightly but the Tiffany lamp on the bedside table cast a soft glow.

He sat on his bed, a black and white wedding picture in his hands. From my position in the doorway, I could see a much younger Mr. Murphy and a plump but pretty blonde wearing a traditional white gown. Obviously in her time, curves were all the rage. They looked incredibly happy, in a state of divine bliss. He wasn't crying, but the hunch of his shoulders spoke of a deep hurt, a loss so yawning that nothing could ever fill the void.

A lump formed in my throat. I'd stared at my own wedding picture like that. The times when I hadn't heard from Luke, didn't know where he was, if he was safe. There were nights when I fell asleep holding it. No matter what anyone says, being a military spouse sucks. But at least I had hope of seeing the man I loved again. Mr. Murphy only had his memories. Maybe allowing him to exist in his delusions, where his wife would arrive at any minute, was kinder.

Shutting the door to give him privacy, I moved into the living room and sat down to wait. The fact that I hadn't kissed Luke goodbye bugged me. After a minute, I whipped out my cell phone and texted him a quick *I love you*.

It didn't make it all better but knowing he was on the other end of the line, that he had that waiting for him, eased my mind a bit.

The backdoor opened and Rebecca Murphy hefted a double stroller into the house. Her twin girls wriggled and squirmed, but were fastened in securely. Her hair was as wild as her dad's and she had what looked like oatmeal smeared on her left boob. Her yoga pants had holes in them. A full blown domestic goddess. No one would ever mistake Rebecca Murphy for a stripper.

"Dad?" she huffed, clearly out of breath.

"He's in the bedroom." I got up off the couch. "Take a second and catch your breath."

She sagged, clearly relieved. "Thanks so much for stopping him, Jackie. And for staying with him."

"That's what neighbors are for." I dug his keys out of my ruined shoulder bag. "I have somewhere I need to be, but keep me in the loop, okay?"

"Will do." She went to hug me, then grimaced at the shmutz on her shirt. "Virtual hug then."

The girls wriggled and made little squeaking sounds, clearly ready to be set loose. I beat feet before their protests turned to full-out caterwauling. Nothing unsettled me more than hearing a little kid cry. And this day had already cornered the market on disturbing.

****

I was greeted by name at the local precinct and shuffled right into the interrogation room where the detective in charge of the Gomez case had stashed the brooding Parker brothers.

"How's it going?" I asked, slinging my freshly duct taped purse onto the table.

Logan made a disgruntled sound. "Well, we told him."

"And?" Trying to get information out of Logan was the verbal equivalent of pulling teeth.

He shrugged. "And he stuck us in here."

At least they hadn't been separated for questioning. Or cuffed. "What exactly did you guys say?"

"That we knew who the dead girl in the Gomez case is." Luke said.

I smacked my palm into my forehead. "But we *don't*. All we know is how Gomez knew her from the video." *Aye yi, yi.*

The door opened and Sergeant Enrique Vasquez entered the room. Though I didn't know

78

Vasquez personally, I'd heard him mentioned several times. Medium height and build with jet black hair and eyelashes any woman would sell an ovary for. He was young, maybe mid-thirties and recently promoted from detective after helping Florida Department of Law Enforcement, or FDLE, bust a child prostitution ring. The fact that he was assigned to the Gomez case didn't surprise me. He had a reputation for relentlessly pursuing people who hurt children.

Vasquez didn't look surprised to see me. Either that or he had one hell of a poker face. He sat down across the table and folded his hands over his notepad. "I was told you have information on the victim in the Gomez case."

Luke opened his mouth but I beat him to the punch. "There's this website—"

He didn't bat a single thick, dark eyelash. "Gomezkinkygirlz.com."

"You know about it?" Well crap, there went my thunder. "That he knew the victim?"

"Is that all you had?" Not a flicker of emotion. Man, he was good.

"Yeah." Sullen, I leaned back in my chair.

"Did you find out who she was?" Logan leaned forward.

"I'm not at liberty to discuss an ongoing investigation with civilians." Though the words were cold, there was actually a spark when he looked at Logan. A flare of interest that had nothing to do with the case. The Dark Prince shifted and Vasquez broke eye contact and focused on his notepad.

"When can we get back in the apartment?" Luke asked.

"Forensics is done with their sweep and we've turned the keys over to the property owner." He rose

79

and headed to the door, paused and then pulled out his wallet. "If you find anything else, anything at all, call me directly."

He handed the card to Logan, who took it.

Never missing a chance to give out one of our cards, I fished one out of my ghetto bag. "In case you need to reach us."

I held my tongue until we were back in the truck. "Well, it looks like my assets aren't going to be any help here."

"Jackie," Luke's tone held a warning, which I ignored.

"What? Maybe Logan should go make nice, meet Vasquez at *La Cantina* after work for margarita shooters. Bet he could wheedle info just as well as me. I'll even buy him some tight pants for maximum effect."

"In your dreams." Logan gave me a withering look.

This was too delicious. "You didn't have a problem flirting with that tart at Cunningham's office when it served your purpose. Why not Vasquez?"

"Because he's a man and I'm not gay." Logan grated.

"Couldn't you fake it?"

"Jackie—" Luke tried.

"You wouldn't take one for the team?"

He actually growled at me.

"So much for your professional commitment."

Logan chucked his thumb at Luke. "Why aren't you hounding him about it?"

I rolled my eyes. "Duh. Because we were wearing matching wedding rings. It would be too obvious. Besides, you're more his flavor there Tall, Dark and Surly."

A vein pulsed in Logan's forehead. "I swear—"

"Let's go to Gomez's place." Luke cut in. "We'll get your car later."

"Why?" Logan turned the engine over and pulled out of the lot.

"We can now, right Jackie?"

I nodded. "The twenty-four hours are up. I haven't been inside yet. I want to get a feel for the place."

Traffic was heavy over the causeway, many of Miami's inhabitants shifting from the downtown work to nighttime haunts out by the beach. By the time we pulled into Gomez's lot, the moon was up, hanging fat and bloated in the sky like an overfed tourist.

Using the key, I ripped the crime scene seal and unlocked the door. It didn't creek open eerily the way I'd imagined and I was a smidge disappointed. "Smells bad in here."

"A dead body will do that to a place." Luke murmured.

I looked over at him. His jaw was set in a grim line and he was poised to spring. Luke had witnessed many unpleasant things in his time in the corps and the stench of death heavy in the stale air probably brought a lot of unpleasant memories to the surface. Logan had found her first, but Luke had seen more than his share of death.

I squeezed my husband's hand. "It's after work hours and all three of us don't need to be here. Why don't you try to talk to some of the neighbors again while Logan and I poke around?"

Both of them stared at me with matching expressions of incredulity.

"I'm serious, Luke. It makes sense. You're easier to talk to. Logan will look out for me." I had the utmost faith in that statement, more than I was comfortable with.

"If you're sure?" Relief mixed with indecision crossed his face.

"We won't be long." I gave him my best reassuring smile.

Logan and I stood shoulder to shoulder and watched him climb the stairs.

"Big of you. Volunteering to be alone with me," the Dark Prince muttered.

"I just wanted to give you more grief about your new boyfriend, Sergeant Hottie. You know he's too good for you." I turned my back on him and tried the wall switch. No lights. "Either the police cut the power or Fester was behind on his bills."

"I've got a mini maglight on my keychain." He fished it out and clicked it on and a thin beam of light illuminated the dark space. "Where to?"

I considered it a moment. "Show me where you found her."

"Bathroom." Logan moved toward the back of the house, through the lone bedroom in the direction of the attached bath.

I gripped his arm in the bedroom, pulling him to a stop and pointed up. "Shine it at the ceiling, please."

He focused the beam upward and whistled low at the missing chunks of plaster. "Didn't even see that before. How did you know it was there?"

"One of the cops I made nice with mentioned the ceilings would need to be repaired. What do you suppose could have done that?"

"Only one thing I know of other than a light or fan that a person would hang from the ceiling in the bedroom." His tone held amusement.

82

There was a pause because my mind was completely blank. "And that would be?"

"A sex swing, one not installed properly by the looks of it." He waited for my reaction.

I didn't give him one, though I cringed on the inside. "Fits with the website theme." I pulled open the folding doors of the closet. "Empty. The police probably bagged and tagged everything in evidence. Do you remember seeing anything unusual?"

Logan shook his head. "I was in the zone, focused on getting to whoever was in here and helping the occupant."

I knew Logan had been a Navy Corpsman, though I'd never gotten a healing vibe off of him, just a dangerous one.

"There must have been something," I insisted "A man needs things to set up a den of iniquity."

Logan shined the flashlight on his own face. "Seriously? Den of Iniquity?"

"Shut up. I read." I moved past him to the bathroom. Medicine cabinets stood empty. "Rats, I was hoping to get a lead on Gomez's doctor."

"The cops were thorough, took everything that wasn't nailed down. Though from what I noticed, there wasn't much to begin with. " Logan shined the light around. "She was there, in the tub."

"So walk me through it. What did it look like when you came in?"

He gave me a funny look. "A dead girl in the tub."

I sighed in exasperation. "We have *got* to work on your communication skills. I mean, what did you see. Was there blood?"

"Everywhere." His tone was even darker than usual.

"Stabbed to death. How many times?" I pressed.

He frowned at me. "You're kinda gruesome, you know that, right?"

"Just trying to figure out if it was a crime of passion or not."I folded my arms over my chest and waited.

Logan sighed. "More times than the job required, considering the mess. She looked like hamburger."

"Now who's the gruesome one?" I studied the white tiles but the cleaning crew had already been through I was no forensic tech. "Was she wearing anything?"

"No, but the shower curtain had been draped over her."

"Over her face, right?"

Logan frowned at me. "Yeah. How did you know?"

"I've worked with enough law enforcement to pick up a few things. Typically a victim is only covered when the killer is someone who knows her, to hide what they've done. Out of remorse."

"You think he'd have found a better hiding spot than this bathtub."

"Maybe he intended to move the body and was just waiting for cover of darkness. Or if Gomez was the killer, maybe he wasn't strong enough to move her by himself. That still doesn't explain why he wasn't paying his rent, though."

We walked back out to the kitchen and I checked the pipes and ran water in the sink. "We'll get a professional cleaning crew in here once the eviction goes through and then Aaron can rerent the place."

"I don't envy him that task." Logan said.

84

Just for the hell of it, I opened the cabinets. "They even took his dishes. If there were any."

"It'll make our lives easier, less stuff to have stored."

I opened the dishwasher. At first glance it appeared to be empty but then I saw something all the way in the back. "Someone left a mug."

Luke brought the light closer. "There's something written on it."

I grabbed a tissue out of my beat-up purse and picked it up. "The 11th Street Diner. Hey, I know that place. It's just up Washington Avenue, not three blocks from here. Big post-clubbing hotspot, traditional blue plate specials, popular with tourists and locals." I put the mug back where I'd found it and made a mental note to call Vasquez.

We met up with Luke in the stairwell. "Any luck?" I was hopeful.

He shook his head. "No one knows Gomez."

"That's too weird, he's been a resident for years." It made no sense to me.

"Maybe he was a loner," Logan muttered.

"People remember loners," I insisted. "That way when a pet or child goes missing, they know who to blame."

"Now what?" Luke asked.

"Feel like grabbing a bite?" Logan asked. "I'm in the mood for diner fare."

Chapter Eight

As far as Miami Beach landmarks go, the 11th Street Diner has the most mileage under its belt. Built in Haledon New Jersey in 1948, the Art Deco Dining Car spent over four decades in Wilkes Barre Pennsylvania before migrating south to the corner of 11th and Washington Ave in South Beach. Its doors stood open twenty four hours a day, seven days a week, serving terrific food at blue plate prices. Aside from the restaurant there's a bar area with a hand painted mural, traditional booth seating and an outdoor patio. My kind of haunt.

By the time we arrived, the diner had hit the lull between early bird specials and the post club hopping crowd. Though I flashed Gomez's picture to every employee there, no one recognized him.

We slid into a booth and ordered coffee and burgers and I called Vasquez. "Hi, this is Jackie Parker. I had a question about the tenant's personal belongings."

There was a pause, "What belongings?"

I blinked. "You know, the stuff your team took out of the place?"

"Mrs. Parker, we only remove evidence from a crime scene."

"You mean Gomez's apartment was totally empty?"

"That's exactly what I'm saying." His tone was brisk.

"What about her stuff?" I pressed, glancing at my sad little purse. "Every woman has stuff. "Did she have a bag or—"

He sighed. "All right, I'll be straight with you. The girl had no belongings, which is why we are having such a hard time identifying her. No I.D. no keys or even a change of undergarments."

"Maybe the killer took her stuff." I was spit-balling, not really sure why Fester Gomez would want to hide his victim's identity when he left her body to be discovered in his own apartment. Unless he wasn't her killer.

"It's possible," Vasquez said, though his tone was dubious. "So far we have no leads. She doesn't match any missing person reports. Her prints and dental records came back, but so far, no match. The trail has gone cold."

"So that's it?"

"It's the best I can do." Vasquez didn't sound happy about it. "There are other cases that need my attention, cases with a real shot at a solution. Mr. Gomez is officially a person of interest and we'll do everything in our power to find him but until we do, we're stuck. If you find out anything else, contact me."

I hung up the phone and cursed. I relayed my conversation to Luke and Logan and summed up. "He didn't come right out and say it, but the police are giving up on discovering her identity."

"It doesn't seem right." Logan said.

Neither of us argued with him.

"So now what?" Luke looked from me to Logan and back again.

"There's nothing else we can do but evict Gomez." I said. It was so anticlimactic and disappointment bogged me down. "I'll call Aaron's assistant tomorrow and see about fixing the damages so he can rerent the place as soon as possible."

Our food arrived and we chewed in silence. For once I wasn't hungry. Instead, I stared out the window, watching traffic—both cars and pedestrian—stream by. The diner was an excellent people watching spot.

My phone rang and I answered without reading the number. "Hello?"

"Jackie?" The nervous warble belonged to the absolute last person I wanted to talk to.

"Mom," My tone was flat. Both the Parker brothers stared at me and I stared at my mug of coffee. "What's up?"

"Honey could you come over?" At least she sounded sober.

I winced. "Kinda busy right now, Mom."

"Always too busy, Miss Too Good for Her Own Mother." Her tone turned snarky.

Way to entice me to see her. Celeste sure knew how to put the fun in dysfunction. "No really, we're starting up our own business and I—"

"Twenty three hours of labor to bring you into this world and now you can't even spare fifteen minutes for me?"

Criminy. "Be there soon, Mom."

88

Luke asked, "What now?"

I shook my head. "She wants me to come over. Really channeling the Blanche Dubois drama tonight."

"Let the good times roll." Logan extracted his wallet. "I've got this, guys."

Luke and I waited for him in the truck, the cab filled with tense silence. "Do you want me to go with you?" he asked.

I shook my head, then realized he couldn't see me in the dark. "No, just drop me off at Bessie Mae and have bail money ready in case I need it."

I was only half joking.

An hour later I was parked in front of my mother's doublewide trailer. It was a pretty nice place, much nicer than anywhere we'd lived while I was growing up. I'd bought it in cash for her a few years ago and held the deed so she couldn't mortgage it and take the money to the dog track.

The dim lighting from inside spilled through the screen and I ducked inside quickly. "Mom?"

My mother scurried from the back room wearing her ankle length silk nightgown. She was an aged version of me. Not even fifty, she was a little shorter and a little wider at the substantial hips, but same chestnut hair, same blue eyes, same traffic-stopping rack. Years of professional partying had added lines to her face, but she was still a good looking woman. Like those dogs that are both cute and useless, the cute saved them from the pound.

"Oh honey, I'm so glad you're here. It's Richard."

I tried not to roll my eyes and failed. My mother was a recovering drug addict and notorious drama queen. I'd asked her not to get involved with the old geezer but once again it appeared she did what

89

she pleased and left me to clean up after her. "What about him?"

She slipped into her raincoat. "I need you to help me carry him home."

"Carry him?" I repeated. "What, is he drunk?"

"No, I'm pretty sure he's dead."

I stared at her. Took in the way she was dressed. The trailer wasn't that big, just one bedroom, the living area, bathroom and kitchen. I could see for myself that he wasn't in the main living areas. I looked at her ensemble again then my eyes went to the hall.

"He's in the bedroom," she wrung her hands, her words confirming my horror. "We were, that is he'd just—"

"Mom!" I made a beeline for the hall. The bedroom door was open. Everything looked normal, except for the corpse in the bed. Dick Stanley hadn't been an attractive man in life and death wasn't an improvement. "Holy fricking hell, you shagged him to death!"

"Keep your voice down," my mother hissed. "You have to help me get him home!"

"Mom, you need to call the police." Dear Lord, the stiff had a stiffy, I could see it tenting the sheet. I tasted bile in the back of my throat.

"Then his bastard grandson will evict me! You know he never liked the idea of me and Richard."

"Neither did I, but obviously that didn't stop you." I waved at the bed. "I'm calling 911." I rummaged for my cellphone. The battery was dead, of fricking course. Pivoting on my heel, I turned for the landline in the kitchen.

"Wait, Jackie, think about this! If word gets out that he died here like that, my reputation will be ruined. Everyone will know. I'll never get married."

90

"Mom, this is no time for maudlin theatrics." Although I did feel for her. My mother was a trophy wife that had never managed to land a rich husband. She couldn't take care of herself or make a smart decision to save her life. I'd been taking care of her as far back as I could remember.

"Please, Jackie, I'm begging you." Tears shimmered in her blue eyes.

I looked from her face to the dead man and back. If we were caught in the act, all my ins with law enforcement, all my years of networking and making connections would be flushed down the toilet.

So we couldn't get caught.

"Get me a tarp and some bungee cords. If we're going to do this, we'd better do it right."

****

"He's one heavy SOB," I grunted as we staggered up the stairs to Richard's trailer. Full rigor mortis had set in and while Stanley was definitely as stiff as a board, he was in no way light as a feather. The random thought about how my mother could've born all his substantial weight on her took root in my brain and I almost gagged. Stupid gray matter, flashing those images. "Get the door."

My mother was huffing and sweating as she dropped his feet.

"Careful! The M.E.s are overworked and because he had a heart attack it should be open and shut, but if we leave any obvious signs the body's been moved, there'll be questions."

"Sorry." She skirted past where I was poised on the stairs hefting the dead man in the blue tarp. "It's locked."

Of course it was. "Go back and get his clothes. The keys are probably in his pants."

91

She set him down, and I followed suit. Sweat dripped into my eyes from more than just exertion in the Florida humidity. This was bad and the longer we farted around, the more likely someone would see us and phone the cops.

I wanted to kick the tarp but thought better of it. "Couldn't you just keep it in your pants, you old fossil?" Luke would probably divorce me if he ever found out about this. Once he stopped laughing, of course.

Mom scuttled back, her white nighty gleaming in the darkness. Real subtle-like. I promised God then and there that if we pulled this off, not only would I go to church, I'd go to all of them in the area to praise His name.

Finally the door was open and the lecherous old hump was back in his bed. We rolled him off the tarp, vacuumed the dirt from the bed, left his clothes in a pile next to the hamper and then scurried like rats back to my mother's trailer.

"You need to burn those sheets. Maybe the mattress, too." I told her as I stuffed the tarp into the trash bag. "Hell Mom, if you want to move and sell the place, I say go for it."

"No, I'll be okay here. Thanks to you."

I felt guilty as sin for more than one reason. I'd staged my first crime scene and I'd done it because I'd rather go to jail than have my mother come live with me.

She poured us sweet tea and we sat at the table to drink it and let the air conditioning swirl around us.

"Do you think we should call the police now?" She asked.

I shook my head. "He's fine where he is. If no one finds him by the morning, I'll call his office with an urgent question about the septic line. When they can't reach him, someone will come looking." It scared me a little how organized I was in this deception.

Mom nodded, accepting my words but then her eyes filled up. "I can't believe he's gone."

"Don't feel too bad for him, that's how all men want to go." I stood up, uncomfortable with her tendency to over emote. "Gotta head home. Luke will be wondering where I am."

"Jackie," she sniffled, took my hand and squeezed it.

"Yeah, yeah, I'm your favorite daughter and all. Get some rest, okay?"

I drove home with the radio on loudly to keep me awake and drown out the thoughts in my head. Our door was unlocked and the Dark Prince was parked on the sofa watching Nick at Nite. "Hey," he said and muted the television.

"Hey," I staggered to the fridge and pulled out a beer. "You want one?"

"Sure," he came over and took it from me. "You're not usually a beer drinker."

"The occasion seems to call for it." I swigged it back. "Luke go to bed?"

Logan leaned against the counter. "About an hour ago. How'd it go with your mom?"

Maybe it was the fact that I knew he could keep a secret, or perhaps because he was the Dark Prince and he ruled the night, but for whatever reason I blurted out, "She screwed her landlord to death and then called me to help carry his body across the trailer park."

Not a sound except Felix the Cat ticking away on the wall. I waited and took another pull off my beer. He didn't make a sound but I saw his chest shaking with silent hysterics.

I punched him on the shoulder. "It's not freaking funny! It was like carrying a beached whale back to the water and the whole time knowing that my mother had delivered the death nookie."

"You're killing me," he wheezed, leaning against the counter for support. "Death nookie, Jesus. That's how I wanna go."

See?

Watching him lose it sent me over the edge and I laughed alongside him. It was ridiculous, absurd. It was my life in a nutshell.

The bedroom door opened and a rumpled Luke stumbled out. "What's so funny?"

Logan and I struggled to regain our composure. "Death nookie," I croaked. And we were off again.

"I don't get it. Glad to see you two getting along though." Luke headed back to bed.

Chapter Nine

The steady buzz of my vibrating cell phone pulled me from nightmares of death and my mother in a negligée. I tugged it off the charger on my nightstand and grumbled, "Hello?"

"Hello, this is Roland Fisk." Some throat clearing "I'm trying to reach Damaged Goods Property Management. I have a job."

"A job?" I sat up, elbowing Luke in the process. "This is Jackie Parker from Damaged Goods. Can I ask where you got this number?"

"Aaron Tanner referred you. I'm in a bit of a bind you see, with one of my tenants on Sunrise Lane...." He went into an explanation of what he needed and my excitement grew.

I kneed Luke in some delicate places as I climbed over him, too wound to stay in bed. Aaron had referred us. Damaged Goods was more than a one shot wonder. I hopped on one foot, covering the mouthpiece so Mr. Fisk wouldn't hear my eager squeaks of joy or Luke's cussing.

95

"Will you take the job?" he asked.

I sucked in air and struggled to sound professional. "As it happens we have an opening today. My email address is on the card. If you send me the rental agreement, we'll get right to work."

"Thank you." Relief coated his tone. "I'll send it right away."

I hung up and pounced on my husband. "We've got another job! Aaron referred us! Which means he's going to pay us! We're officially in business!"

"That's great." He wrapped his arms around me, dragging me to him for a tight hug. I felt the tension he'd been carrying since finding the dead girl seep away. The Gomez case had felt like such a dead end but here we were with a new job.

"We've got so much to do." I hopped up again and dashed into the bathroom to start the shower. My hair stuck out every which way, defying all natural laws since I'd gone to bed with it wet. As tired as I'd been, no way would I have climbed into bed until I'd scrubbed off Dick Stanley's death cooties.

Luke followed me into the bathroom. "What's the job?"

The water was still cold, but I was too impatient to wait. "A house condemned by the county. All the other tenants in the area have relocated, but this guy refuses to go and the owner is collecting fines while he's waiting on the courts. He wants us to go in and convince him to leave. Tennant's name is Horace Cooper. I'll do a little digging after breakfast so we know who we're dealing with." Thank God for Google because it allowed me to be a socially acceptable stalker instead of a creepy lurking in the bushes sort.

"I'll let Logan know." Luke flushed the toilet and I yelped as my shower turned frigid. "Sorry."

"You don't sound the least bit sorry," I grumped.

I finished up quickly and pulled on a pair of jeans and a lightweight blouse. Before joining the guys, I telephoned Mom. "Just checking in. Anything new today?" I'd told her the night before not to say anything over the phone just in case the NSA had a satellite trained on her trailer park.

Her drama queen tendencies could always be counted on in a pinch. "Oh Jackie, you'll never believe it, but my landlord, Mr. Stevens, was found dead this morning."

"Oh no," I gasped as though this was the first I'd heard about it. "What happened?"

"His grandson came by for breakfast and found him naked as a jaybird in his bed."

"Do they know what happened?" I held my breath.

"Heart attack. Looks like it hit him while he was sleeping. They're taking him out now. I can see them from my bedroom window."

No investigation, hurray! I'd drink to that.

"It's so sad." Mom sniffled dramatically. "He was such a nice man, always so considerate."

He was a vile old letch and I was sorry I hadn't kicked him while he was down. "I've got to run, we have a job. I'll stop by later to check on you if you want."

Please say no. Please say no.

"That would be great." Drat. "Maybe we can finish that movie you fell asleep watching last night."

I rolled my eyes. "The one about the beached whale that went out with a bang? Thanks, but I'm not

97

a fan of nature films." I heard the doorbell chime. "Got to run, Mom."

I jogged out of the bedroom and opened my door to my mother-in-law. "Mom, what are you doing here?"

Marge bussed my cheek with a powdery kiss and pushed past me with all the authority of a drill sergeant. "I told you we were coming on Friday. You didn't forget, did you?"

"Next Friday." I went to the calendar hanging on the wall. "See, I even wrote it down. Friday the 26th."

She clucked like a chicken. "Today is the 26th, Jackie."

"Say what?" I'd lost an entire week?

Marge's crayoned eyebrows pulled together as she surveyed our space. "Where's your dining room table?"

"In the second bedroom."

She grabbed the handle of her rollerboard and dragged her huge bag in. "Well, that's a hell of a place for it."

"Long story," I said as Luke strolled in, followed by Logan.

"Hey Mama," Luke picked her up in a bear hug. Logan skirted the happy reunion and made tracks for the coffee pot.

"Look at you, so handsome." She cooed with pure adoration. "And with your hair growing back, finally. I hate those buzz cuts, you have such gorgeous hair, just like your brother."

A grunt of acknowledgment from the Dark Prince. He didn't take compliments well.

Luke set her carefully back on her feet. "Where's Dad?"

98

"Oh you know he stays at that hotel on the golf course the week leading up to the vow renewal."

Luke took her bag from her. "Why, when he can stay here?"

Logan and I exchanged looks, wondering where exactly. The livable space in our bungalow was already maxed out. He mouthed, "I'll take the couch." One problem down.

She waved the offer away. "It's good for him to have a taste of single life. He'll play a few rounds, order room service and appreciate me all the more come next Saturday. Anybody hungry?"

Without waiting for an answer, she strode right into the kitchen and pulled eggs and oranges from the fridge and bread from the cabinet. "Where's your juicer, Jackie?"

"At the store, waiting to be purchased."

"Smart ass," she winked at me, an affectionate gesture. "Okay, well I suppose we can make do with the prebottled stuff. How does French Toast sound?"

"Freaking fabulous." I watched in awe as my kitchen was transformed into a real working food preparation room.

"Mom, we've got work to do." Logan interrupted.

She actually rolled her eyes at him, the only woman who he'd let get away with that sans comment. "I know, but you still need to eat. Help your brother drag the table back out here where it belongs."

Logan looked at me.

"I'm hungry," I said with a shrug.

He shook his head and went to help Luke with the table.

Real cooking in my kitchen and Logan doing what he was told. I hugged her. "I love you Mom.

99

Don't ever leave us." Even if the timing was inconvenient, having her around was always a blast. She drank and cursed and criticized and accepted me in the same breath, the way only a mother could. I never had to be the grown-up with Marge. And she had yet to ask me to help her move a corpse.

Once we were all seated around the table, my mother-in-law rubbed her hands together. "So, we've got a lot to do. There's the shower tonight and the bachelor party and the bachelorette party next week, plus fittings and whatnot. I know you're all busy, but boys, try to be back by five for your fittings and you can go right from there to the club. Don't keep your father out too late. He needs his rest."

"Um, where's the shower?" Crap, I really thought I had another week.

Marge stared at me as if I'd lost my mind. "Here, of course."

I choked on my not so fresh squeezed orange juice. "Here?" I looked around at the construction zone, the spackled and unpainted walls, the bare light bulbs, and piles of sheetrock dust. "Oh, Marge, I don't think that's a good idea. We only have one working bathroom." And many of her friends had needs that required several trips to the loo.

"We'll just have to make due. Who's catering?"

I shifted as two generations of Parkers fixed their eyes on me. "Um, well, you see, I didn't exactly know I was in charge of this." As excuses went, it was lame as all get-out and their expressions told me they thought so, too.

"You're my matron of honor." Marge said slowly, as though talking to an idiot.

"I'll fix it, I promise." Even if I had to call in every IOU floating around the greater Miami-Dade

100

area, I wouldn't ruin this for Marge. She was too good to me.

Too bad she didn't have any dead bodies to carry, because that might be simpler. And I already had practice.

****

"What do we know, Jackie?" Logan asked me as we drove out to Sunrise Lane.

I dug out my notes. "Horace Cooper, age forty two. He has a vlog on being a prepper."

"A what?" Logan asked.

"A survivalist who thinks the End of Days is coming and they need to be ready for it." Luke answered. "Preppers are getting ready for the post-Apocalyptic world. Stocking up on canned goods, batteries, weapons and whatnot. A couple of guys from my platoon went that route. It's a slippery slope from prepared to complete nutjob."

Couldn't have said it better myself. "From the vlog entries, it looked like Cooper is in the second camp. Whatever the case, we have to do our level best to convince him to leave, before the property owner receives any more fines for unlawful inhabitance."

Sunrise Lane was in an all but abandoned area in the western part of the county, just shy of the Everglades. No sea breeze here, just a constant pressing humidity and the twisted, broken remnants of humanity. Moss crept over broken cinderblocks and tall grasses sprouted up through cracks in the concrete. Judging by the state of the area, I had no problem seeing why the place was being condemned.

We pulled up in front of the rental house, a drab little shotgun style with a sagging front porch and peeling salmon paint. Half a dozen burned out cars had settled around the place, missing obvious

101

parts. A ragtag chain-link fence held a pair of Dobermans who growled at our approach. It looked like a crack den.

"If the Apocalypse hits, how the hell will he know?" I asked.

"You going in hot?" Luke asked his brother.

"If this guy is stockpiling weapons, I think it's the best plan." Logan had a concealed carry permit and I saw him open the glove box and retrieve his 9mm. Luke was still waiting on his paperwork to go through.

"Jackie, wait in the car this time." Logan said.

"Good one." I popped the door and slithered to the ground, radiating a bravado I didn't feel. Male cursing drifted to me.

Luke sighed. "Just keep back a little. Make sure he has to go through us to get to you."

I didn't bother arguing but I had to admit I was in no hurry to get too close to Cooper. From the vlog, I knew he had crazy eyes and some pretty whacked out beliefs to go along with them.

Luke knocked on the front door. "Mr. Cooper? My name is Luke Parker. We work for your landlord."

The sound of a shotgun being ratcheted back was not at all reassuring.

Logan shoved me behind him, but Luke didn't budge. "We only want to talk."

"Go to hell." It was Cooper, I recognized his voice "You're on my property. I have the right to shoot you all where you stand."

"It's not your property," I bravely called out from my position behind the wall of Logan. "It's Mr. Fisk's house and the county says you can't live here anymore. I know it sucks, but no one in this situation has a choice."

The door opened and Horace Cooper appeared. Same salt and pepper crew cut, same crazy bloodshot eyes. He wasn't the kind of unstable that ranted and raved at random people on the street. No, his crazy held a glimmer of sanity, just enough to make him extremely dangerous. It was like staring at a King Cobra in a man's body. I shivered when his gaze landed on me.

"Get back in the car, Jackie," Luke murmured too low for Cooper to hear as Logan slowly reached for the handgun he had tucked in the waistband of his cargo pants.

"Hands where I can see 'em!" Horace leveled the double barrels at Logan's chest.

I swore under my breath and gripped my brother-in-law's wrist. He was a narcissistic jackass but I didn't want to see him get shot. "We're only here to get your side of the story."

His eyes lit up and I knew I'd hit pay dirt so I pressed on. "Would it be okay if we came in to see what's what?"

His eyes narrowed. "You don't work for the government?"

I shook my head. "No, Sir. We represent your landlord. He's had to pay a lot of money to the city because you won't leave. Let me come in and we'll see if we can come to a mutually beneficial understanding." If I could gain entrance to his house and find out what he was so protective of, maybe I could figure out a way to solve this dilemma.

"Jackie," Logan's tone held warning but Cooper lowered the shotgun.

"Just you." He waved at me and disappeared back inside.

"No." This from, Luke, firm but definite.

103

I turned to him, put a hand on his arm, glad I wasn't shaking. "We don't have a choice. Let me try and talk him down."

"Take this." Logan slipped the handgun beneath my waistband at the small of my back. I bit my lip, more afraid of shooting myself in the butt than anything else. "Call out if you need us."

And have the prepper and his arsenal take them both out? Hell no, but I nodded, figuring it wasn't really a lie if I didn't say it out loud. "I'll talk to him, gain his trust and be back in a jiff."

And if not, well, then I didn't have to worry about how to pull a bridal shower out of my ass.

Chapter Ten

"**W**ow." It was the only thing I could think to say to Mr. Cooper, or as Luke had deemed him, the nutjob. The entire building was lined with shelves and gave off the sense of organized chaos. Food in cans, boxes and vacuumed-sealed bags, probably several years' worth. Car batteries lined one wall and gas cans marched precisely along the other. Mountains of firewood stacked up the back wall. Weapons everywhere, munitions boxes of bullets ranging from shotgun shells to clips for a glock and magazines for the semi-automatic rifles. I spied a bow and a quiver of arrows as well as hunting knives, machetes, even a medieval ax.

Cooper was opening canned dog food into stainless steel dishes. "Have a seat."

Hell no, I was too afraid to breathe with that handgun in my waistband, never mind sit. I cleared my throat. "Mr. Cooper, you're a survival expert, right?"

Cooper grunted. "Ready to go completely off the grid. That way when the world ends, I'm not gonna lose a wink of sleep."

There seemed some holes in his plan, but I wasn't about to point that out. He opened the fridge and I pushed on. "I respect the way you're living, obviously this took years of work and—is that urine?"

Pint sized Mason jars filled with yellow fluid were stacked up in his fridge.

He nodded and I threw up in my mouth a little. "I'm boiling it down to the point where it's safe to drink."

My stomach flipped over. "Why?"

He looked at me like I was the nutjob. "In case the water table is contaminated. I got to get it right, to make sure all the bacteria is gone."

"And if it isn't?"

He unscrewed a cap and dumped it on the Alpo. "I test it on the dogs first."

Yuck, yuck yuck. Okay, obviously reason wasn't going to work here. Time to get tough. "Mr. Cooper, your landlord is willing to pay for a moving van to help you clear out."

He slammed the dog food can down on the cracked Formica counter. "I'm not leaving. They won't let me take it all."

He was right, most moving companies wouldn't transport gasoline, car batteries or ammunition.

"You don't have a choice here and neither does your landlord. This place isn't safe. The roof is about to cave in and the foundation is crumbling. What would happen if something landed on one of those gas cans? You're a survivalist, Mr. Cooper, but you won't survive in this place."

106

He stared at me so long I wondered if he was contemplating hacking me to little edible Jackie pieces and feeding me to his dogs. Then slowly, he nodded. "How long have I got?"

I already had my cell phone out. "Just let me make a few calls." If I could get the landlord to agree to compensate him for whatever he couldn't move, it'd be that much easier.

"I'll go feed the dogs," he said.

Poor creatures. I shook my head and dialed Luke. "We're good here. He's set to go. Call B-2 moving and storage and ask for Raul. He'll hook us up with a van, just move the truck out of the way. I'll call Mr. Fisk and see if he'll agree to sweeten the deal."

"You're a miracle worker," Luke breathed. "We'll move the truck and be right back to help."

"Approach cautiously, he's still pretty squirrelly." Not to mention batshit crazy. "I'll see you in a few." Unspent adrenaline jangled around in my system like loose change in a jogger's pocket. I shifted my weight as I scrolled through my cellphone history, searching for Mr. Fisk's number. I dialed but the cell phone beeped, telling me I'd lost my signal. Oh what the hell? I'd just been talking to Luke. I took a step back to see if I could find it again and tripped over a gas can. Gasoline spilled out all over the threadbare carpet, the stench heavy in the confined space.

Cursing, I scrambled to regain my purchase and knocked over the shotgun propped in the corner, the loaded one Cooper had held on us. It hit the floor and discharged, the safety having never been reengaged. The trail of fuel ignited, leading straight for the munitions corner.

I ran, not waiting to see if I could put it out in time because the place was going to go up like a

107

Roman candle. I didn't want to be anywhere near it when that happened.

Booking toward the front door, I jumped off the rickety porch and hit the ground, still in motion. Luke and Logan jogged toward me, but I waved them back, flapping both hands like I was a giant bird trying to take off. "Get back!"

A roar filled the background and I saw the Parker brothers stop in their tracks. Shouting could be heard from the left of us, but I didn't turn around. The worst was yet to come.

I hit Luke square in the chest just as the massive explosion engulfed the condemned bug out house in a fiery inferno.

"That's one way to get him out." Logan said.

We watched as flames busted out the few remaining windows and licked their way up to the roof.

I panted, struggling for breath. "Better back up in case there's another—"

A second explosion caved in the roof, consuming the shingles in a massive fireball. In the distance, sirens grew closer.

"Jesus," Luke said. "What the hell did he have in there?"

"You bitch!" This from Cooper who stormed around the side of the house, mangy looking dogs in tow. "You destroyed my stuff!"

"It was an accident," I wheezed. "I'm so sorry."

"You're sorry?" Cooper waved his hands around, the crazy no longer contained just to his eyes. His face was covered with soot and even his dogs looked wary. "That took me years to accumulate, years! Gone in a second. I'll make you pay for this!"

Luke and Logan boxed him in. "Stand down now."

The livid tenant shoved at them, trying to get through them to me. Luke had him down on the ground with his arms pinned behind his back while Logan wrapped the flexicuffs around his wrists. Cooper rolled in the dirt, wriggling like a snake, still vowing all sorts of doom on me.

"Jackie, call 911, tell them what happened. And give Logan his weapon back so he can stow it before the cops get here."

I'd forgotten all about the 9mm in my waistband. After carefully handing it over to Logan, I called 911 and filled them in. The sirens drew closer as the house continued to burn.

The fire truck was first on the scene and as they uncoiled their hoses, the cops pulled up. Luke and Logan and I all raised our hands and explained who we were. Cooper writhed around in the dirt, still promising vengeance.

"He's the tenant," I said. "This place was condemned."

"Call the owner," The officer advised me. "Find out if he wants to press charges."

I dialed Mr. Fisk's number

"Is it taken care of?" His question was full of anxiety. "He won't try to come back, will he?"

I looked from the fuming Cooper to the smoldering remains of the house. "Pretty sure that won't be a problem."

****

"Why do you three smell like smoke?" Marge frowned when we trooped back into the house.

109

"Just work stuff," I said and turned to Luke. "Go ahead and shower, you have to go get measured in an hour."

"I'll be quick." He headed into our bedroom.

Marge's purse rang. "That'll be the florist." She grabbed it and headed out to the verandah, leaving me alone with the Dark Prince.

"So," I said, fully prepared to get blasted on the Cooper house situation.

"What are you doing about the bridal shower?" he asked, surprising me.

When I raised my eyebrows he waved around the living room. "Separate work and personal lives, right? We're in the personal space."

"Ah." I had to admit I was impressed with his restraint, I didn't think he had it in him. "Well, I've got it handled." I hoped. I'd arranged it this morning and been texting nonstop at every chance I got but hadn't seen the progress yet.

"Good." Awkward pause. "Jackie, I want to tell him."

I'd opened the fridge and grabbed a hold of two bottles of water, but was stuck in the bent over position, unable to believe what he'd just said in his smoke roughened voice. Felix ticked on the wall while I tried to get my brain to work.

Logan didn't move either. "It's not right, the three of us working together and him being in the dark. We've got to tell him."

I swallowed and stood up. "Tell him what, exactly? That you and I collided in a one night stand a million and a half hours before I even met him? How will that help him, Logan?"

110

"It's not right." He took the bottle of water from me but set it down on the counter unopened. "If I were him, I'd want to know."

"Would you really? You'd want to know that your wife had slept with your brother? You want to know what I think?"

A muscle jumped in his jaw. "Probably not, but go ahead anyway."

I ignored that. "I think you're sick of feeling guilty."

"Exactly," he nodded. "We're both guilty."

"Of what? Being young and stupid? If that were a crime, everyone would be locked up."

Not even a ghost of a smile.

I sighed. "Logan, I'll be honest. I don't like keeping secrets from him and at times I do feel guilty about it, especially when you imply that I'm a liar and a whore."

He winced but kept quiet.

"But I deal with all of that crap because keeping this secret isn't just to protect me, or you. It's for him. Knowing would only hurt him and drive a wedge between the two of you and upset our marriage. I just got him back and we're still adjusting to being together full time. Is easing your conscience really worth all that collateral damage?"

He looked away and I could tell that for him, this wasn't over. At least he was listening to what I said. I touched his hand lightly. "I'm sorry that this is so hard on you, I really am. The last thing I want is for you to hate me."

"I could never hate you, Jackie." He looked back at me, dark eyes filled with emotion. His Adam's apple bobbed as he reached to push a sooty lock of hair away from my face. "Never."

111

"Yes, Lorna, cocktails at seven. See you then." The backdoor slammed and we both jumped as Marge bustled back into the kitchen.

Logan cleared his throat. "I better go get ready."

"You do that." Never mind that he'd have to either crawl in the tub with Luke or use the hose out back to clean up. I was ready for the awkwardness to end.

Alone with Marge, I forced a chipper smile. "So, you ready for your shower?" If it was anyone else in the world I'd blow it off to make another ice cream baby, but Marge deserved my all.

She glanced around my train wreck of a bungalow and forced a smile. "I'm sure it'll be great."

"Oh, we're not having it here."

"Thank God." Immediately, she looked apologetic. "That is, I'm sure it'll be a very nice house, when it's done."

At the rate we were going that would be about quarter past never. "It will, which is exactly what I wanted to show you."

She frowned. "I'm not sure I understand."

Eh, my actual shower could wait, I was too excited to see what my friends had pulled off. "If you'll follow me."

I led her out the back door and into the humid evening air. We navigated down the unfinished steps and squished across the lawn to Mr. Murphy's house. Rebecca saw us coming and opened the door to the Florida room with a big smile. "Right on time."

"Oh my," Marge blinked, clearly stunned.

I grinned. Her reaction was the perfect reward for what was sure to be an astronomical cell phone bill. But my friends had come through.

112

Marcy stood on a ladder, hanging gauze from the doorway. Silver and white balloons floated up to the glass ceiling. Twinkle lights wrapped around the pillars and a white bouquet of roses stood perfectly arranged in a bowl on the glassed-topped table. A wishing well made of cardboard covered tulle had been erected in the center of the room, right next to a chaise lounge for our guest of honor. A portable bar took up one wall and Shonda and Gertie talked to the young mixologist who'd be concocting what was sure to be a bazillion chocolatinis. I was afraid to touch anything so I stood and admired my friends' handy work.

"Oh Jackie." Tears welled in my mother-in-laws eyes. "Oh honey, it's lovely."

"I'm glad you like it."

"How on earth did you do all this in one day?"

"Magic." Plus the best friends and a stellar credit card. "Rebecca, would you mind showing my mother-in-law the house before her guests arrive? I want her to see why I'm living in the middle of renovation purgatory."

"Sure thing."

"Thank you, sweetie." Marge stayed down wind as she left.

"Kudos to the decorating committee." I said.

Marcy climbed off the ladder. "Thanks. It was fun actually. I've got the cold cuts platter and potato salad in the fridge, and a chocolate mousse cake that I'd sell a limb for in the freezer."

"The guests?"

"All but three said they'd come."

"The gifts?"

She winked. "I know a guy who owns an adult book store. You ever hear of Jenna McCormick? These old broads are in for quite a thrill."

"You are a bloody miracle worker. What do you want, my firstborn?"

"Put in a good word for me with your brother-in-law and we'll call it square."

I choked a little on my own spit.

"Jeeze," Marcy said, looking me over from head to toe. "You look like you could use a drink. Come on."

"When you said you'd buy me a drink, I didn't think you'd go to such extremes. And just what the hell happened to you now?" Shonda asked as we sauntered up to the bar.

"I blew some guy's house up." I smiled at the bartender, who must be Shonda's cousin, Deborah. She wore a professional smile, though her eyebrows went up at my comment. "Thanks so much for doing this on such short notice."

"No problem. Can I get you a drink?"

She could get me a tanker, but I shook my head. "I'm going home to get cleaned up first."

"Honey, you're gonna need a sandblaster to get rid of that stank." Shonda waved her hand in front of her face.

"You're right, she smells bad," Gertie agreed. She wore lime green knee socks and penny loafers under a paisley dress that was at least six sizes too big for her, but at least there were no Post-it's in sight.

I was surprised to see her out. And here. "How you doing, Gertie?"

"Better than you, obviously." She turned back to her drink.

Well if that didn't just say it all.

114

Chapter Eleven

Squeaky clean and loaded down with a mudslide, I watched my mother-in-law open her "gifts". Since this was a yearly event, her friends had long since resorted to giving donations to various charities in Marge's name. A few more risqué items like a red peignoir and fuzzy purple handcuffs added to the fun. Overall, the shower was more an excuse to get together, have a few drinks and gossip, a real girl's night in that profited the dogs and the dolphins.

Marcy's chocolate flavored penis pops were a big hit, though I could have lived a long and happy life without seeing Gertie noshing on one, and the sight of Ethel Kramer, my former home economics teacher, removing her dentures before inserting the phallic-shaped treat would haunt me forever.

I followed Rebecca into the kitchen to help clean up the food trays. "Thanks again for letting us do this here."

"No problem." She stretched some plastic wrap over a tray. "Dad would have gotten a kick out of it."

"How is he?" I bent to load empty plates into the dishwasher.

"Safer, if not happier. He's so forgetful. It's like I have three kids to keep an eye on now, not just two."

"I know exactly what you mean." I thought about my mother. Shoot, I'd forgotten that I'd promised to stop by and now that I'd been drinking, it was too late. She was probably out, trolling for a new man to help fill the void Richard left.

No pun intended.

"Anyway, do you know anyone who might want to buy this place?" Rebecca stowed the leftovers in the fridge.

"You're selling?" I don't know why that came as a surprise to me. It made sense. Mr. Murphy couldn't live alone anymore and Rebecca had her own place.

She nodded, expression stressed, though she hid it well. "Have to in order to get him into a decent nursing home. I just can't take care of him and the girls fulltime."

I squeezed her arm reassuringly. "I'll spread the word—see what we could come up with." It'd be nice to have a say in who bought this beautiful house, since they'd live next door to me and all.

Shonda poked her head around the corner. "Deborah has to get going—she has an eight o'clock class tomorrow. The bar's all packed up."

"Shame." I wasn't nearly as toasted as I deserved to be. Then again it was my responsibility to make sure everyone got home safely, which I couldn't do if I was passed out drunk. "I'll see her out."

Deborah drove an ancient VW bus that was parked at the curb. She was struggling to shove the portable bar up the ramp and not having much success.

"Can I give you a hand?"

She sent me a relieved look. "That'd be great. I usually have a co-bartender to help me out, but he's in the Keys on vacation. Just hold it still so I can straighten out the wheels."

116

I slid into place in front of the portable bar and she moved around it and kicked at the little mechanical wheels until it was in position. She pulled, I pushed and the cart creaked and groaned up into the back of the bus.

Deborah locked the wheels and strapped it into place with a series of bungee cords. Wire mesh separated the bench seat in front from the hodgepodge of stuff in back. There was a great deal more than just bartending supplies. A battery powered lamp and an armchair took up one corner, and a crate of texts sat next to it. A mini fridge, toaster and a hotplate sat beneath a fold up table. Several duffels had duct taped labels marked, work, school, other and laundry. "Wow, you could practically live out of here."

"I do." Deborah finished strapping down the bar. "At least during the week. Then I drive to my parent's house in Sarasota on the weekends when I don't have a gig. Saves on rent."

I'd been kidding and her answer took me aback. "What about a bed? And a bathroom? Electricity?"

"Chair folds out into a single. And everything is battery powered, charges when the engine is on. As for bathroom, either the school locker rooms or I park at a friend's place and use theirs. I tried keeping an apartment, but I was never there and it was such a waste to spend that kind of money on rent. This way, I can live at the beach for next to nothing."

Sounded a little scary to me, but I lived in a construction zone and had no room to judge. "Just be safe, okay? Lots of whackos out there that would carjack you in a heartbeat."

She shrugged. "I've got a gun."

117

Was I the only Florida resident who didn't? I'd once had a blue hair with glasses thicker than an old-fashioned coke bottle pull a .22 on me at a stoplight for breaking at a yellow. Seemed I made her late for the early bird special.

I handed Deborah her fee plus a hefty tip and we both exited the back of her van.

"Besides, it's not like four walls and a deadbolt could really stop them if they were determined. This way at least I'm always on the move and it would take them a while to track me down."

I watched the VW's taillights disappear around the corner, but my thoughts were out on South Beach. Had Fester Gomez thought along the same lines as Deborah? The medical examiner stated that the girl with the purple nail polish had been dead for days, but what if Gomez had moved out weeks before and was living out of a vehicle somewhere, oblivious to what had happened?

Before I thought it through, I dialed Luke's cell. He picked up on the first ring. "Kill me now."

In the background men shouted angrily or laughed loudly. "Let me guess, sports bar?"

"You know dad, he's a creature of habit. We always end up at *Racks* for stale beer, bumpy pool tables and girls in low cut tops. Why bother going out when I've got the best set in town at home?"

"Flatterer. Listen, I have a theory on Gomez."

Luke groaned. "Jackie, let it go. Aaron's got his place back, our job is done and the police have an APB out on Gomez. There's nothing else we can do, babe."

"But what if it wasn't him? You and I both know that the solve rate for homicides in this county is less than one in four. Considering they still haven't I.D.ed the victim, I don't have a lot of faith. Luke, you

118

saw that girl. Doesn't her family deserve to know her killer has been brought to justice?"

"Of course. But Jackie, you're not a detective. This isn't your job."

He was right but that didn't mean I had to admit defeat. "Will you just hear me out?"

"I can barely hear anything, it's so loud here. We'll talk about it when we get home."

"Have fun, and don't overspend. I'm going to have to sell a kidney to pay for your mother's shower as it is."

"So, I guess you're out of the favor business?"

Gertie waved to me from the front window and I turned away so she wouldn't see me grimace. "Permanently. See you soon."

"Not soon enough, hot stuff." Luke hung up.

I sat down on the curb and jiggled my phone. Though he hadn't said anything, I could tell Luke was still affected from discovering the murder victim. It was wrong to keep bringing it up with him when he just wanted to move on. But I knew someone who would be up, thinking about the purple nail polish wearer the same way I was.

I scrolled through my recent contacts until I found Vasquez's number. "I have a theory," I said when he picked up.

"Mrs. Parker, I don't have time for idle speculation."

"Just hear me out. You told me yesterday that Gomez's apartment had nothing in it when you found the girl. Doesn't that seem weird to you? I mean, it's right across the street from the beach, you'd think we'd find some towels, suntan lotion, a change of skivvies. Our property owner hadn't been paid for

119

three months. So what if Gomez had moved out before the mystery woman moved in?"

"And then the killer took all her stuff, other than the diner mug you found? What does that prove?"

"That whoever killed her knew her and knew that her identity could lead the police back to him." I was proud of myself for connecting those dots two drinks in. "Which matches the fact that she was covered when she was found."

"So, you're saying the killer knew her personally, but it wasn't Gomez? I don't buy it. What about the website?"

I'd forgotten about that. "Maybe he sold it. Had a sick girlfriend or whatever, sold the business, complete with the website address, kissed off his security deposit and took off. He was making money from that website, right? And part of that money would be linked with the domain. So Gomez puts up a for sale sign, new guy buys the brand, promises to take over Gomez's lease, and Gomez rides off into the sunset, oblivious to what went down. Either way, he didn't kill her."

Vasquez was quiet for a moment. "It's thin."

"Anorexically so. But you've got to admit it's possible."

"I won't admit to anything until I talk to Gomez. And I can't do that until he surfaces."

He wasn't saying no, and that was a good sign. "Thank you for listening."

"May I ask you a question?"

"Logan's single."

That earned me a deep laugh. "And as straight as an arrow, no doubt. But that's not what I meant. Why are you so invested in the Gomez case?"

120

I wasn't really sure. "Maybe because once upon a time, I wore purple nail polish and would have done almost anything to keep a roof over my head. Good choices are for people who *have* choices. My team found her and this feels personal to me."

Vasquez seemed to accept that. "I'll let you know when I find Gomez."

"Thanks." I hung up and rejoined the party.

****

Marge had the coffee already made by the time I got up the next morning. Logan was sprawled on the couch, snoring like a moose in full rut.

"It's not too hot yet. Let's take our coffee and sit on the verandah so we don't wake the boys."

"Just promise me you'll chase away any gulls that try to nest in my hair." I pointed to my rat's nest 'do, which was really more of a don't.

I had a pair of bedazzled flip flops by the back door that I slid my feet into before moving out to the humid morning air. I left her the slatted sunbather and perched against the railing, furtively hoping I wouldn't end up with splinters in my butt.

"Did you have fun yesterday?" I asked and sipped my coffee, barely stifling an orgasm. I don't know what she did to a pot of java, but I'd sell my left boob for the secret. That's my favorite boob, too.

Marge beamed. "I really did. You didn't have to go to all that trouble."

A snort escaped. Of course I did, she wouldn't have let me live it down otherwise. Marge may be awesome, but she's still my mother-in-law. "Glad you liked it."

She smiled, but then looked away. "Jackie, is everything okay with you and Luke? I'm not trying to invade your privacy, I'm just concerned."

121

Had Luke said something to her, mentioned something that he didn't want to say to me? Luke was in no way a mama's boy, but after he snuck Logan in behind my back, I was beginning to realize just how little we truly knew about each other. "Is there a reason it wouldn't be?"

Her foot, shod in a fuzzy pink slipper, jiggled nervously. "Well, I'm curious as to why Logan is staying here."

Was that all? I could've keeled over in relief. "He's just crashing here while his apartment is fumigated."

Those bright green eyes fixed on me. "I heard you two talking yesterday. It sounded...intimate."

Oh *shit*. So not what I'd expected. My stomach flipped over like a griddle cake. "We were just...that is...um...?"

Way to be articulate, Jackie.

Marge's shrewd eyes fixed on me with laser-like intensity. "I'm going to ask you point blank. And please don't insult me by lying. Are you sleeping with Logan?"

"*No.*" The delicious coffee churned to sludge on my tongue and I set my cup aside. "No. Marge, I'd never do that to Luke. Never." It hurt that I'd even have to convince her. I thought she knew me better than that.

She cast a sidelong look to the door. "But you do know that he's in love with you."

I stared at her for a full minute, breath frozen in my lungs. I somehow managed to exhale a succinct. "No."

"No, you weren't aware or no—?"

"No, he's not in love with me." I shook my head, to get the thought out. "He hates me, most of the time and barely tolerates me the rest of it."

"I know my sons," Marge insisted. Christ, she was like a dog with a bone. "They're so very much alike and yet so different. It makes sense they'd fall for the same woman."

A nightmare. That had to be, it was the only explanation that I could wrap my head around. I had eaten one too many slices of pepper jack before bed and dreamed this whole clusterfuck up. Damn tasty party tray.

I licked my lips, oddly dry considering nothing stayed dry long in Miami. "Logan and I have a complicated history. I met him before.... " I waved my hand because I didn't know how to finish that sentence.

"Before? Before what?"

"Before Luke."

"And by 'met' you mean, 'slept with'?"

My heart pounded so fast I felt dizzy. I'd never confirmed this to another living soul and now my mother-in-law was asking me if I'd slept with one of her sons then married the other. I could give her a billion excuses, God knew I'd come up with a boatload of them over the years, but that wasn't what Marge deserved.

"Yes." I looked away, unable to meet her eyes.

She touched my bare knee. "Does Luke know?"

Wordlessly, I shook my head. It was too early to cry, I'd be puffy all day long. But the tears were thick in my throat, stinging behind my eyeballs.

But her next words, delivered with absolute conviction, knocked me flat on my ass.

"Good. Don't tell him."

Chapter Twelve

I wasn't always a well-adjusted certified process server. In high school I'd been voted most likely to appear on *Jerry Springer*. The trailer parks Celeste and I inhabited back then was more the stereotypical white trash sort, complete with rusted-out car parts that littered the cracked asphalt and each and every shabby abode packed to the gills with drunks and drug addicts. Mom was a younger, slimmer version of her drama queen self and most of the time I was the one putting *her* to bed.

Ah, memories.

The summer after graduation I had one goal—to find my bio dad. Like any kid who grew up never knowing her father, I envisioned some sort of superhero. I even had a list of characteristics in my head to help me keep a hazy mental picture of what he was like—strong, loyal, handsome, patient and responsible. Somewhere deep inside me I understood that if my father really *had* been all those things, he would still be with me and my mom, but that annoying little truth had no place in my fantasy world. I told myself he didn't know about me, that if he did he'd swoop in and take me away to his castle in England or a ski resort in the Swiss Alps, or beachfront mansion in Barbados. I wasn't fussy about the particulars.

As usual, Celeste was no help. I don't know if she truly didn't remember him or if she intentionally tried to keep me in the dark. No father had been listed on my birth certificate and my last name was Drummond, just like hers. When I asked about him, she'd say something like, "Oh, it was such a long time ago." Or, "I really didn't know him very well."

"What was his name?"

"Jesse? Or maybe Jeremy? Or was it Jamie?" She'd shrug and go back to painting her press-on nails.

"Where did the two of you meet? High school?"

She nodded. I'd known my mother had dropped out of high school to concentrate on partying, but again, the details were unclear. She surprised me though. "Round about that time, though I don't remember ever seeing him at school. We met on the beach, I think."

"Which beach?" I grilled her like a steak.

"I can't remember." She got that glassy look in her eyes and I knew Q&A time was over.

Finally though, I caught a break, in the form of her high school yearbook. I'd never seen it before, probably because she'd used it to balance the legs of her off the truck special nightstand.

Because she was thirty four, I knew she'd been seventeen when she got pregnant with me and dropped out of school, though I'd never know if that had been the chronological order of events. Celeste wasn't big on reliving the past, more interested in where the next event would be held.

I found her picture first, Celeste Drummond. Despite her hardcore partying, she hadn't changed much, at least in looks. The black and white photos

126

were a passport to another time, where the hair was longer and smoother, the jeans were flared beyond belief and glasses were small, rounded and though I was guessing, probably colored.

I flipped through, fascinated. Though she'd been a member of the sophomore class, she had well over one hundred signatures. Obviously Mommy Dearest was the life of the party, even back then. One candid caught my eye and I stared at the names, unable to believe my luck. Right under the photo of my mom talking to a bare chested man.

Celeste Drummond and QB 1 Bradly James at Homestead Bayfront Park.

Could it be? My mom, a lowly but pretty sophomore and the senior quarterback? The timing and place was right. Homestead Bayfront Park was a locals beach and judging from the body language of the candid, they were engaged in a heavy flirtation. Sure, the James part was in his last name, but considering the source could I really rule it out?

At that time, we didn't own a computer, so I'd taken the bus to the public library to do some research on suspect dad. Bradley James had been given a full ride football scholarship to Notre Dame and was expected to return home to Miami and bring the Dolphins back to the NFL championships. It'd never happened, though. He'd been in a car accident during his junior year at college, messed up his rotator cuff and lost his scholarship. The Dolphins had ended up with Dan Marino instead. Poor dad.

I bit my lip, thinking it over. Celeste and Bradley had a summer fling, and then he went off to college, never knowing about me. Could I really blame him for putting some distance between himself and

Celeste when I wanted to do the exact same thing every second of every day?

And wonder of wonders, he owned a car dealership in Miami. I read until my eyeballs stung, absorbing every tidbit I could unearth. He was married with two kids. A devoted dad, just as I'd suspected. I printed his home address as well as the one for his dealership and plotted our reunion.

Choosing the right time was crucial. I didn't want to put him on the spot in front of his employees or his family. That could lead to awkward explanations and I wanted him to be at ease, receptive to what I had to say. For the first few weeks, I staked out the dealership to get a feel for him.

My first impression of the man who'd contributed half of my DNA was a nice guy. Sure, life had given him plenty of lemons, and some people would be angry or bitter that it wasn't going the way they'd planned. But not Bradley James. He had the build of an athlete who still ate like one but didn't exercise the way he used to. Soft, squishy even. Very dad-like. His hair was thinning but his smile was always bright and absolutely genuine. I liked that about him.

Being way too young and white trash to pull off the pretense of looking for a car, I sat at the bus bench across the street and watched him operate. Business was slow, but dear old dad was always friendly and engaging. It broke my heart to watch him smile and shake some guy's hand and then watch the customer drive off in the same old jalopy he'd arrived in.

I liked that he kept a routine, it made it easier for me to spy on him. At exactly twelve fifteen, he'd flip the sign to read *out to lunch* and walk down the block and around the corner to a little Mom and Pop

128

style restaurant. His meals varied from meatloaf and mashed potatoes to chicken-fried catfish and collard greens drenched in butter, but at least the walk was giving him a little cardio.

I'd just made up my mind to introduce myself to him that day when he beat me to the punch. I sat on the bus bench and gawked with my mouth hanging open when he approached me.

"I've been watching you. You sit here all day but never take a bus. Don't you have any money, sweetheart?"

"Not much," I admitted, half ashamed, half in awe. He really was a nice guy. A hero even.

"I have an idea. Why don't you join me for lunch?"

I'd love to go to that cozy little restaurant and sit across the table from my dad. Maybe order an ice tea instead of pretending to stare at the menu so I could keep tabs on him.

"What's your name?" he asked as we strode along.

"Jackie. Jacqueline actually." I didn't want to divulge my last name, in case he recognized it and put two and two together.

"Pretty name to match a pretty face," he said simply, as though stating a fact.

"Thank you." I'd never actually felt pretty before. Stacked, yes, but never genuinely attractive. But he was saying it and he didn't even know he was my dad so it must be true.

We sat down at his regular booth and the gnarled-old waitress made a fuss over me. "Is this one of your daughters, Mr. James?"

My heart stopped.

He laughed, waving it off. "No, Grace, I'm not as old as all that. Just a new friend."

Her demeanor cooled somewhat but I was too full of nerves to pick up on the weird vibe. We ordered, or rather he ordered two plates of steak and eggs and she shuffled off.

"So, Jackie," he smiled.

My knee bounced and it took all my effort to still the frenetic movement. "Yes, Mr. James?"

"Mr. James is my father. You can call me Brad."

Funny, I'd never thought of him as a Brad.

"I'm concerned about you, honey," he continued and I jumped when a hand landed on my knee. "It seems like you have nowhere to go. No one's looking out for you."

Uncomfortable, I shifted away from his touch. "No, I have someplace. I live with my mom."

His eyes narrowed as he scrutinized me. "How old are you?"

"Twenty one." I knew for a fact I could pass for drinking age and I had the fake id to prove it.

He relaxed visibly. "That's great. So, do you know anything about computers? I just got one for the dealership and I don't know what I'm supposed to do with it."

"I know some stuff."

"Good. I'd like to offer you a job as my secretary."

"Really?" Did he sense the connection between us? Was that why he was making this overture when, based on his sales lately, he probably couldn't afford it?

"Sure." Grace set our plates down and he dug into his steak with relish. He didn't have great table manners but after Celeste, I wasn't about to be fussy.

"Oh, that'd be great." Working side by side with my dad, sharing more lunches and taking our time while we got to know each other. I wouldn't have to blurt out the truth right away, I could work up to it, ease it into a conversation when the time was right.

He put his fork down, staring at me with eyes the same exact color as mine. "And of course, when it's slow you could keep me...entertained."

The hand was back on my knee.

I stared at him for an endless moment, not wanting to admit to myself that what he was implying was the truth. But the look on his face, the familiar way he touched my leg under the table, all of it was unmistakably obvious.

This guy didn't want a daughter, he wanted a mistress.

No loyal, doting father, no king or even a decent man sat across the table from me. The gauzy veil of hope was lifted and in that moment I saw him for what he truly was.

A selfish, cheating has-been turned used car salesman.

I set my napkin down beside my untouched plate and rose slowly to my feet. Rebuffed and visibly confused he frowned. "What's the problem?"

I leaned in close, one hand on the table, the other balled into a fist at my side. Celeste would have screamed the place down but I didn't operate that way. The unappetizing steak congealed on the plate in the thick silence.

131

"The problem," I said clearly, concisely while looking him in the face for what I hoped would be the last time. "Is that I might be your daughter."

I turned and left without a backward look.

****

A thunderstorm was brewing. The air became unbelievably muggy and difficult to breathe.

Stupid, stupid, stupid, stupid. The mantra resounded with every step I took. I wasn't really angry at Bradley James. After all, he was just being himself, the pig. No, my ire was focused inward, self-loathing like a living thing that wrapped around me and took up an entire seat on the bus next to me.

There's no greater disappointment than shattered expectations. And I had no one to blame but myself.

And Celeste. Hell, I didn't even know if Bradley James was actually my father. But even if he wasn't, it didn't matter. Celeste didn't bring home decent guys. If she had, one of them would have married her by now. No, whoever my real father was, he was a user and a jerkoff and I was better off without him. It was the dashed hope that stung like I'd stepped on a jellyfish.

The storm broke at my stop and I was drenched to the skin by the time I made it to the front door. Thunder rattled our single pane windows and the bucket in the living room was filling up fast. For once, I ignored it.

Luckily, Celeste wasn't home. I raided her closet and snagged her most reveling clubbing clothes and her wallet. Most of the money that was in there was mine anyway, from the waitressing job I'd had until Celeste had called me up drunk and crying one time too many.

I showered off the stick of the humid day and dressed in my mother's party duds. I was taller than she was and the skirt revealed a lot more than it hid. Perfect.

I waited only until the thunderhead rolled on through before I strode back out to the bus stop. The ride was longer this time, down to the club scene near the beach. It was time to put my fake I.D. to the test

It was early at the first club I hit, but the bouncer let me in. The wedge heels hurt my feet but a few vodka and cranberries in and I didn't notice the pain anymore.

Hours later I was still moving and shaking it and accepting drinks from every man who sent one, rewarding him with a smile and a wink, sometimes a dance. More guys asked me to dance because obviously, I was the life of the party.

Like mother, like daughter.

I lost myself to the music, the lights, the energy. It was fantastic, exactly what I needed. I had no mother, no father, no past and no future. I was just this moment and it was me.

A hand landed on my ass, breaking my Zen.

"Back off." I shoved the hand away hard.

"Tease," the hand's owner grabbed me again.

"I said let *go*." I pushed him again, though the wall of bodies kept him on the rebound.

He got in my face. "Do that again, bitch. See where it lands you."

The guy had bad breath and was killing my buzz. I turned and walked toward the door, fully intending to continue my partying elsewhere.

133

He grabbed me for the third and final time and my reaction was pure instinct. My knee came up, catching him between the legs. He grunted and cupped whatever sensitive bits my strike had damaged, falling down like a sack of coconuts.

I had no coat and my purse was more for show than anything so I abandoned it and squeezed past the crush of bodies at the bar, bee-lining to the door.

"Watch it," I snapped as some skirt tottered on her six-inch heels and knocked me into another person. The impact was hard and I expected to go down but strong hands held me up against a solid wall of a chest.

"Are you all right?" A deep voice asked.

"Why wouldn't I be?" His heat amazed me. *Me*, a Miami native. It was neither oppressive nor sultry like the air around us, but engulfing. Consuming. I hadn't even realized I was cold until he touched me.

These were stupid drunk thoughts. Though I'd never been drunk before, Celeste had slurred enough nonsense at me to make the signs clear. Thankfully, I managed to keep them to myself as I turned to face the man who caught me. His gaze had locked on my face, his expression surprised, but not annoyed as I'd expected.

"I saw what happened over there. With that guy." He gave a head jerk in the direction where the grabby bastard still cupped his bruised bits. "I was coming to help."

"I can handle myself." It would have been more believable if I didn't slur.

"I saw that." He grinned down at me and I lost a bit of my soul in his sinful eyes.

"I'm Logan," my rescuer offered his hand.

134

Unlike the earlier scene with Bradley James, I recognized his look for what it was. In his head, Logan was removing my skimpy clothing and imagining all the things he could do to my naked body. Despite the heat, the blare of music, the crush of bodies, or maybe because of them, he held me in thrall with an unspoken sensual promise. He could provide the escape that all the liquor and the music and the people failed to do.

Come with me if you want to forget every other man you've ever known, that look said.

He was exactly what I needed.

"Jackie." I said. "You wanna get out of here, Logan?"

Chapter Thirteen

"**W**hat are you two talking about out here?" Luke asked as the Parker brothers joined us on the verandah. He was sweetly rumpled and hadn't shaved yet. Logan appeared hung-over and grouchy.

"Girl stuff." Marge patted my knee. "We didn't want to wake you guys after your wild night."

Logan snorted. "After Jackie blew up that house, watching dad drip barbecue sauce on his shirt was anticlimactic."

"I hope he remembers to pretreat the stain. Eh, who am I kidding, I better call him and make sure he packed a bleach pen." Marge scuttled inside.

"You're awfully quiet this morning." Luke kissed me on the top of my head. "Feeling okay?"

I felt as though my insides had been put through a wood chipper. I still forced a smile for his benefit. "Fine, just a little tired."

"Babe, you've been burning it at both ends. Maybe you need a day off." He rubbed my shoulders while Logan looked on.

I closed my eyes, feeling like a heel. Shit, now their mom knew and Luke didn't, the guilt was getting harder to shoulder, especially with Logan looking at me that way. She was wrong, she had to be. He wasn't in love with me—he could barely stand being in the

136

same room with me most of the time. "I'll be fine, just need a little more coffee is all. What time is it?"

Logan dug out his cell phone. "A little before nine. Why?"

"I want to call Mara Young, Aaron's property manager, and ask her a few questions about Gomez."

"Jackie," Luke looked pained, "I don't think that you should keep involving us in this. We need to separate our business from the Gomez case."

"I disagree," Logan spoke up, surprising us both. "Despite the murder and the investigation, we got the job done and quickly, too. Aaron's already recommended us so think how grateful he'd be if we unearth a few answers. Even if we can't, what could it hurt to cover our bases? Besides, it's not like we have anything else to do."

As if on cue, his cell phone rang. He frowned but answered it. "Logan Parker."

"For Damaged Goods," I hissed.

He rolled his eyes and then turned his back. "Right. We can do that. What's the address?"

Luke and I followed him inside where he moved into the office and wrote on the side of a box. "504? Got it. We'll check it out."

He hung up and I groaned. "Did you get his email so I can send him our contract?"

Logan's expression was smug. "He already emailed you yesterday and was concerned because he hadn't heard back from you."

Crud. I had been crazy distracted. "Okay, what's the job?"

"Mr. Esposito owns a building in Wynwood. The bottom half is rented to a retail shop and the top is an apartment. The downstairs tenant is complaining about an awful smell that's driving his

137

customers away. He's blaming the upstairs tenant for it and threatening to withhold his rent if the landlord doesn't handle it."

"What kind of smell?" Luke asked.

Logan shrugged. "Dunno, he just said it smells like shit."

I headed back into the house. "I'll go get ready so we can smell it for ourselves. Mara Young will just have to wait."

Half an hour later we were in the truck heading north of downtown toward the neighborhood known as Little San Juan, for the large Puerto Rican population. Wynwood is divided into two sections, the Wynwood Art District in the north and the fashion district along West 5th Avenue. I'd spent a considerable amount of time serving notices in this neighborhood. The push towards gentrification had displaced many of the poorer tenants who couldn't pay increasingly raised rents. Some displaced tenants had a habit of causing trouble for their former landlords.

Luke pulled up to the curb and we all got out and assessed the building. The downstairs boasted a small gallery featuring what looked like urban graffiti art prints. The sign read *Fredo's Fine Art*. It wasn't one I'd ever heard of before but considering the square footage of the building and the location in the heart of the art district, the tenant had to be doing pretty well to afford it.

"Let's talk to the downstairs tenant first," Luke suggested. "Get his side of the story and see if we can locate the smell. It might be something as simple as trash that fell behind the dumpster out back."

The smell hit us the second we walked through the glass front door. "Holy frijoles, it reeks in here." I

138

did my best to breathe through my mouth. It would be unprofessional to speak with the tenant who'd registered the complaint while holding my nose.

"May I help you?" A man in his late sixties wearing faux crocodile shoes, black slacks and a purple button up shirt with the top three buttons undone approached. His skin was darker than mine, but light for this neighborhood.

"Alfredo Cruz?" Logan asked.

"You have found him." His voice was heavily accented, which may or may not be authentic to Puerto Rico. It was all in the presentation.

"We represent your landlord. You registered a complaint about the property," Logan continued.

He turned his head and I saw the diamond stud at least twice the size of my engagement ring in his ear catch the overhead light. "Are you here to do something about that smell? It chases away all my customers. No one wants to shop in a place that smells of shit. I will to leave if it is not removed."

"You have a lease, Mr. Cruz. You can't just turn over the keys," Luke said.

"Here's what I think of the lease." He spat on the floor. "I cannot pay my rent if nobody buys my prints. And no one will stay long enough to buy if it stinks of shit in here. I spray and spray and spray the air cleanser and still, shit you smell."

When I first heard the description, I thought he'd been overly dramatic and nonspecific. But it really did smell like a truck stop restroom. I cleared my throat. "Do you know where it's coming from?" Perhaps the septic line was broken.

Cruz looked at the ceiling. "The upstairs tenant. He is a strange one, does not go out much. I had no problem with him, until the smell."

139

"We'll check it out," Logan promised.

The three of us trooped outside, inhaling the relatively clean air that smelled like nirvana after the stink. We circled the building, a much more industrialized version. Obviously, all the money had been spent on the front street facing portion of the building. Scrubby weeds poked up through cracks in the concrete.

"It's not the sewer line," Luke said. "We'd be able to smell that out here."

All of us looked toward the upstairs apartment. A rickety set of wooden open back stairs led to a small deck outside the apartment. I doubted it'd hold all of our combined weight at the same time.

"What do you think he's doing up there?" I asked.

"One way to find out. You two stay here." Logan moved toward the wooden stairs.

I wanted to protest but didn't want to be any closer to the source of that smell.

Logan knocked. No answer. No windows on that side except for a small arrow slit, too high to see in. He knocked again "What's the tenant's name?"

I checked the email from my phone. "Estaban Martinez."

"Mr. Martinez!" Logan shouted.

"Do you hear anything?" if we suspected the tenant might be hurt we had the right to enter immediately.

"Not a peep." Logan shook his head.

I prepared a 24 hour inspection notice, citing a bad smell as the reason for entering and carried it up to Logan. "Paste one side on the doorjamb and the other on the door itself. That way if the seal is broken, we'll know he got it."

We trudged back down the stairs.

"That's it?" Alfredo Cruz had abandoned his stinky print gallery to watch what we were doing. "You said you'd fix it!"

I patted the air in the classic calm yourself motion. "He's not at home. We can't enter the residence without the owner's permission or twenty four hour's warning. We'll come back tomorrow."

"Tomorrow does me no good for today. This stink drives away my customers. No one will buy art from a store that smells of shit."

He was right. I hadn't noticed the art, my only thought on how quickly I could get out of there. "Maybe you should close down for the day. Go to the beach."

"The beach?" His eyes went wide. "You want me to disappoint my customers and abandon my art and just go to the beach?"

Jeeze. "I didn't mean to offend you. I was just suggesting—"

But Cruz was on a roll, waving his arms around and ranting for all he was worth. "I'm not some lazy slut that can just go to the beach and have a man buy her a drink."

"Hey!" Again with the assumption that I was fast and loose. What was up with that? "It was only a suggestion."

"I spit on your suggestion." A lugie hit the ground. "And I spit on you."

He tried, but I scrambled over and into the truck. The door slammed and a big wad of saliva hit the rolled up window and slid down, leaving a slimy snail trail in its wake.

I contemplated giving him the finger, but didn't want to agitate him further. Luke and Logan were propping each other up, they were laughing so hard. If I'd had the keys I would have taken off, leaving them with the mad spitter and his gallery of shit.

Note to self: carry extra keys from now on.

****

"Come on Jackie, you got to admit it was funny." Luke said.

"Maybe if I wasn't the one he was about to spit on." I slammed the door and strode over to Bessie Mae. "I'm going to meet with Mara Young." I'd called her earlier and set up an appointment to talk with her.

"Want some company?" Luke offered.

He just wanted to talk me out of it. "Thanks, but I won't be long, and I'll probably swing by Celeste's on the way home." I was already late on my promise to visit with her.

I rolled down the windows to combat the oppressive heat and turned back toward the downtown. Mara Young's office was actually a boat based at the Miami Yacht Club on Watson Island, the manmade island connected to the mainland and South Beach by the MacArthur Causeway.

Traffic was heavy through downtown and I was about forty minutes past my scheduled appointment by the time I made Watson Island. I hoped she'd still be able to talk with me.

Poor old Bessie Mae looked sad and completely out of place snuggled between a Mercedes and a Porsche, but there was nowhere else to park. I slipped my sunglasses up and scanned for slip C-17, where Mara Young both worked and lived.

A couple of guys in khaki shorts with sweaters tied neatly around their polos pointed me in the right direction. Mid-day, mid-week and they're just being seen at the Yacht Club. Compared to them, I looked

142

like a lost dock worker. If Alfredo Cruz ever came down here, he'd have a spitting-conniption.

A large sign hung off the port side of Mara's boat, *Forever Young.* "Young Real Estate, finding the lifestyle you aspire to."

I wasn't overly impressed, mostly because she ended her slogan in a preposition. But I guessed being based in the yacht club forgave all sorts of sins in the eyes of the consumer.

"Ms. Young?" I called from the dock.

A woman with curly blonde hair and big blue eyes appeared out of the cabin below. She wore a complicated outfit that looked to be part halter-top, but covered with a gauzy flowing sheath dress. Shoes by Manolo Blahnik, which should have appeared obscene on the boat, but didn't. Both her jewelry and her makeup were impeccable, creating a classy effect. She may not have been an English major, but I had to give her props for curb appeal. "May I help you?"

"We spoke on the phone. I'm Jackie Parker from Damaged Goods. Sorry I'm late but traffic was a beast. I was wondering if I could ask you a few questions about Fester Gomez?"

She didn't invite me aboard as I'd expected. In fact, her gaze skittered away in a nervous gesture. "I'm sorry, Ms. Parker, but I'm expecting a client soon."

Crud. "I'll be quick. How did Gomez pay his rent every month?"

She shifted her weight. "I honestly couldn't say. Probably an auto draft, that's how most of my properties are handled anymore. I collect from every tenant in Aaron's South Beach Rentals and keeping their payment methods straight is impossible."

Why the hell was she so jumpy? "Do you know which bank? You must have records. You get a

143

percentage when you rent one of Aaron's spaces, right? There's got to be a paper trail a mile long."

"Yes and I have no time to go through it all right now. Please, I have a client coming in a few to tour a home in Coconut Grove. You need to leave."

I dug through my shoulder bag and fished out a business card. "Please call me if you find the information I'm after."

She took the card and shooed me off.

On a scale of one to weird, that took the damn cake. With nothing else to do, I returned to Bessie Mae and waited to see who the client was that had made Mara Young so squirrelly. Maybe it was someone famous. Coconut Grove was one of the original and relatively unchanged Miami neighborhoods and it took some serious financial resources to buy a place there.

A few people came and went while I baked in my car, but no one moved toward slip C-17. Starving, I dug through my bag, searching for stray edibles. I came up with a pack of orange Tic-Tacs and when I looked up, the *Forever Young* was moving out to sea.

"Shit." I got out of my car and watched the yacht get smaller and smaller.

What the hell was going on?

Chapter Fourteen

"**M**om?" I called out as I entered Celeste's trailer, a bag of groceries tucked under one arm. "Are you here?"

"Jackie?" A thump from the partially closed bedroom door. "I'll be right out."

Fudge, I hoped she didn't have another geezer with cardiac issues in her bed. I unloaded the milk, cheese, crackers, cereal, nuts, cookies, fruit and box of wine so she didn't need a bottle opener. Everything a grown culinary challenged woman needed to get by. "Are we alone?"

Luckily she came out of the bedroom fully dressed in shorts and a tank top. "Yes, I was hanging my new curtains."

"Oh, well, just making sure." I stowed the cheese, milk and wine in the fridge.

Mom dumped the grapes in a colander and turned the tap on. "Why do you always think the worst of me?"

Um, because the worst was usually accurate? She'd boned a man to death, for crying out loud. "I just know you, Mom. I know your patterns."

"How come you didn't tell me you threw a party for your mother-in-law yesterday?" She shut off the water and braced her hands on either side of the sink.

How did she find out about that? I rubbed my temples, not wanting to get into it with her. I'd spent all afternoon in a hot car, already headachy from the excessive heat and dehydrated from the dregs of my alcoholic romp the night before "Honestly, it was no big deal, a last minute thing."

Her hands went to her ample hips as she turned to face me. "A wedding shower was no big deal? Are you ashamed of me?"

How to answer that honestly without hurting her feelings? "I swear Mom, last time I talked to you I didn't know about it or I would have invited you." Maybe.

That seemed to mollify her a bit.

She opened the cardboard wine and reached for two plastic juice glasses. "You want to stay for dinner?"

I shook my head and snagged a bottle of water. "No thanks. Marge called, she's making veggie lasagna."

The cups slammed down. "Marge, Marge, Marge! Is she all you can talk about?"

"Mom, what's the problem?" Celeste was always touchy, but her outburst seemed extreme.

"The problem, Jacqueline," she said tartly, "Is that my own daughter would rather bond with some strange woman than give her own mother the time of day. I swear, sometimes I doubt you'd spit on me if I was on fire."

"Sure I would." Or if not, I knew a guy that would gladly step up to the plate. "I helped you carry a dead body the other night, remember? That's not exactly a sign of indifference."

"Oh, here we go." Celeste threw her hands up in the air. "I make one lousy mistake and you're going to hold it over my head for the rest of my life."

Exhaustion had broken the leash on my temper and I snapped, "*One* mistake? Try a baker's dozen, and that's just this calendar year. Mom, I've always cleaned up your messes and when have you *ever* been there for me, huh? When my husband was away for months on end? Or how about when I was a teenager and wanted to know who my father was? Marge has been there for me since Luke and I got married. She's been a source of support whenever I needed it. So excuse me if I like the fact that I don't have to be the adult all the time with her or that I get to have someone step up and make me a damn veggie lasagna and take care of me for a frigging change."

Celeste stared at me, unblinking. Hurt flashing in her big blue eyes. She looked younger without her war paint, softer and more vulnerable.

I felt like a jerk and my shoulders slumped. "Sorry."

She cleared her throat. "Don't be, if that's how you really feel."

I wanted to protest and make a boatload of excuses. I'd had a rough week, was under a ton of stress and all that garbage people spouted when they behaved badly and felt guilty about it. Unloading both barrels on Celeste wasn't nice or fair, but damn it, something had to give, and soon.

She sniffled. "Go on with you then. I don't want you to be late for your lasagna because of me."

I picked up my purse and then turned to the door, but hesitated. It wasn't in my nature to wound and run. "You should come over. Get to know Marge. I think you'd like her if you gave her a chance."

147

"I don't know." Celeste fiddled with a bunch of grapes. "You sure you want me there?"

No, but this wasn't just about me. Maybe if she met Marge she'd get over her resentment and stop haranguing me all the time. "We'll do a wine and cheese thing. It'll be fun."

"I'll think about it." She offered me a small smile and I had to hug her. She stiffened but eventually wrapped her arms around me. Celeste was many things including self-centered, clingy, needy and irrational, but she was still my mom.

I drove home through the early evening traffic, thinking about family. Usually, it was a total pain in the ass, but people went to extremes for their families, even if they were certifiable.

Rosie Harris's house wasn't exactly on my route home, but it wasn't too far out of the way either. I had plenty of time for a few questions before veggie lasagna.

Rosie wore a canary yellow sweat suit and smoke billowed out around her when she opened the door, like she was opening the gates of the inferno.

"You again," she greeted me.

No way was I crossing that threshold into glassy eyed doll territory. "Hi, Ms. Harris. I won't keep you long, but I need to ask you something. The last time I was here you kept calling Mr. Gomez a pervert, but you never said why."

"If it walks like a duck and quacks like a duck, it's probably a duck, right? Fester was all about the younger women. Even my sister, God rest her soul, was ten years younger than him."

"Do you know what Fester did for a living?" I fished, wondering if she knew about the website. The

148

dead girl was connected with the website and if Rosie knew something about it, I wanted to know what.

Rosie scratched one of her chins. "Investments, mostly. He did lots of work on the computer, day trading and the like."

"Day trading? Like stocks and stuff?"

"Beats the snot outta me. All I know is that man had money to burn. Look sweetie, I got my Bingo ladies coming soon so I have to get ready."

"Just one more thing. Did Fester ever go looking for his daughter?" It was a longshot, but if he hadn't confided in Rosie, maybe he had in his long lost daughter.

She cast me a dark look. "How the hell would I know?"

"Thanks for your time." I headed back to my car, wondering if Fester had lied to Rosie or if Rosie was lying to me.

And if I'd ever find out the truth.

****

"Great dinner, Marge." I discreetly reached under the table and popped the straining button on my waistband.

Marge pushed away from the table and began collecting plates. "Thank you, Jackie. I can teach you how to make it if you'd like."

"Give it up, Mom." Luke took my hand and brought it to his lips. "Jackie's not interested in learning how to cook."

"It's not a lack of interest. I'm cursed."

Marge waved me off. "Phooey. There's no such thing as a curse."

149

"I'm serious. The one time I tried to make toast I accidentally toasted my braid. Our place smelled like burnt hair for a week."

"I've seen you use the microwave." Logan teased. "You lived on those frozen dinners while Luke was away. Does the curse not extend to that?"

"No, the technology is newer than the curse, so the curse doesn't apply. And how do you know what I ate while Luke was away?"

He shrugged and pushed back from the table. "I'll get the dishes, Mom."

Marge waved him away. "Oh honey, let me get those. You've been working so hard."

"What was that abrupt change of subject about?" I asked Luke.

Luke jerked his head toward the office. "Not here."

Curiouser and curiouser. I followed him in and shut the door. "Spill."

"No family talk in the office, remember?" He winked and sat down behind—hallelujah—the desk they'd picked up from Marcy's that afternoon.

Mental forehead smack. Me and my stupid rules. "Didn't take long for that one to bite me on the ass and you know that was about him, not us, right?"

"No trying to wiggle out of it now. Besides, we have another job."

I perched on the edge of the desk so I could see the computer screen. "Really? Where?"

Luke jiggled the mouse to wake my snoozing laptop. "A warehouse/loft apartment rental in the design district. The tenant has refused to let the electric company inspect the property for the source of a huge power drain and we need to go convince him

150

he has no choice before the city makes good on its threat to fine our owner."

I studied the location. The design district was originally part of the Buena Vista neighborhood, but in typical Miami style, reinvented itself after urban decay had almost annihilated it. Made up of mostly low rise warehouses, the neighborhood was home to architectural firms, art galleries, antique dealers, eateries and bars. Not too many residential spaces, especially for rent. "What do we know about our tenant?"

Luke ran a hand through his hair. "Tennant's name is Chris Collins. There's no written lease, just a verbal agreement."

Frick. That made things more complicated. If there was no lease it was harder to prove a violation of the rental agreement and it made the eviction process that much trickier. "Does the owner know why the tenant is blocking the inspection?"

Luke shook his head. "No. Just that he's refusing to open the door. He's never been late on his rent either, so this is the first offense."

"We need to get in there, inspect the property if we can. If he's damaged it in any way, we have grounds to start the eviction process."

"My bet is that he's got a pot farm going." Logan leaned against the door frame. "Those lights drain the grid and a warehouse space would be the perfect place to set up an operation like that."

I crossed my arms over my chest. "A power drain could mean anything."

"It's weed." Logan mimicked my closed off body language.

"Twenty bucks says it's something else." I didn't care what was gobbling up electricity the way I

151

shoveled in veggie lasagna, I just wanted the Dark Prince to be wrong.

"Easy money." He extended a hand and I shook it.

"If he's doing anything illegal, the cops will take care of the problem for us." I said.

"Only one way to find out." Luke grabbed his truck keys and we set off.

Other than a few crowded bars, the design district was a virtual ghost town after dark. We parked the big black truck in front of the warehouse and looked up to the flickering blue lights on the second story of the squat cinderblock building.

"I don't think grow lamps flicker like that." I said. "You owe me twenty bucks, Logan."

"Not until we know for sure." Logan stepped inside the old elevator car, too intent on proving himself right to order me to stay in the BBT.

We all squeezed into the car and Luke slid the metal gate over the lift. Someone had gone hog wild with the garlic bread at dinner—probably me—and we were all relieved when the lift stopped on the top floor. There's something downright unsettling about being sandwiched between the Parker brothers.

Luke knocked. "Mr. Collins?"

"Go away!" The metal door muffled the voice but the message was clear enough.

Logan gave it a whirl. "Mr. Collins, we work for your landlord. If you would just open up—"

"Fuck off already!" The shout was louder this time.

I raised my eyebrows to see if the big strong goons had had enough. "May I?"

"Go ahead," Logan grunted.

152

Luke tossed me a wink and gestured to the door. I cleared my throat and unbuttoned the top two buttons on my sleeveless top and aimed the girls at the small camera perched in the corner above the door. With a little extra ditz in my voice, I called out. "Mr. Collins? My name is Jackie and I *need* to talk to you."

If he was straight and not terrified of my lurking cohorts that door would be creaking open in three...two...one...

Right on time, the scrape of a floor bolt being released was followed by a rush of arctic air as Chris Collins appeared. He had a long, horsey pimple-covered face and lank brown hair badly in need of a shampoo and cut. His glasses were held together with masking tape, but he was all man as he gaped at my exposed cleavage.

"This really isn't a good time," he murmured, not looking at my face.

Sometimes being mistaken for a stripper came in handy. I angled my body until I was leaning in the doorway one arm braced against the frame, and my foot positioned so he couldn't close it in my face. "We represent your landlord. He's received a fine from the city because you refused to let the electric company in earlier." I didn't add, you naughty boy you, but it was implied in my breathy tone.

Since no more buttons were being undone, he looked over his shoulder at whatever the hell was so captivating in his place. "I really can't talk now." The door started to swing shut.

Logan put his hand over my head, bracing the door open. "This is serious, Mr. Collins. If the power company can't find the source of the drain they may shut off power to the entire building."

153

Panic flared in Collin's eyes, followed by a healthy shot of anger. "They can't do that! I pay my bill on time."

"We don't want that to happen either. Do you mind if we come in to have a look around?" Luke asked, the good cop to Logan's bad. "Maybe if we knew what's been going on—"

"Fine, I just gotta get back." Collins left the door standing wide open as he rushed out of sight.

We followed. Logan took point with Luke close behind and me bringing up the rear. The place was dark, and cold, like a mausoleum and I shivered. "I've got a bad feeling about this."

"Why would anyone pay to live here?" Luke murmured. "It's like a cave."

"Logan, can you see which way he went?" I squinted into the dimly lit space.

"No but there aren't too many options."

We were drawing closer to the flickering blue light. Up ahead there was an enormous doorway, big enough to drive a truck through. What looked like mist coated the floor so I couldn't see anything below my knees. Mist in a Miami warehouse? Shoot, maybe I should consider waiting in the car because I really didn't want to go through that doorway. "Guys?"

"Holy shit." Logan stopped so suddenly that Luke crashed into his back.

"Dude, what the—" Luke cut off on a sharp inhalation.

"What is it?" I sandwiched myself between them, standing on my tiptoes so I could see whatever they did.

At first, I couldn't make out what I was seeing, they just looked like giant silver cylinders. But then I caught sight of Collins messing around with an open

154

one. More specifically, what he was stuffing inside it

"Oh my God, is that a body?"

Chapter Fifteen

"**D**ude. What. The. Hell?" Logan said at the same time Luke asked, "Did you kill her?"

And wouldn't that be just my luck? If the press caught wind of this dead body streak Damaged Goods was on, our reputation would be toast. I could see the headlines now. *Dishing out death: Jackie Parker certified process server or grim reaper?*

"No. It's a cryonics lab," Collins wheezed as he positioned the corpse of a hefty woman inside the silver cylinder. "People pay me to freeze them at the point of death and store them until science comes up with a way to cure whatever fatal disease killed them."

"Is that legal?" Luke whispered to me.

Yes, but not the way the creepy tenant was doing it. "Mr. Collins, you can't do this in your residential apartment. There are zoning laws and regulations, procedures that need to be followed. What if one of your clients has a communicable disease that gets out into the general population?" The CDC fines alone would cost our client the building.

Now that I was no longer playing the bimbo, Collins waved me off. "No one here died of anything like that. Mostly it's heart disease, aneurisms, cancer, things like that. And I have all the proper permits." He shut the lid and connected a tube from a tank that read liquid nitrogen.

"If you did, the city wouldn't be asking questions." Logan stressed.

"It's my building—I can do what I want." Collins connected the tube to the metal coffin and turned a valve on.

Sometimes when a renter had lived in the same place for a while, they forgot that they don't really own the property. "No, it's not your building and even if it were, you can't just run a cryonics lab out of it without informing the city." I was pretty sure about that much, anyway.

Collins threw up his hands. "What do you want me to do? Let them all expire after they paid me for a second chance? It's unethical."

Through the small Plexiglas window, I could see the features of Collin's latest client. Round face, apple cheeks, eyelashes frosting over. She looked like somebody's Mom. "All I'm saying is you can't do this, here."

"I'd like to see you stop me." Collins the creep smirked.

I was ready to break his beaklike nose but Luke grabbed my arm and jerked his head at Logan, dragging us to an impromptu powwow in the corner. "What are our options here, Ace?"

I sucked in some meat locker air, cooling my temper. Bodies freaked me out under normal circumstances and the fact that people paid Collins to do this to them was beyond belief. "Seven day notice to cure. I serve him now and he has a week to remove all this stuff and restore the property or face eviction."

"We're talking about more than a few equipment items being unplugged." Luke stated.

157

"Those are human bodies. Can we transport them without doing irreparable damage?"

"They're already dead." Logan said. "It doesn't get much more irreparable than that."

I was busy filling out the seven day notice. I tore it from my clipboard and handed it to Collins. "This is a seven day notice to cure the breach of the lease."

"I don't have a written lease, so how can I be in breach of it?" The way Collins smirked clued me in to the fact that this probably wasn't his first rodeo.

Damn it, I'd forgotten about that. I hid my surprise and put my hands on my hips. "We'll be back in a week so you'd better make other arrangements by then."

We left him there and strode down the hall and out the door to the elevator.

"Parasite," Logan muttered once we were all back in the truck. "He knew he had us by the short and curlies, too."

Despite the sultry night air, I was still chilled. "Luke, call the owner and let me talk to him."

Luke scrolled through his contacts and handed me his cell. "His name's Joel Amony, and he's a Haitian immigrant. English is his second language."

"Hello?" A musical Creole cadence infused the simple greeting.

"Mr. Amony? My name is Jackie Parker and I'm with Damaged Goods Security. I'm calling to let you know what Mr. Collins is doing in your building." I succinctly outlined what had gone down.

Joel was silent for so long that I checked to make sure I hadn't lost the signal. It was still live so I waited patiently, letting him absorb the news.

"That is disgusting," he said. "What do I do?"

158

I liked this man, no cussing or raging, just straight forward to the solution. "I served him with a seven day notice to cure, so he has a week to return the apartment back to its original condition and let the electric company in to inspect or we can move forward in evicting him.

"However, because you don't have a written lease with Mr. Collins, he could decide to challenge the eviction. Drag out the process, while you continue to collect fines. We need to report him to the proper authorities, to make sure you are not implicated in this. I'll make some calls, find out if he has the right to do what he is doing. I'd also recommend giving him a financial reason to leave. Offer him five thousand dollars and perhaps even assist him in finding a legal place to operate his business. In the end it'll cost much less than taking him to court. It's the best solution for everyone involved."

"You are a smart young woman," Mr. Amony told me in his deep, musical baritone.

I almost believed it when he said it in that rich voice. "Does that mean you'll authorize us to make the offer on your behalf?"

"Yes. I rent to the living. To rent to the dead is bad juju."

"My sentiments exactly. I'll call you back and let you know what he says."

"Thank you, Ms. Jackie." He hung up.

"Okay, that's step one." Not knowing who else to call, I phoned Enrique Vasquez. "I'm calling to report a...something."

Logan snorted and I covered the phone to hiss at him, "It wasn't marijuana so pay up."

The Dark Prince had many faults but he didn't welsh on bets. He grumbled as he forked over my

159

twenty but I refocused on Sergeant Vasquez, who was making impatient sounds.

"Mrs. Parker is there something I can do for you?"

"I'm not sure," Briefly I explained the situation and then waited for Vasquez to stop laughing. Cop humor, go figure.

"Sweet Baby Jesus," he wheezed "Cryonics in Miami. I'll bet his electric bill sucked canal water backward."

That was putting it mildly. "So, what do I do?"

"Well, unless your tenant is killing those people, it's not a homicide case. Being creepy isn't illegal. Sounds more like a health department issue. There are laws about the handling and storage of the dead for funeral parlors and crematoriums, but this is out of my depth. I have a contact at the board of health, let me call him and see about getting someone over there to make sure your guy is following all the proper procedures. We'll take it from there."

I hung up and then brought the guys up to speed while I waited for the call back.

"It's a hot button issue, no pun intended." Luke said. "Do you think it will work?"

"No." Logan shook his head. "When you're dead, you're dead, no second chances. That reanimation stuff is just wrong."

"Spoken like a good Catholic boy." I muttered. The Parker family was of the A&P Catholic variety, only attending church on Ash Wednesday and Palm Sunday. "You forgot the burn in hell part."

Logan turned to face me. "You can't sit there and say with a straight face that you weren't completely freaked out by what he was doing."

160

Actually, I was more concerned with what Collins had been doing *before* we arrived. His zipper had been down and the woman's body was nude. Like Rosie Harris had said, if it looks like a necrophiliac.... And he'd been ogling my cleavage. Ick ick ick. Luckily the phone rang, stopping that downward spiral in its tracks.

"My guy is on his way to check out the set-up." Vasquez said. "If it meets regulations, you're free to make the offer for your client."

"Thanks, Vasquez. Logan owes you two drinks now."

Death glare from the Dark Prince. Luke's shoulders shook as he laughed silently.

"One last thing. You have any idea how we could transport the bodies?"

"Try renting an ice cream truck," he said. And he hung up.

****

It was after eleven when we dragged our sorry carcasses back into the house.

"Anybody else hungry?" I beelined for the fridge, then screamed as Marge popped up from behind the counter. She wore a housecoat and spongy pink curlers and her face was clean of her typical war paint.

"Sorry, I didn't mean to scare you. I was just organizing your Tupperware cabinet."

I made my eyes go wide. "We have a Tupperware cabinet?"

She swatted at me playfully with a blue lid. "Wisenheimer. Can I fix y'all something to eat?"

"Just beer for us." Luke kissed her on her cheek then retrieved two bottles from the fridge.

161

"Jackie?"

I made it a policy to never turn down someone else's home cooked meal. "How about another slice of that veggie lasagna? I need something hot to fill me up."

Luke choked and Logan snorted, but I ignored them. They wouldn't say anything lewd in front of their mother.

Marge extracted the Pyrex dish from the fridge and cut off a square of lasagna and set it on a plate. "How did the job go?" She asked as my food nuked.

"Odd," Luke said. "Do us a favor and don't ever consider being frozen. It's not pretty."

"When your number's up, it's up, no second chances." Marge said as the microwave dinged.

I shot Logan a smirk. "Pretty sure I've heard that somewhere before."

I poured myself a huge glass of red wine and sat down to enjoy my second dinner while the Parker boys told their mom about our mad scientist tenant.

"Believe it or not, the creep was doing everything he was supposed to, except for storing the bodies on his property without his landlord's knowledge. We couldn't get an ice cream truck at this time of night, but Jackie did find a refrigerated meat truck for rent, along with a proper climate controlled commercial warehouse that would house his "clients" and fit his equipment a few miles from the port." Luke smiled and took my hand.

"He's upset though, that he now has to pay rent along with the new storage fees. I guess that's why he wanted to live there in the first place, he thought no one would notice," Logan added with a shake of his head. "It takes all kinds."

"We're going to oversee the move tomorrow." I drained my wineglass. Really, there was nothing a good meal couldn't cure. "Right after we check on the mad spitter and his stinky upstairs neighbor."

"Don't forget the engagement dinner," Marge reminded us.

Shoot, I'd forgotten about the other vow renewal stuff. I'd counted on having a little more time to nose around and dig up the dirt on Mara Young, maybe find out why she'd lied to me and sailed off into the sunset.

Luke faux yawned, an obvious ploy, especially when he followed up with, "Boy, I'm beat."

"Lucas, if you want to take your wife to bed, just say so. We're all adults here." Marge winked and took my plate to the dishwasher.

I snuck a glance at Logan who was staring at his beer bottle like the secrets of the universe were trapped inside. I'd never really considered how weird it was for him to know that his brother and I were getting biblical. I mean of course he knew it, but he didn't really know when or how.

Jeeze, I hope he didn't know how.

Luke pulled me to my feet. "Come on, wife, you heard the woman."

"Night," I spoke to the room at large. Logan nodded, but Marge's eyes went from me to her oldest son then back.

Oh shit, she wasn't going to talk to him about me and what I'd told her earlier, was she?

Granted, I didn't know Logan well, but I knew enough to accept that he was a private person, someone who played his cards very close to the vest. I seriously doubted he'd appreciate that I'd confirmed his mother's suspicions regarding our past connection. In fact, it may even push him back into thinking we had to tell Luke.

No way I could concentrate on a happy ending knowing that conversation was taking place in the next room.

Luke locked the bedroom door and pulled me into his arms. "Alone at last."

His kiss was magical, like always and before I knew what had happened I was stripped down to my bra and panties.

"You're amazing, you know that?" he murmured as he worked the hooks free of my bra. "I always knew you were good at your job, but the way you handled everything tonight...we would have been lost without you. You just make everything better, Jackie."

And no way was he not getting laid after a speech like that. I forgot all about whatever might be happening in the kitchen and gave myself over to the moment.

Chapter Sixteen

"What's wrong with these pants? Did they shrink in the wash or something?" I struggled to make the connection between button and button hole but my capris weren't having it. "Damn it."

"Uh, Ace, I don't think it's the pants." Luke was toweling his hair dry and watching my battle with a grin I wanted to slap off his handsome face.

I gave up on the pants and put my hands on my hips, partly to demonstrate my annoyance but mostly to keep my ass covered. Pissed off in a thong just couldn't be taken too seriously. "What's that supposed to mean? Are you saying I'm getting *fat*?"

"No, I'm not an idiot." Luke dropped the towel and pulled on his own pants without a problem. Showoff.

I turned back to the mirror and scrutinized my reflection. What had been an hourglass shape had taken on more of a padded bench effect. I poked at my gelatinous middle and grimaced. "I am. I'm getting fat. It's your mother's fault. Her cooking is too good. I don't overeat when we're living off of cereal and bad Chinese."

Still shirtless, my hard-bodied husband pressed himself up against my back and wrapped his arms around my cushy midsection. "Hmm, think I could get used to being a chubby chaser."

"Jerk," I laughed when he tickled my exposed belly.

"What's that expression? More cushion for the pushin'?"

"I'll hurt you," I smacked his shoulder but the effect of my threat was ruined by my breathless giggles.

He picked me up and plopped me on the bed. "I can still toss you around with no problem. We just have to make sure you get more exercise is all." He sprawled on top of me, his weight pressing me into the mattress. He was hard *everywhere.*

"Have a few ideas on how I could go about that, do you?" I asked as he kissed my neck.

"Mmm, definitely." His hands were busy worshiping my flesh. "Aerobic sex, just what the doctor ordered."

I was about to kick off the treasonous pants shackling my ankles so I could wrap my legs around him when someone started hammering on the bedroom door.

"Come on you two, don't make me whiz outside." Logan yelled through the door.

Luke dropped his head onto my chest. "We need to make that second bathroom a priority."

"Or evict some of our own tenants."

Luke rolled off of me "They aren't tenants, they're *cockblocking squatters."* He raised his voice enough to be heard through the door.

"Don't make me get the hose," Logan threatened. "Or Mom."

I got up, kicked off the useless capris and scurried into the closet. It was a tight fit, especially because I was taking up more real estate than usual,

166

but it allowed Luke to open the door, so the Dark Prince could use the facilities.

"Elastic is my friend," I muttered as I searched through the closet, finally settling on a pair of tropical print palazzo pants and a braided orange tube top with enough flair to disguise the blubber. I hated dieting, and saying no to a Marge cooked breakfast was a sin but these were desperate times and I had a matron of honor dress to slither my expanding backside into.

"Just coffee for me, thanks," I practiced saying it. Practice made perfect. I made sure all the important bits were covered and then exited the closet.

And walked smack into Logan.

His hands landed on my shoulders, steadying me. "Morning,"

"Just coffee for me, thanks." Gah, I was such an idiot.

The corner of his mouth kicked up. "Kay, but we have a great house special—"

I walloped him on the shoulder, almost the same spot I'd hit his brother not even ten minutes ago. "Shut up, jackass."

He laughed, his eyes sparking. "Never a dull moment with you, Jackie."

"Come on you two, breakfast is getting cold." Marge poked her head in the room. "Busy day!"

I followed Logan out into the dining room where a wave of hunger at the smell of bacon and German oven pancake made me dizzy. My mouth watered and I wiped my face to make sure no drool had trickled out. What was my line again?

"Sit down and eat." Marge clucked around us.

"Jackie's just going to have coffee this morning, Mom." Logan said as he cut a huge wedge of the fluffy oven-baked pancake for himself and doused it liberally with powdered sugar.

"She thinks she's getting fat." Luke put in.

"I hate you both," I grumbled as Marge set a steaming cup of coffee in front of me.

Marge took her own seat and helped herself. "Nonsense, a woman your age is supposed to spread out a little."

"My age?" Great, first I was fat and now I'm old? What was next, varicose veins and warts?

My mother-in-law tapped her chin. "Of course, usually pregnancies and children are the cause of that, so at least that's an excuse."

"I wonder what the weather's like in Nova Scotia today." I mused aloud.

Marge made a face. "I'm just saying. Don't be so touchy."

I flinched. Great, was I turning into crazy Celeste to boot? This day was off to a roaring stop. "You know what? I've got some work to do in the office. Enjoy breakfast."

I grabbed an orange and as I made my way to the office I heard Luke mutter, "Mom, you hurt her feelings."

"Balderdash," Marge said. "Jackie's made of sterner stuff than that."

I smiled at both my husband's defense and my mother-in-law's confidence in me. I knew it was rough on her, that she had two grown sons and no grandkids to spoil, but I was in no way, shape or form a baby factory.

Thirty four wasn't *that* old. Of course when my mother was thirty four, she had a seventeen-year-old

168

daughter, but no way was she a shining example of maternal fitness.

I peeled my orange and broke it into sections as I waited for my laptop to boot up. I'd just swallowed the last segment when Logan entered the room. "Any new developments?"

"A couple of potential clients, one in Coconut Grove, another in the Omni neighborhood."

The Dark Prince lowered himself into one of the chairs on the other side of the desk. "Luke's on dishes detail, he'll be in soon and we can come up with a plan of action."

I checked the time on the computer. "We've got the meat truck at ten and the 24 hour inspection of the stinky apartment is up at noon, so we should check back in on that. I don't want to overcommit us and either have to split up the team or fall behind."

"I agree," Logan said, startling me. He folded his hands so his fingers were steepled together in a powerful and sinister pose. "We're most effective as a team."

I smiled at him over the laptop. "Logan, I just want to say thanks."

One eyebrow went up. "What for?"

"For giving me a chance to do this with you guys. For sticking with the separate work/ personal life thing. I know it's hard but I think we'll all benefit from the structure."

His demeanor shifted, growing darker, more intense. Less joking brother-in-law and more Dark Prince. "Jackie, you have no idea, do you?"

"About what?" he seemed aggravated for no reason, and that threw me. "What did I do wrong?"

He closed his eyes and inhaled, his hands curling into fists. "It doesn't matter how much we

169

separate work from family. I don't want you on this team."

It felt as though he'd slapped me across the face. "Still?" I thought I'd proven myself on the last two outings. Luke had definitely been impressed with my mad skills, but Logan was the most stubborn man on the face of the planet.

His eyes opened and his pupils dilated, as though trying to suck me in. "That's not something that will change."

"Why?"

He just shook his head.

I shot out of my seat and leaned over the desk, sloshing coffee onto the floor in the process. "Damn it, tell me why. Don't I deserve to know why you think I'm such deadweight?"

Logan's eyes narrowed. "You blew a man's house up! You could have gotten yourself killed!"

True, but I wasn't about to concede the point. "It was a bizarre set of circumstances, it won't happen again."

He leaned in closer until we were a hairsbreadth from each other, almost nose to nose. "And you're still snooping around with the murder investigation, right? Even though Aaron's happy, he's paid us and we've moved on, you're still acting like you have something to prove about Gomez."

"It's not about Gomez." And here I'd thought he'd understood. I had been more open to him because I thought he accepted it as something I needed to do. "You said I should talk to Mara Young."

"To get closure so you could move on. But you haven't, I can see your wheels spinning, can see you plotting. Look me in the eye and tell me you've given up on finding Gomez."

"If we find him we could—"

His empty laughter cut me off. "Don't you get it? You have this quality about you that gets under people's skin and drives them nuts. Tenacity is overrated and one of these days you're going to piss off the wrong person, ask the wrong question at the wrong time and maybe even get yourself killed. Did you ever think what that would do to Luke? He'd be devastated."

Thunderstruck, I sat back down. "Is this really about Luke? Or is it about you? Did you come up with this laundry list of excuses because you're uncomfortable working with me."

Logan looked out the window. "If that's what you think, you don't understand me at all."

I closed my eyes, unable to look at him any longer. "I never claimed otherwise."

****

Logan and I did our level best to avoid each other for the remainder of the morning. We silently watched Chris Collin's "clients" being loaded into the refrigerated meat truck then went through the apartment, making sure all the modifications had been removed before letting the electric company in to do their thing. By the time it was over, my stomach growled loudly, complaining about my lackluster breakfast.

"Hey," Luke touched my arm. "You okay?"

"Fine." I said tersely. "Just tired."

He nodded, accepting my explanation. "Your body needs fuel, Jackie. We'll stop and grab something before we deal with the next one."

"Something light." It was hot out and heat plus a car ride and possibly getting stuck in midtown traffic would probably equal vomit. "We need to bring water

171

with us too, maybe a cooler if we're going to ride around all day."

We stopped into a little Mexican place that made the best tortilla chips this side of the Rio Grande. The Parker brothers ordered sodas. I asked for a bottle of water. They pointed to giant platters of meat and cheese and creamy rice that made me drool. I ordered a single bean burrito, no guacamole, no sour cream. It took all my willpower but I managed to push the basket of fresh baked chips and salsa across the table. Luke took a chip but Logan just stared at me. I squirmed under his scrutiny, then intentionally stilled my motion and defiantly met his gaze.

"Why the hell aren't you eating?" Logan growled.

"I'm fat," I snarled before I thought better of it. Damn my need to meet his every challenge. It would have been better to spit out a "None of your business" or something instead of saying what was on my mind.

"You're not fat, Jackie." Luke said like a well-trained automaton husband.

"It's your mother's fault. She's always cooking and now I don't fit into any of my clothes with waistbands." Was there an echo to this day?

He popped another chip in his mouth and winked at me. "Waistbands are overrated. You look great, babe. Tell her, Logan"

Logan's response wasn't nearly so sanguine. At Luke's invitation he took his time and perused my body like I was part of the all you can eat buffet. My muscles tensed. I ground my molars together and did my best to ignore the rush of heat that followed every flicker of his eyes on me. His expression didn't change but I knew in that primal way that some call women's intuition, that my brother-in-law liked what he saw.

172

And wanted to see more.

"Ignore her, Luke," he said after a leisurely inspection. "She's doing that stupid girl thing, fishing for reassurance."

"Ignore him, Luke," I mimicked his matter of fact tone. "He's doing that stupid guy thing and talking out his ass."

"What the hell is wrong with the two of you?" Luke glowered from his brother to me and back. "I thought we'd solved this."

"Logan doesn't want me on the team." I tattled like a four-year-old. "He told me so this morning."

Luke frowned.

"And since when has what I wanted mattered?" Logan said.

Before Luke or I could respond he pushed his chair back from the table and stalked toward the restroom. Maybe I'd get lucky and he'd flush himself back down to the underworld.

But even my mental criticism lacked its usual rancor. It must be the after-effects of that heated look, the one that said he'd rather have me for lunch than anything on the menu.

The thought made me uncomfortable for several different reasons.

Luke took my hand in his and squeezed. "He'll come around. You're invaluable to us and eventually he'll figure that out."

"You keep on saying that." I smiled though. "Do you genuinely believe it or are you doing your peacemaker thing?"

"I believe it. Logan fights everything, he always has. Even stuff he genuinely wants, he fights on principle. We're not ignoring what he wants. He

173

doesn't tell us and then gets pissed when we don't read his mind."

Luke released my hand when Logan returned to the table and they ignored the blow up, as men so often do. Instead they talked tactics for the next stop. Our meals arrived and I messed with my bean burrito, what little appetite I had all but gone.

Logan Parker had once told me what he wanted. In no uncertain terms, with no room for doubt.

Me.

And I'd run screaming in the other direction.

Chapter Seventeen

I didn't mean to break him. In my saner moments, I almost convinced myself that it wasn't possible for someone like me to actually break a man like Logan Parker. After all he was built like a Grecian marble, shoulders like Atlas, built to carry the weight of the world. And he had the forceful personality to match the stellar bod.

But every now and then I'd catch him looking at me with a certain expression on his face. With *longing*, of all ridiculous things. That look pissed me off, made me want to run, to hide, to grab hold of his massive shoulders and shout that I wasn't special, that he should just go pick up another babe at a club, take her home and move the hell on already.

I didn't because he'd tried. *Everything*. Deep down I knew it, though it wasn't a thought I wanted to dwell on. If it was in the realm of possibility, Logan had attempted it. He'd tried to hate me, to forget me, to drop kick the past back where it belonged instead of toting it around like a set of designer luggage. There had been women, scores of them probably. But no repeat performers, no one that he looked at the same way he looked at me.

Like I was a light to his the darkness.

I hated that look, hated the mix of emotions it poured into a blender and hit frappe. Guilt predominated, though logically I knew I had nothing to feel guilty about. People had random hook-ups all the time. Maybe not with their future brother-in-laws but still, how was I supposed to know?

Granted at the time, I'd been too drunk and too desperate for acceptance to imagine the future consequences. I'd been the weak one, the needy one. If someone told me the events of that night would ruin the man beside me for all other women, I would have laughed in their faces. I didn't want it to be true and denial was my friend. Better to believe he hated me and had ever since that fateful night.

After we'd left the club, by mutual consent we'd turned toward the nearest beach. The moon was a large, pale orb floating overhead so close I could almost reach out and touch it. In my drunken brilliance, I might have tried.

"Do you do this a lot?" Logan asked me.

"Do what?" I blinked at him, surprised that he hadn't kissed me yet. Was I going to have to do everything? "Getting stupid drunk or picking up random hot guys to walk on the beach with?"

He grinned, his teeth a flash of white in the moonlight. "Both."

I turned to face him fully. "Would you believe me if I said no?" Considering the way I was dressed and my aggressiveness so far he probably thought I was a veteran of the walk of shame.

But he surprised me. "Yes." No reasoning, no I was watching you before and you looked innocent. No BS lines at all, just unwavering faith in a total stranger.

Those eyes seemed to look past my trashy club clothes, the body glitter which looked idiotic in retrospect and seen the broken heart I'd been trying to

176

forget. Drunk thoughts again. Before I could rein in my tongue I blurted, "I've never done this before."

He nodded once, accepting my words as though they were gospel and took my hand in his. "It's not usually my scene either."

It was probably the cheap vodka, but his words made me giggle. "No, so what is your *scene*?"

He shrugged. "Just hanging out with my brother, I guess."

There are two of them? I sent up a quick prayer of thanks to the benevolent deity who had concocted that scheme. "So why isn't he out with you tonight?"

"He's deployed overseas." The breeze intensified and a lock of dark hair was tossed over his eyes. He ran his free hand through it. His words revealed a world of loneliness but he smiled. "Some friends convinced me I should go out tonight and I'm glad they did. I would have missed out seeing you hand that grabby bastard his nuts."

I snorted. "It wasn't that much of a scene. I doubt anyone noticed."

"I noticed." The words were spoken quietly, but still crystal clear. "I was all set to play the hero but you handled it well all on your own."

I shrugged, discomfited by his praise. "It's what I do. Handle things, I mean."

It was his turn to snort. After I realized how that sounded I bust out laughing. "That's not what I meant," I wheezed.

I half expected him to make some lewd comment. H*ere baby, I've got something for you to handle*, or even to take the hand he'd trapped and put it on his crotch, but he didn't. Instead, he laced his

177

fingers through mine the gesture both sweet and intimate.

"So, what drove you to it?"

"Hey, if he'd grabbed *your* ass what would you have done?"

Another laugh. "No, not that. I mean why are you out doing the club thing?"

My smile faded and I turned away, tugging my hand back. "Trying to forget the shitty day I had." More like the shitty life I lived.

He let go, but matched my stride. "It's okay if you don't want to talk about it."

Of course I didn't want to talk about it, not with anyone I knew and especially not with a man I'd just picked up for a quick nail and bail. But for some reason the words, "I met my bio dad and he tried to get in my pants," slipped out.

Damn booze. I was never gonna drink again.

Logan swore under his breath. "Yeah, that's....shit I don't know what that is."

"Fucked up?" I offered.

He nodded, "Completely."

"In his defense, he didn't know who I was when he made the indecent proposal, but still. He's married and he's got a few kids and he didn't know me. I was just some trailer trash blowing along in the wind and....it was just so seedy, you know?" To my horror, a tear escaped, followed by another. Damn it, crying was *not* part of the plan.

Poor Logan just stood there, dark eyes wide, expression poleaxed.

I sniffled and turned away so he couldn't see my mascara run. Celeste always came home with mascara tear stains and the thought of looking like her...I had no idea what the hell I was doing. "Sorry.

178

This is probably heavier than you bargained for, huh? I wouldn't blame you if you want to cut and run."

"It'll be okay, Jackie." He pulled me into his chest and wrapped those strong arms around me. His hands rubbed my back in slow, reassuring motions. That unearthly heat seeped into me, warming all the cold places inside me and melting the ice around my battered heart. "It'll be okay."

It all came out then in great racking sobs, a torrent of emotion too much for any one body to handle. He held me as I shook and cried and basically lost my shit all over the beach. It seemed to stretch out as though time slowed and drew out as it reached for the distant horizon.

He murmured soft nonsensical things, telling me repeatedly that it would be all right. His kindness was too much, the safety too alluring, too close to what I'd been looking for with a father I'd never known. Protection, comfort, just someone else to lean on so I didn't have to carry it all by myself. His shoulders were so broad, surely he could carry me for a while. I clung to him, both grateful and afraid that he'd disappear. He couldn't though, I *needed* him.

And that was the scariest drunk thought of all.

The tears slowed and finally stopped. My body quit shaking. The white linen shirt he wore had big blotches, wet spots from where I'd leaked all over him and streaked with black from that bride o' Frankenstein mascara.

I looked at them and didn't know what to say, what to do. He was supposed to be my pick me up, like the vodka and cranberry or a bar of chocolate or a guilty pleasure movie marathon on Skinamax. Under no circumstances was he supposed to be the rock for me to cling to in the middle of my emotional breakdown. He wasn't supposed to see me like this, to hold me or encourage me to let it all out and have a good cry and ruin his shirt.

He wasn't my damned boyfriend.

A thumb brushed over my cheek. "You okay?"

I looked up at him. The expression he wore was one of concern. What were the chances I'd stumble across a guy like him, tonight of all nights? Women who picked up strange men in clubs were supposed to get screwed in one way or another. Anything from an unsatisfying nail and bail to having their kidneys carved out in a bathtub full of swiftly melting ice. Those men weren't supposed to be tender and consoling.

They weren't supposed to care.

"Jackie?" The concern morphed into worry. "Should I take you home?"

Take me home? So I could pass out beside Celeste and know that all it would take was another few nights like this to transform me into her clone? I'd gleefully sacrifice a kidney if it meant I didn't have to feel for another miserable second. I ruthlessly tamped all those nasty emotions back down, wiped my eyes and met his gaze. "Yes, take me to your home."

Those sinful lips parted. "I don't think—"

I kissed him. It was more of an assault than anything soft or sweet. My desperate gamble to get this night back on track. My body plastered against his as I focused on seducing him out of his heroic mindset.

He held out longer than I thought he would, not kissing me back or grabbing at the goodies I thrust unmercifully against him. But in the end he was a man and I was an insisting woman. His lips parted and he gave in with a groan so hot and desperate I

180

knew I'd won. He held me to him, not in the soft way from before but in answering demand, fingers digging into my hip, hand gripping the back of my neck so I couldn't get away.

It was all there, all the heat and promise I'd sensed at the club radiated from him like a sun. He stole my breath and promised me the oblivion I craved all at once.

"Take me to bed, Logan," I urged when we parted long enough for breath.

He studied my face as he panted, dark eyes assessing. Whatever he saw there must have reassured him because he nodded once and muttered, "It's not far."

Chapter Eighteen

"Earth to Jackie," Luke nudged me under the table. "You okay, babe?"

His words woke me from my little side trip down memory lane and both Parker brothers were staring at me intently. I forced a smile. "Fine. Just spacing out."

Luke smirked with pride. Logan glanced away. I gave in to temptation and ate a chip. There's only so much willpower a girl can be expected to show in a twenty-four hour period.

Luke signaled for the check. "We'd better get a move on, we need to get back to check on the tenant living over the mad spitter."

"Skippy." Could this day get any better?

We piled into the big black truck and sat silently in midday traffic, ignoring the giant fuchsia elephant squeezed into the vehicle. Logan's knuckles were white on the steering wheel as he executed each turn. Luke's shoulders were tight, though I didn't know if his tension was in anticipation of what we'd find in the upstairs apartment or the hinky vibes from his coworkers.

This time we didn't bother to check in with Alfredo Cruz before heading up the back stairs to Estaban Martinez's apartment. The 24 hour inspection notice was exactly where I'd left it. The door hadn't been opened since our visit yesterday.

"Maybe he stunk up the place then left town." Logan suggested without much feeling.

"I hope he's not dead." Even as I said it I had my cell phone poised, ready to call the police.

The Parker brothers exchanged a speaking glance. "Only one way to find out. Jackie, stay here. " Luke said as he headed for the stairs.

"This time, I actually will." I had no desire to be any closer to the source of that smell.

He nodded and used the key he'd procured from the landlord. The door opened and he removed the inspection notice. I stood on my tiptoes as if that would give me a better look as two broad sets of shoulders disappeared into the smelly apartment.

"What the hell...?" That was Luke.

Logan swore, coughed then added, "Do you see him?"

"What's going on?" I shouted.

"You!" Cruz appeared in the alley behind me, eyes narrowed in menace.

I squeaked and then scurried for the stairs before he could hock any phlegm in my general direction.

With the door opened the smell wafted out like a mushroom cloud. Stuck on some rickety stairs between a lugie and a rank place, I went up, my desire to stay spit free driving me onward. Cruz stood, hands on hips and eyes narrowed, but didn't follow.

The smell was overpowering on the landing and after the bright afternoon sunshine the inside of the apartment had a new moon darkness. I moved forward without giving my pupils time to dilate and tripped on something. There was a clang and a slosh as the bucket I'd just knocked over splashed across the ground. Part liquid but a good bit of mass spread out at my feet. Dear God, the *smell*. There was no way to categorize it as anything other than bad. My olfactory sense shut down in self-preservation.

A light clicked on, not an overhead light but the intense beam from a flashlight. The wielder shone it right in my face, ruining my night vision again. "Jackie?"

I threw my arm up, like a vampire caught in a ray of sun. "Damn it, get the light out of my eyes."

Logan swept the light off to the side. "Sorry. Why are you up here?"

"Because Cruz is down there and I didn't want to get spit on. Why didn't you turn the lights on?"

"His power's been shut off. I'm looking for the windows so we can air this shithole out. Watch the buckets."

"There's more?" Dread seeped into me as whatever had been in the bucket I'd tipped over seeped into the carpet. "Is the tenant okay?"

"Depends on who you ask. He's high as a kite."

Explained why his power had been turned off. "And the smell? Is his plumbing backed up?"

"If only." Logan located a window overlooking the street and yanked the shade until it retracted. He threw open the window and stuck his head out.

With the influx of light, I could see our surroundings. Though I'd half expected squalor, empty beer cans and pizza boxes, the interior wasn't

184

too bad. Except for where I'd knocked the bucket over, the place was halfway decent.

I stared down, unable to comprehend what I was standing in. "Is that a turd?"

"Afraid so."

I gagged and stepped back, bumping into yet another five gallon bucket of human waste. It tottered but didn't go down, thank all that was holy. They were *everywhere*, on the coffee table, beside the threadbare couch, on the kitchen counter. Several weeks' worth of preserved fecal matter.

"Why...?" My brain couldn't even finish the question, the words, this is wrong on so many levels spinning around and around the inside of my head.

"Come on." Logan took my arm and steered me around the bucket obstacle course toward the lone bedroom. "He's in here."

The bedroom door stood open and the window was already up. More buckets strewn around the room, these only half full. Or half empty, depending on who you asked. Obviously works in progress.

Luke looked slightly green as he crouched beside a semi-conscious and fully naked man sprawled in the doorway that separated bedroom from bathroom. His fingers were on the man's neck, timing his pulse. The man's head lolled and his eyes were rolled back in his head. "Jackie, call 911 and report a possible overdose."

I'd been breathing through my mouth and choked out, "Do you know what he took?"

The tenant lunged up suddenly, slipping Luke's hold in a flurry of frenetic struggle. "You can't have it, it's mine!" he darted to the nearest bucket and stuck his head in, inhaling deeply.

Bile rose in my throat and I swallowed hard.

185

Logan took the phone out of my numb hand and dialed. Distantly I heard him talking in a low voice to the operator. My eyes were glued to the naked maniac breathing in his own feces.

Martinez's slim shoulders relaxed and he rolled away, giggling.

"Jenkem," Luke said. "He's huffing fermented shit."

"That's an urban legend." I said, none too sure of my facts when the evidence splattered my pants.

"Tell that to Martinez," Logan hung up the phone. "Paramedics are en route."

"Let's bring him outside. Jackie, see if you can find a towel or something so he doesn't get arrested for public indecency."

"We already have enough shit to deal with," Logan deadpanned.

I giggled. The pun was incredibly bad, the situation so whacked out and just plain sad it was ridiculous. We *literally* had massive amounts of shit to deal with. I couldn't help it and couldn't seem to stop once I'd started. A hysterical note escaped and tears streamed down my face as I laughed.

"Uh oh. Ace, you better get outside, pronto." Luke said as he hefted Martenez's deadweight over his shoulder. "Logan, help her."

Logan moved toward me and manhandled me over to the window. He popped the screen free and his warm hand pressed against the back of my neck to hold me still while I sucked in some fresh air.

My head started to clear and gradually, the giggling subsided. I blinked, then shook my head.

"Better?"

I looked over into bright blue eyes, shaded with concern. "I'm not high." Just borderline hysterical.

I expected a quip, but he simply stared at me. His scrutiny was uncomfortable but after an apartment filled with human excrement, my tolerance for discomfort had no limits. I let him look, closed my eyes and just breathed.

"I'm sorry," he said quietly.

My eyes opened. "For what, exactly? You're gonna have to be more specific."

Though my tone was light, he winced. "That bad, huh?"

"No," I said, surprising us both. I took his hand in mine and squeezed it once. "You're really not. And even if you don't want me here, I'm glad you have my back, that you have Luke's back. I wouldn't trust anyone else this way."

"Thanks for that." He offered me a weak but genuine smile. "It's not that I don't want you here, but you shouldn't have to see stuff like this."

Could it be he was being a protective big brother sort instead of a raging dickweed? I decided to give him the benefit of the doubt and offered a smile. "I've seen worse." Maybe.

"Really?" One eyebrow went up.

"Okay, maybe not *quite* this bad."

"Didn't think so. We need to go help Luke."

I stood too quickly and cracked my head against the window frame and let out a yelp of pain. "Son of a motherless goat!"

"Easy," Logan cupped the back of my head and massaged my scalp, checking for lumps. I winced when he found the sore spot and he murmured

187

soothing sounds. "You're always in such a hurry to escape my company. It'll give a guy a complex."

"You are not any guy, you're Logan Parker." Though I'd be hard pressed to think of a less appropriate setting, with his hands in my hair and his fingers massaging my scalp and our eyes locked, that thing passed between us.

Our thing, mine and Logan's. The one we fought so hard to ignore, to pretend it had never existed, like a creature from myth. In that moment it was very real and about to wipe out a village.

He didn't say anything, just looked at me and let me see all the feelings he hid behind snark and menace. Heat of remembrance, the longing for a future we'd never have, the anger at me for taking it away, the hurt because I hadn't chosen him. And the guilt, for still wanting me in spite of my relationship with Luke.

I wanted to reach for him, to acknowledge his feelings. But I'd made my choice years ago and being close to him wasn't in the cards. In the end all I said was, "I'm sorry, too. For everything."

He looked away first, breaking the connection. "Come on, let's get the hell out of this shithole."

It would be a miracle if I survived the puns.

We made our way back through the bedroom and into the hall when the sounds of shouting reached us. Luke's steady drawl was drowned out by a series of curses.

"Crap," Logan hurried forward.

Alfredo Cruz stood on the dinky porch and ranted in rapid-fire Spanish at the unconscious man slung over my husband's shoulder. His arms waved as though he was trying to land several planes on an aircraft carrier at once and his face turned bright red as he unloaded his wrath.

"He needs medical attention." Logan put himself in the line of fire so Luke could slip down the stairs with the unconscious tenant. "We'll get the place cleaned up and you'll never know it was here."

His promise seemed somewhat grandiose. My guess was that the stench had invaded the sheetrock. I wanted to help but three people standing on that rickety stairwell didn't seem wise. That, plus I really didn't want him to spit on me.

Cruz's dark eyes swung toward me. "And what do I do while I wait for the shit smell to clear away? I tell you it is shit I smell and you leave!"

"There's a process we have to follow," I tried to explain. I should have saved my breath, tainted though it was.

"Process," he spat, literally. What was it about the tenants of this building and their bodily functions? "I spit on your process! And I spit on you!"

Oh no. My hands went up and I tried to babble out something. Logan grabbed hold of his arm to keep Cruz from coming after me. Cruz ducked, wild eyes fixed on his target.

Me.

He lurched forward and I stumbled away, tipping a bucket and landing flat on my back in a puddle of fermenting excrement. Cruz loomed over me and spat again. It struck me right between my eyes with the impact of a spent bullet, like he had a freak spitting superpower. Logan hefted him bodily upward and wrestled him out the door.

I lay on my back in the squishy mess and stared at the ceiling.

Worst. Day. Ever.

189

*****

We cleaned the buckets out of the apartment and called the sanitation department to remove them. The upstairs apartment desperately needed to be aired out but we couldn't leave with the windows open, so Logan guarded the steps while Luke helped me strip down to my bra and panties and hosed me down in the alley like a stray dog. Logan had procured a blanket from the paramedics who'd taken Mr. Martinez away for whatever treatment a shit-high warranted. The blanket was scratchy, but it covered my mostly bare ass after the makeshift cleansing. My clothes had gone into the Dumpster because as much as I'd adored that outfit, there was no way I could ever wear it again.

"The cops want to know if you want to press charges against Cruz. Apparently spitting is assault and the fact that he hit you with his lugie is battery."

I was tempted but I doubted that filing a misdemeanor against the downstairs tenant would endear me to our client. "No. But if he does it again, I'll have 'em throw the book at him." I'd always wanted to say that though I wished the circumstances would have been different.

"At least it wasn't in your hair." Luke shut off the water.

"Thank God for small favors. I would have had to shave it all off."

"Have you ever seen anything like this?" Luke asked as he used the blanket to dry me.

Despite the intensity of the sun, I shivered and tugged the blanket tighter over my bra and panties. "No."

"I keep going over it all in my head. First tenant's AWOL with a dead body in his place, next

190

one's house blows up, then the freak show cryolab and now an apartment full of shit. I'm beginning to think our venture is cursed."

I frowned and looked up at him. "What are you saying? Do you want to give up on it?"

"Why would I?' He looked genuinely surprised at my question.

I grinned. "I love you."

"Enough to still go to the engagement dinner?"

I blew out a breath. "Can't I skip it on account of having been covered in fecal matter?"

"If you really want to. But Jackie, you know how Mom is. You could show up still covered in fecal matter and she wouldn't care as long as you were there. It's tradition."

Damn it, if it had been anyone else on the face of the planet I could have bowed out. But Luke was right, Marge would expect me there. "Fine. As much fun as this has been, I need a real shower first. Possibly with bleach. How long until we can leave?"

He looked like he was about to kiss me, then thought better of it. "I can have Logan drive you home and then come back for me."

Which was more uncomfortable, swathed in only a blanket and my underwear in a back alley or more alone time with the Dark Prince? "I'll wait. The owner should be here soon, right?"

"He's en route as we speak. Oh, and the paramedics said it's highly unlikely you could have contracted anything just from rolling around in the shit. Or being spit on."

I forced a smile. "Must be my lucky day."

"The owner just pulled up. Is she safe to transport?" Logan called from around the corner.

Sheesh. "I'm not toxic waste," I shouted.

191

"Your stench says otherwise, oh Queen of Putrescence."

My eyes narrowed. "He's slamming me via *The Princess Bride*? He's doomed."

Luke looked like he was choking. "Ignore him."

"Are you laughing at me, too?"

"Trying really hard not to. I'll just go update the owner. Go wait in the truck."

I rolled my eyes, secured my blanket and marched over to the truck. Logan's lips twitched as I dripped on the superheated sidewalk. Passersby stared open mouthed at me but quickly averted their gazes from Logan's glare.

"Windows already down in preparation for your arrival, your majesty."

And here I'd thought we'd had a moment and declared a truce. "Get bent."

His eyes softened. "Jackie—"

I scowled at him. "I'm about five minutes away from total meltdown. If you knew what was good for you, you'd grab your brother and get this truck in motion, ASAP."

"Drinks are on me tonight."

I wanted to say something about dumping them over his fool head, but didn't want to prolong the verbal sparring match. He was trying and my bad mood was no reason to needle him. I stared out at the lively street silently until Luke returned.

Traffic was bumper to bumper all the way back to Coral Gate. Both the Parker brothers agreed I should have the first shower and I didn't feel even a little bit bad about using up all the hot water as I practically parboiled myself clean.

"Shower free?" Luke poked his head into the bedroom.

192

"I'll take it out in the skin trade," I quipped.

He kissed me quickly and disappeared into the bathroom while I poked through my closet.

Though I wanted only to slither into some sweats and veg out in front of the DVR with some takeout, I forced myself into the standard sleeveless LBD, with a scoop neck to accentuate my cleavage and a swishy skirt to disguise my thighs. Hair got pulled up and twisted into a chignon and I lined my eyes, applied mascara liberally and glossed my lips. No necklace to distract from the girls, but I did insert diamond stud earrings that Luke had given me on our last anniversary. I slipped my feet into sandals with little wedge heels, sent up a quick thanks that my pedicure was holding up and exited the bedroom.

Logan sprawled across the couch facing the T.V. He had a bottle of beer in hand and was just raising it to his lips as I sauntered out of the bedroom. He glanced my way, then did a double take and put his feet down, squaring his shoulders. His posture gave new meaning to the phrase, *sit up and take notice.*

"You look...." His voice was hoarse and he let the sentence trail off as though words escaped him.

"Ready for a drink?" If it was Luke I would have swiped his beer, but I knew better than to cross that line with the Dark Prince. Instead, I made my way to the refrigerator and made a screwdriver, trying to ignore the feel of his gaze glued to my back.

"Beautiful," he finished, surprising us both with the admission.

"Thanks." I sipped my drink. "Queen of Putrescence cleans up right decent then?"

"Like no one else." Logan said.

193

Chapter Nineteen

Marge and Gerald had reserved a private room on the upper floor of a fabulous restaurant in South Beach for their "reengagement" party. The view was magnificent, overlooking the ocean—the atmosphere lively with candles in little glass jars on every table and slow jazz crooning from the speakers. Classy, just like my in-laws.

I looked around for the bar, determined to take Logan up on his offer to buy the drinks as soon as humanly possible. There were at least eighty people in the room, most of whom I didn't know. Gerald always invited his clients and their significant others to the party. Marge waved when she saw us come in. My mother-in-law was dressed in a lightweight mauve pantsuit and matching pumps and wore a white fringed shall to combat the restaurant's subarctic air conditioning.

I waved back. "Should we go say hello?"

"Don't you want a drink first?" Luke asked.

"Every time I see your mother lately, I have a drink in my hand. I'm surprised she hasn't suggested I join Alcoholics Anonymous yet. It's bad enough I don't cook and she can't pin me down about the grandchild thing, but I don't want her to think I'm a lush."

I shifted nervously beside him. It was more than that, so much more. Never mind that I'd rolled around in excrement earlier, parties of this magnitude unnerved me. In a glittering crowd it was impossible to forget that I was Celeste Drummond's trailer trash daughter.

Luke shook his head. "Why are you worried? Mom thinks you hung the moon. After all, you got the coveted matron of honor gig. Women have scratched each other's eyes out over that role."

I didn't know if he was kidding or not, but Marge and Gerald were notorious for their nuptials and all the events that surrounded them. Gerald's father had been a rancher and my father-in-law was a financial genius who turned the family's land wealth into serious money. He worked part time as a financial advisor for the nation's elite.

Now that I thought about it, I had been on the receiving end of some pretty dirty looks at the bridal shower, but had chalked it up to the smell of burnt house.

Marge appeared at my elbow, still the same warm woman who cooked us breakfast, now glammed up for society. "Jackie, don't you look gorgeous? So elegant. And your skin is absolutely radiant. What's your secret?"

"You wouldn't believe her if she told you." Logan appeared and handed both me and his mother a glass of champagne.

Marge turned toward Logan and fussed with his perfectly straight black tie. "Logan, would it have killed you to get your hair cut? You're starting to look like the Wild Man of Borneo."

I thought he looked more like a successful drummer, what with the diamond stud in his ear, the

195

unkempt locks and the all black suit. I glanced away because no one asked me.

"Just the look I was going for." Logan winked.

Luke nudged his brother in the ribs, and then stooped to kiss his mom on the cheek. "Where are we sitting?"

"With me, your father and your grandmother, right over there." Marge's smile looked a little forced.

"Granny's here?" Luke's eyes went wide at the news.

I exchanged a glance with Logan. Granny Ursula didn't get out much, but when she did there was always drama. She was probably at least partly responsible for why Marge was such a considerate mother-in-law to me. Ursula Parker had been the very definition of a harridan to her son's wife for four decades.

Marge downed her champagne and upped the wattage of her smile. "Your father's idea, he claims she's depressed and needs to spend more time with the family. God help us all." The last bit was delivered under her breath.

Over the music and the din of voices came an accusatory, "Are you lazy or just stupid?"

"Speak of the devil." Marge plucked my glass out of my hand and downed that one too.

"Paper rock scissors you for who carries Mom out of here," Logan hissed to Luke.

I elbowed him that time. "That's your *mother*."

"And she's not as light as she used to be," he shot back.

"Logan, why don't we make ourselves useful and fetch a few more drinks?" Luke steered his brother away.

I called out. "And don't think I haven't noticed that it's an open bar," before turning to Marge.

"How was work?" She asked, her tone distracted.

My teeth sank into my lower lip as I considered telling her about the cryonics removal followed by the shithole. Definitely a discussion for another time, like a quarter past never. "Fine. Is everything all right, Marge?"

"Fine." Her answer was as false as mine, her smile just as brittle. The Parker boys returned, liquid offerings in hand. We both nodded our thanks and drank.

"There you are." Gerald approached his face lit up at the sight of his bride.

Even after I met Luke, I never thought I could handle being married. Having to take care of Celeste had soured me on the idea of tying my happiness with someone else's. But seeing Marge and Gerald together had altered my perception. There was no obligation in their relationship and even forty years in, a shared look between them still produced enough heat to light up all of Miami. Both the Parker brothers made gagging sounds whenever I voiced that opinion, but they knew it was true.

Gerald Parker was as fit and trim in his late fifties as his sons were in their thirties. Same lean build, same chiseled jaw and though his hair had more salt than pepper, I caught a glimpse of my future with Luke every time I looked at him. Though somehow I doubted Luke would ever look as comfortable in a suit and tie, never mind the horn-rimmed glasses that were Gerald's trademark.

He leaned in and kissed my cheek. "Jacqueline, you look lovely as always."

197

"You wouldn't say that if you'd seen her earlier." Logan, who else?

Gerald shot his son a confused look, then refocused on me. "Come, sit. Mother is dying to see you."

"We aren't that lucky," Marge muttered. Then louder, "Gerald, for heaven's sake, don't call her mother like that. You sound like Norman Bates."

Gerald blinked his big blue eyes, appearing even more owlish. "What else would I call her?"

Marge's lips twitched and I could only imagine the temptation she resisted. Gerald was a sweet, although somewhat naïve creature who excelled at making money and possessed all the social skills of a mop. He was perpetually caught between the rock and the hard place of the formidable women in his life and was blessedly ignorant of it.

Luke took my arm, propelling me forward to the table where Ursula Parker sat, glowering at anyone who dared to stop by. She was lean and meticulous, not a strand of white hair out of place. Her posture was perfect, her eyes the same icy blue as Logan's, a startling contrast next to her paper bleached skin tone. She too wore all black, like she was attending a funeral rather than a reengagement party.

"Good to see you, Granny," Luke dropped a kiss on her heavily powdered cheek.

Her spidery eyebrows contracted as she frowned up at him. "Which one are you again?"

"That's Luke, Mother." My father-in-law raised his voice to a near shout.

Her displeasure moved from her grandson to her son. "For God's sake Gerald, I'm old, not deaf."

Marge picked a seat several away from Granny Parker and held up her glass to her husband. "Be a dear and get me another."

Ever solicitous, Gerald Parker courted his mother's wrath. "Can I get you anything, Mother? Another drink, perhaps?"

Those steely blue eyes narrowed. "Just because your wife overindulges doesn't mean I will."

Luke and Logan flanked their grandmother, creating a human shield between the senior Parker women. I sat between Luke and Marge and tried to be as inconspicuous as possible.

It didn't work.

"You're still here?" Ursula didn't bother to hide her surprise. "Would have thought my grandson would have grown bored with you by now."

I never had any idea what to call her. Beelzebub maybe. "No, Mrs. Parker, I'm still here."

"Jackie and I are married, Granny, remember?" Luke passed the dinner rolls to me. "You came to our wedding?"

"Give it up Luke, her memory is selective." Logan took a long drink.

Ursula sniffed. "It takes some doing to hold a man's attentions, you know. Back in my day, women practiced the feminine arts."

"Eye of newt, wing of bat," Marge muttered.

I choked on my next swallow of champagne and Luke pounded me helpfully on the back.

Gerald returned with a fresh drink and handed it to his wife but didn't sit. Instead, he tapped a knife against his champagne flute. The room quieted quickly and he called out. "Thank you all so much for coming and sharing this special event with us." Slight pause accompanied by a sheepish grin. "Again."

199

Laughter.

"Before our dinner is served I'd like to make a quick toast." He turned to face his wife.

"There are two kinds of romantic love. The kind you can share with anybody you're attracted to if you both want it badly enough. Many people live and die only ever experiencing love like that. But then there's the special kind that is between you and one other person. The kind of love that you bask in because you know deep down that your life would never be the same without that person in it. That you are better, not because of anything that they do, but because they simply are. Between you and your soul mate and you only get one. I have been fortunate enough to share a life with mine. To Margie."

We all raised our glasses and chorused, "To Margie."

Tears were in her eyes and from a distant corner I heard Granny's distinctly disgusted harrumph as the happy couple shared a kiss.

Luke took my empty champagne flute from my hand, set it down on the table and leaned in to murmur in my ear. "Will you dance with me?"

I shivered at the warm breath on my neck and my lips parted in surprise. "Really?" Luke was not a cut a rug kinda guy, which I accepted. Maybe it had something to do with the sentiment he'd seen his parents share. Or maybe it was because I both looked and smelled halfway decent for the first time in what felt like days.

He grinned and rose, offering me his hand. "Really."

I followed him out onto the dance floor among the other couples canoodling in elegant splendor. I always associated dancing with foreplay, bodies moving in rhythm with one another, touching, scenting, and experiencing something beyond their own mental diatribe. Maybe it was just me.

One of Luke's hands gripped my waist, the other clasping my hand. His lips twitched as he pulled me close. "You gonna let me lead this time?"

I shrugged. "Anything is possible, but I wouldn't count on it."

We managed an awkward adult version of the eighth grade shuffle. I was happy just to be close to him, to stare up into his melted chocolate eyes and imagine what would happen once we were shut up in our bedroom for the night.

A shiver stole over me and I rested my cheek against his chest in contented anticipation. All sorts of hijinks would ensue once we ditched the extended family.

He kissed the top of my head. "You're gorgeous, you know."

"And you always know exactly what I need to hear."

He pulled me in a little tighter. "I was thinking about what Dad said, about soul mates."

"Yeah?" I had a good idea where he was going with this and tried to ignore the heat on my back. Without looking I knew Logan was staring at us.

Someone tapped Luke on the shoulder. I stiffened as a male voice asked, "May I cut in?"

I looked up and smiled in recognition. "Aaron."

The two men shook hands. If Luke was disappointed he hid it well. Instead, he dropped a kiss on my cheek. "I better go check on the family."

I put a little more space between myself and Aaron. He was a much more skilled dancer and I enjoyed falling into step with his easy confidence.

"So, how's the job going?"

"It's moving along. I spoke with Mara Young the other day."

"Oh?" His smile was polite, if a tad disinterested. "I hope she was helpful."

"Actually, she seemed distracted, like I caught her at a bad time. And I'm pretty sure she lied to me."

Aaron frowned. "That doesn't sound like the Mara I know. She's as focused as a laser beam. It's why I've utilized her so many times in the past."

He looked so concerned, I instantly regretted bringing her up. The last thing I wanted to do was cost Mara Young Aaron's business. I, of all people, knew just how important professional reputations were. Damn it, why did I have to go and open my big, stupid mouth?

"I'm sure she was just having an off day. Maybe family issues. God knows we've all been there. I'm there right now." I waved a hand around to encompass the room.

Aaron's eyebrows drew down at my inane babbling, clueing me in that he didn't know what the hell I was talking about. That made two of us. I was too tired to do the small talk thing properly.

Luckily, his cell phone rang, saving me from more awkward prattle. "Excuse me," he turned away to take the call.

I glanced around, looking for a ladies room so I could hide when someone gripped my hand and whirled me back into motion.

I jolted as I realized who my new dance partner was. "What are you doing?"

Logan looked down at me, blue eyes intense. "Luke lost the coin toss and he's helping get mom into the car. She's toasted."

202

I sagged against him, relieved. "So, we're going?"

"Yeah." But he made no move to leave.

"Logan," I said, not sure what to tag on after. We shouldn't, I don't want to fight with you. When the hell will this get any easier?

"Ssshh. Just enjoy the dance, Jackie." He spun me out, then pulled me back in. Unlike Luke, Logan relished dancing on the same primal level as I did. Not as an art or a formality, but as an experience. Though I wasn't at all comfortable with him the way I was with Luke, I'd be hard-pressed to find a better partner.

Taking his advice, I leaned back and enjoyed the dance.

Chapter Twenty

I rose early the next morning, thought about going for a jog, then decided I'd rather have coffee. I took a shower first, climbed into some yoga pants that had yet to see a day of yoga and pulled on a tank top.

Luke was still asleep when I tiptoed from the bedroom. The clang of a pan on the stove told me Marge was already up and bustling about the kitchen. After her night of imbibing, I was seriously impressed with her stamina. "Mom?"

Logan's dark head appeared through the opening between the kitchen and living room. "She's still sawing it off. Sounds like a pack of wildebeests crank starting a model T."

I stifled my laugh. "What are you doing up?"

"Making omelets. What with all the crazy I didn't get anything to eat last night. You hungry?"

"Starving." I'd planned on just pouring myself a bowl of cereal but an omelet sounded infinitely better.

He pushed a red bell pepper in my direction. "Can you manage to chop that up without losing a finger?"

Maybe. "I'll do my best. You can reattach it if I do though, right?"

"Not before I eat."

We worked in silence, though I stayed well back from the stove, the coffee pot or anything else that might explode. Though the pieces were all different sizes, the pepper got chopped and my fingers stayed attached. He took the cutting board from me and dumped the pepper into a sizzling frying pan along with a minced red onion and mushrooms. He did that little thing cooks did where they rotated the stuff in the pan by just yanking on the handle. Veggies flipped in the air then landed neatly back on top of less well cooked veggies. I winced when I imagined the carnage if I ever tried a stunt like that. Logan cracked several eggs into a bowl, added spices and whipped it all frothy.

"So Logan," I began as he poured his egg concoction into the heated pan.

He groaned. "Knew it was too good to last."

I poured myself a cup of coffee, intentionally keeping my back to him. "What?"

"You, digging at me."

"I don't dig at you." I might dig at him.

He just looked at me.

"Well, you say stuff sometimes and it makes me curious. Sue me."

He sighed and added shredded Monterey Jack cheese, then folded half the omelet expertly on top of the other half.

"No bacon?" I sipped my coffee. Damn, that was the good stuff.

He glanced at me over his shoulder, one eyebrow raised. "No diet?"

"You're mean."

"Sue me."

He split the omelet down the middle and slid half onto my plate and half onto his, then put the pan in the sink to soak. "Fine, I'll answer your damn question if you answer one of mine."

205

I pulled a face. That could get dicey but the only other option was to let my curiosity go unchecked and sit with him in silence. "Agreed."

He topped off my coffee and poured a mug for himself as I carried our plates to the table. I dug in, and just bit back a moan of bliss. Magic. He'd definitely traded a piece of his blackened soul to cook so well.

"Okay, so ask your questions." He rose and popped two slices of whole wheat into the toaster.

"Who taught you to cook? Your Mom?"

He blinked, obviously surprised that was the question I'd picked. "She didn't used to cook, at least not the way she does now. We had a housekeeper when we were young and she kept the place well stocked, but family meals weren't the big deal back then."

I frowned and set my fork down. "Luke never said anything to me about that." As close as I was to both Marge and Luke, neither one had ever suggested that their current way of life was different from the ways things had been when the Parker brothers were children.

The toast popped up and Logan buttered both slices and passed one to me. "Didn't you ever wonder how he could be so content with a woman who was kitchen cursed?"

"No," I deadpanned. "I didn't."

His lips twitched. "Well, he was trained for it. Uniquely suited. First, at home and then the military. Food was fuel. We always had enough, but it wasn't gourmet or anything."

I loaded a hunk of my yummy omelet onto the toast. "So, back to the original question. Who taught you to cook?"

206

He shrugged and finished the mouthful he'd been working on. "It was kind of a fluke thing. I stumbled across a cooking show and watched the chef prepare a meal. It wasn't anything fancy, just stuffed pork chops and almond roasted green beans but I was watching and I thought, hey, I could do that."

"And you did?" My coffee cup was empty, but I was too riveted to his fascinating tale to get up for a refill.

Logan grinned, that deep disarming smile of his flashing out like a shooting star. If I'd blinked I would have missed it. "Hell no. My first attempt was awful, my second was worse. Ask Luke, he'll tell you the horror stories. I probably scorched every pot we owned at some point."

"So when did you get so good?" When I realized how that sounded, I made a face. "That didn't come out right."

He leaned back in his chair. "I'll take the compliment. Well, to tell you the truth, it was just like anything else. You work at it and get better over time. Of course, when I worked as a sous-chef in that pub a few years ago, my skills got a boost. I learned a lot there."

My fork clattered to my empty plate. "You were a *chef* in a *pub*?"

"Sous-chef. One below the guy in charge. In that particular kitchen there were only three employees, so the title was really just a formality." He shrugged like being a frigging chef wasn't such an unbelievably awesome accomplishment.

"That's incredible," I breathed. I knew a lot of people, but never an actual chef before. Chefs were the miracle workers who we paid for culinary delights. Yes, some were better than others but all were better

207

than me and my sad little kitchen curse. "I never knew that about you."

His gaze trapped mine. "You never asked."

Why did I feel guilty all of a sudden? Maybe because I never thought about what Logan did when he wasn't acting as my personal tormentor? "I guess I haven't been the best sister-in-law."

He shrugged, eyes fixed on his plate. "Don't worry about it."

"I'll do better going forward. I promise. After all, we're family." I rose, collecting our plates. "I'll clean up."

"Jackie?"

"Hmm?"

He seemed to be struggling with something.

I let the hot water run to fill the sink, checking to be sure there weren't any sharp objects waiting to gore me. "Fair's fair, you answered my question so I have to answer yours."

"Do you ever regret marrying Luke?"

I froze, hands immersed in hot, soapy water. "Why would you ask me that?"

He got up, moved beside me. "What I mean is, with him in the military, you've been alone a lot."

Forcing my hands to scrub I murmured, "That was my choice. I could have gone with him but I needed to be here for Celeste and for my career. Sure, I missed him, but I have friends, a job. I kept busy."

"Eating microwavable meals and watching T.V." he grumbled. "That's not living."

I whirled to face him. "How the hell would you know what I was doing?"

His expression was a mixture of incredulity and pity as he murmured, "He asked me to look out for you."

"Look out for me? You mean *spy* on me?"

He turned to the side, giving me his profile. "It wasn't like that."

I ran a hand through my hair, too late remembering it was full of soap suds. "So what was it like, huh? Were you or were you not parked outside this house staring at me through the windows?"

His jaw hardened into a stubborn line.

I shoved him in the chest. "Frigging hell, Logan! Did you drive-by to check for my car? Did you follow me when I went out at night? How many places have I gone to that you were there and I didn't even know it? Do you have any concept of how creepy this is to me?"

Blue eyes flashed from ice to fire. "I won't apologize for looking out for my brother's wife when he asked me to. Like you said, we're family."

I wagged a finger in his face, soap flying off the end of the digit. "He meant for you to drop by and ask if I needed anything and you know it! Luke would never—"

"Don't tell me what Luke would never do. I did the best I could in a shitty situation." He turned and strode toward the door, his body posture screaming end of discussion.

Part of me wanted to fly after him, to beat on his back and kick and yell at him some more. Instead, I turned around and plunked my mitts back in the sink. Damn it, this was so unsettling. How many nights had Logan watched me, followed me? Hell, call a spade a spade, frigging *stalked* me? Was it any wonder none of his relationships had worked out when he felt obligated to watch over me while his brother was away?

209

Luke had no idea of what he asked with his simple straight-forward request. He'd inadvertently asked his brother to fixate on the woman Logan was desperate to forget.

Though I didn't want to, maybe I *needed* to tell Luke about what had happened, if for no other reason so that he'd never ask his brother to watch out for me again. But if I did, what would happen to Damaged Goods? Would we all be able to continue working together? Somehow I doubted it.

I scrubbed and stewed and muttered to myself. Something had to give. Soon.

A door opened down the hall and Marge shambled in, looking much the worse for wear. "Dear God, why did you let me drink so much? And what's with all the shouting?"

Had we been shouting? "Oh you know, just me and Logan at it again."

She rolled her eyes but then winced as if the motion pained her. "You two go at it like an old married couple."

I blanched at her word choice. After a moment's consideration, she did, too.

"Sorry, I didn't mean it the way it sounded."

"Believe me, I'm the last person who'll take you to task for misspeaking."

Marge poured a cup of coffee. "Do you want to talk about it?"

I dried my hands. "Not right now. I'm going out for a drive."

"Remember the dress fitting today at three," she called.

I offered her a sincere smile. "Will do."

My Dolphins cap hung on the antique coat rack which was a ridiculous piece of furniture for a Miami resident, but I liked it all the same. I plunked it on my head, slid my feet into sneakers and grabbed my purse.

I had no real destination in mind when I started out, other than away from Logan. Bessie Mae chugged through the early morning traffic. I flipped through a few radio stations but didn't find anything to take my mind from my troubles. The gas light came on and I drove up to the nearest gas station.

Though I winced at the fuel prices, I filled the tank. Given my current mood I might drive around all day and have to fill up again. Though I was tempted to hop on the interstate and see how far I could get from the Parker brothers, I knew I'd have to go back eventually and deal with them all.

Anxiety knotted my guts. I didn't know what to say to Luke. Marge had agreed with me, telling my husband about one night of ancient history would only hurt him, but Logan was hurting too. For the first time, I considered our situation from his point of view. All he'd done was meet a girl he liked only to have her vanish the morning after. Nailed and bailed he probably would have dealt with, but then he finds out I'm engaged to his brother...that was the textbook definition of awkward.

I could clearly recall the look on his face the first time Luke had brought me home to meet the family. The stunned expression, the dawning horror that a woman he'd wanted for himself had instead picked his brother. Talk about a kick in the crotch. Was it any wonder he vilified me?

The tank was full so I reapplied the cap and headed back out into traffic. The little light was blinking on my phone, indicating I had a text but I ignored it, too caught up in my own head to deal with the outside world just then.

So what if Logan had wanted me? I hadn't wanted him. Didn't that count for anything?

Damn it, I wasn't fooling anybody with that lie, not even myself. I *had* wanted Logan, desperately. Hell, I could even admit that I'd needed him the night we'd met. He'd been kind and generous and attentive and...perfect. But the timing for a real relationship had been horrific. I couldn't let myself depend on a man, not if I wanted to avoid turning into Celeste 2.0, the damaged daughter edition.

So I'd slipped out while he was asleep, never to return. Though that wasn't the whole story, not by a long shot. I'd been tempted to go back, had driven by his apartment building, checked for his car. Okay, I'd admit it, I'd spied on him the same way I'd accused him of spying on me. The irony wasn't lost on me.

"What a mess," I said to Bessie Mae. She didn't answer of course but it helped to feel like I wasn't all alone rattling around inside my own head.

But where was I? Frowning, I scanned the street for landmarks. Near the yacht club. Good, I could pop by Mara Young's office and give her a head's up that I might have accidently cost her a big account. Wasn't exactly the mood lifter I'd been hunting for, but it was something to do.

I parked and climbed from the car, wincing as I realized I was the embodiment of dressed down. Not even wearing a bra for crying out loud. Why couldn't I have been in the LBD from last night instead of my bag lady garb? Maybe I should go home and change into something a little less slacker-casual. But then I'd be running from the frying pan into the fire, wouldn't

I? Besides, that was just an excuse to put off the conversation I didn't want to have with Luke.

Decided, I pulled my ball cap low and donned my oversized sunglasses. The morning was hazy, but the relentless south Florida sunshine would prevail as it always did. I ignored the odd glances at my wardrobe choice and headed to Mara's slip, relieved to see the *Forever Young* was in. I called out as I approached but no one answered.

Looking like I had the right to climb aboard, I scurried up the steep stairs. Maybe Mara was out, grocery shopping or whatever. I scanned the parking lot, but it was wasted effort since I didn't know what kind of vehicle she drove.

So, I'd just wait. Inside the cabin so none of the neighboring yacht owners could get a look at my outfit. Was it breaking and entering if it was a boat and a place of business? Probably only if it was locked. If not, it would just be entering. Worth a try.

The door to the below deck cabin was closed, but pushed open with a simple turn of the handle.

The smell hit me hard. Same wretched stank as at Fester Gomez's place.

Death had been there.

I almost dropped to my knees, no longer worried about my plebian ensemble because Mara Young's sightless eyes wouldn't notice anything ever again.

Chapter Twenty One

"Tell me what happened?" Sergeant Enrique Vasquez pulled me off to the side of the slip while the medical examiner did his thing inside the cabin of the *Forever Young*.

"I stopped by to see Mara. She was responsible for collecting the rent on Gomez's place. We'd talked a few days ago but I showed up late and she had another appointment...." I trailed off as my eyes locked on the black body bag being lifted from the belly of the yacht.

Vasquez blew out a breath. "Mrs. Parker, why are you still asking questions about the Gomez case?"

That snagged my attention. "Why shouldn't I? Our team was responsible for the property."

"Was being the operative word. The property has been cleared and handed back to the owner."

I blinked at his abruptness. "Did you ID the Jane Doe yet?"

His lips twitched. "You watch a lot of crime and punishment television, don't you?"

"I prefer *Bar Rescue*. Seriously though, do you know who she was? Or did you find Gomez?"

Vasquez looked pained. "I really can't discuss this with you."

"But you're still looking, right?"

A muscle ticked in his jaw and he wouldn't meet my gaze. Answer enough.

I stared at the gurney as it was wheeled up off the docks. "They have to be related, the deaths I mean."

"It could just be a coincidence," Vasquez said.

I glared at him. "You don't believe that any more than I do."

"You're right, I don't. What I do believe is that it's time for you to get past this, Mrs. Parker."

No way was he serious. "Get *past* this? Tell me, how is finding two dead women like the flu?"

The sergeant's dark brown eyes hardened. "If you're right and these cases are connected, that means Mara Young was killed over the Gomez property. Two women are dead. Fester Gomez is still missing. My guess is his body is somewhere in the Everglades, being slowly digested by the local fauna. Now, you've found two out of the three bodies. Asking questions could get you killed. You aren't a trained law enforcement officer so it's time you back off."

My mouth hung open and I blinked twice, stunned. He thought I was right and he still wanted me to stand aside and just do nothing, to stop digging. "But—"

"Understand me, Mrs. Parker. I'm under no obligation to provide you with information and I will formally charge you with interfering with a police investigation if you don't let this go. Do I make myself clear?"

I shut my mouth and nodded once.

215

Vasquez nodded crisply. "Good. Then you're free to go. I'll call you if I have any further questions."

Feeling like an indignant child who'd just been spanked, I slogged back to Bessie Mae. I was so lost in thought that I didn't see him at first. A man, lying on the ground by my car. I sucked in a sharp breath when I saw the garden hose snaking out of my gas tank and feeding into a little red carrier. The son of a gun was siphoning gas out of my car. "Hey!"

He turned to face me and I stopped when I recognized him. Horace Cooper, the survivalist whose bug out house I'd exploded. How the hell did he find me? The fact that he'd do this right under the nose of several of Miami's finest meant he was even crazier than I thought.

"Sergeant Vasquez!" I shouted and jumped up and down, waving my hands to get the cops' attention. My target was too far away but several uniformed patrolmen looked my way. One smirked as I bounced again, ogling the unfettered girls. "Yo, crime in freaking progress here!"

Quick as a striking snake, Cooper yanked the hose from my car, spilling gas all over the ground. He picked up the gas can and leapt into a nearby van. The door slid shut behind him.

The police had finally figured out I wasn't just showing off the goodies for their viewing pleasure and were running, but it was too late. The van roared away, going up on two wheels as it took a corner too fast.

I swore and looked at the mess I'd been left with. That nutjob had violated my Bessie Mae!

The police officers stopped beside me. "What happened?"

"Someone just siphoned gas out of my car."

The taller of the two officers had a confused look on his face. "This car? That tank is fifteen gallons, tops. Why would anyone bother to siphon gas out of this car?"

"Because I blew up his bug out house. It was a vengeance thing."

Both officers looked at me like I was crazy.

I sighed, then explained what had happened with Cooper.

"And he just happened to be here?" the shorter officer said.

"He was probably following me, waiting for the opportunity to snag my gas."

They exchanged a look. "So you're telling us some guy was burning all of his gas out of a big V-8, just following you around waiting to steal your measly fifteen gallons worth?"

"Did you miss the part where I said he was bugfuck crazy?"

"Lady, guys bent on revenge slash tires or key the paint. They don't siphon off gas."

I threw my hands in the air. "So he's a pragmatic nutjob."

Vasquez had arrived and one dark eyebrow went up. "Problem?"

I turned my back on the skeptical uniforms and retold the story.

Had to give the sergeant credit, he tried really hard not to laugh. Ultimately failed, but A for effort. The two uniforms joined in. I crossed my arms over my breasts and waited him out. I had a good sense of humor, but this was a bridge too far.

Vasquez sucked in a deep breath. "Damn, I needed that. Okay, do you want to file a report?"

"What will that accomplish?"

217

"Not much, but we'll have Cooper on file in case he strikes again. Any chance you caught the plate number?"

"I never think to look for them. It was a big white van. Chances are he's living out of it now, since his house is toast."

"Does anybody like you?"

I ignored that last comment and snagged my phone and purse from Bessie Mae. Three missed texts, all from Luke. Damn. "Any chance you can drop me at a gas station?"

Forty five minutes later, I was back on the road, late for my dress fitting. Marge was gonna kill me. The parking lot was full to bursting and some jackass in an SUV had straddled the line between his space and the only available one. Luckily, Bessie Mae was bitty, though if another oversized vehicle encroached on the other side, I'd be forced to re-enter the car through the window. Was it worth the risk of having the car stolen to leave the window down? Convinced whichever decision I made would be the wrong one, I hurried into the store.

There are times when I like to make an entrance. This wasn't one of those times. The dress shop's patrons looked up and a few sniffed delicately. I was too busy enjoying the efficient air conditioning to care, at least until my mother-in-law marched up.

"What happened to you?" Marge's brows pulled together in concern.

"It's a long story." Great, my tank top had pit stains and the cuffs of my yoga pants were spattered in gasoline. Delicately, I pushed my wind-tossed hair back from my face and settled my sunglasses atop my head to keep the mess at bay. I gave my mother-in-law a reassuring smile. "Better late than never, right?"

218

Marge blinked, but shook it off when a woman scurried forward with a zipped garment bag. "Are we waiting on anyone else?"

"One other." Marge turned to face her.

That was news to me, but it was Marge's vow renewal so I kept my trap shut.

Marge took the bag from the woman and passed it to me. "This is yours, Jackie."

"Fitting rooms are just through there." The clerk indicated a curtained off portion of the store.

I'd never been in a wedding before, other than my own. And Luke and I had kept it simple. A brief ceremony and a beach party, just our speed. I hadn't even worn a real wedding dress, just a white halter sundress that worked my cleavage to its best advantage. No appointments, no big to-do, no stress. After the week I'd had as matron of honor, I was double glad my wedding had followed the KISS credo. Keep It Simple, Stupid.

A sense of foreboding rippled through me as I eyed the garment bag. It was way too similar to the body bag Mara Young had been zipped into as the medical examiner hauled her off to the morgue. Dizziness washed over me and I put my hand out to steady myself so I didn't keel over in a dead faint.

"Keep it together, Jackie." I huffed and puffed like I could blow the dress shop down, then jumped when someone knocked on the door. Damn it, I needed to get a freaking grip already. "Just a second."

"Did you need anything? Undergarments maybe?" the saleslady asked.

"I'm good." What I needed was a shower and a fifth of vodka. And maybe a time travel device so I could literally unscrew an extremely screwed-up

219

situation. Somehow I doubted this dress shop had either in stock.

"Jackie, honey?" Marge tapped lightly on the door.

My sanity was dangling over a pit of acid by a frayed thread. I needed to bulldoze my way through this dress fitting and get somewhere I could go insane without making a public spectacle and embarrassing my mother-in-law.

"I'll be right out." With a shaking hand, I slid the zipper down to reveal the horror within.

"Um...?"

"Do you like it?" Marge asked anxiously.

I poked at a pastel ruffle. "It's mint."

"No, it's sea foam. Those are our colors, sea foam and silver."

Sea foam, my dimpled ass. Reluctantly, I shed my clothes, daubed at my underarms with a tissue from my bag and pulled the frothy mint confection off the hanger.

"What do you think?" Marge sounded excited. "Come out here. There are more mirrors."

The lone one in the stall was bad enough.

I exited the dressing room. "It fits." If by fits I meant me being shrouded in ruffles until I resembled a seasick cloud.

Marge scowled. "You're right, it's mint. It makes you look green."

Skippy.

The attendant who'd handed me the garment bag of doom hurried over at my mother-in-law's wave. "Is everything all right?"

Though my mother-in-law was no bridezilla, she didn't get pushed around either. Marge put her

220

hands on her hips and scowled. "No, I ordered sea foam but this dress is clearly mint."

The woman whipped a tablet out of God alone knew where and pulled up Marge's order. "No, ma'am, you ordered the mint."

Marge looked indignant at that. "Why on earth would I order mint, when my colors are sea foam and silver?"

"I have the order right here." The other woman said.

Marge's eyes went wide as she saw the order. She looked at me with something near panic. "Oh, no, she's right. I checked the wrong box."

"If I had a dollar...." I grumbled but was ignored.

Marge scowled at the tablet as if it had done her dirty. "And now we don't have time to order a new one."

Having seen a great deal of sea foam in my life I wasn't sure that it would have been much of an improvement. "Mom, it's okay. The bodice fits and it's the right length."

She shook her head. "But you look ghastly."

"It'll be better with make-up and jewelry." And a few cocktails. "Besides, it's your day. People won't be looking at me."

"Are you sure?"

Considering my life lately, this dress was the least of my problems. "Positive."

"All right. But I'm paying for it."

"For the rest of your natural life," I teased.

"I love you." She pulled me in for a hug.

"Love you too, Mom."

That was the exact moment my mother walked in, a stricken expression on her face.

221

"Mom?" Celeste whispered, turning the same color as my dress. "You call her mom?"

I so could not deal with her drama right now. "What are you doing here, Celeste?"

"She called looking for you earlier and I invited her." Gracious as always, Marge held out her hand to my mother. "Glad you decided to come."

For her part, Celeste appeared to be seriously regretting her decision. She shifted from foot to foot, clearly uncomfortable.

"I thought the three of us could go out for drinks after this? There's this terrific little martini bar right around the corner." My mother-in-law said. She was either oblivious to the awkward vibe in the small space or intentionally ignoring it.

Going out drinking with Celeste was the absolute last thing I wanted to do on an average day, never mind the bitch of one I'd endured. "Thanks, but I need to get home. Luke's been calling me all day."

"Just one drink?" Marge coaxed.

In my ratty clothes with my mother, the borderline alcoholic who I'd put to bed for most of my life. "How about coffee, instead? There's a diner not too far from here."

The Eleventh Street Diner, the one Fester Gomez hadn't frequented. Because no matter what Sergeant Vasquez said, I couldn't just let it all go. Someone had snuffed out Mara Young before I could talk to her and my gut told me it had something to do with the dead girl in Fester Gomez's apartment. And because I loved that diner and needed a pick-me up in order to deal with sea foam and Celeste.

Marge's face lit up. "Oh, a diner. It's been years since I've been to a diner. I'd love a piece of pie, though one of you will have to split it with me. I have

222

a wedding dress to fit into after all. Should we drive together then?"

And if Vasquez was keeping tabs on me, it'd look like I was out for coffee and pie with the women in my life, not scouting for clues. Multitasking. Who could argue with that?

Chapter Twenty Two

"**W**ell, that was... nice." Celeste said as I pulled up in front of her trailer.

"Yeah," My tone was distracted. I kept checking the rearview mirror for signs of Cooper and his van. Though I'd searched for a tail so far, nothing.

Celeste turned, folding her arms over her breasts and glared at me. "All right, what's wrong with you today?"

That snapped me from my surveillance. "Wrong?"

"You look awful." She gestured with distain over my outfit. "And I don't just mean your clothes. You're all distracted like."

I blinked at her, surprised she'd picked up on my unease. "It's nothing."

She bit her naked bottom lip. Her cherry red lipstick was long gone, staining the diner's coffee mug. Or maybe it had been eaten away with her key lime pie. I hated that lipstick, it made her look young and naïve, easy pickings. Seeing the garish color always reminded me how many men's shirt collars it had

imprinted over the years. I'd paid the check and
hustled her from the diner before she could reapply it.

I cleared my throat. "It's been a rough couple
of days."

"Do you want to stay for a spell?"

Though I fully intended to say no, a faint yes,
slipped out. Huh. Celeste appeared delighted that I
was coming in without the necessity of corpse
removal. Guilt ate at me for minimizing the time I
spent with her. Sure, on paper it looked like I took
care of her, paid her bills when she was between
hairstylist jobs so the power didn't get shut off. In
reality, I avoided her like white pants after Labor Day.

A paper plate of brownies sat on the counter,
covered by plastic wrap. I frowned at the unusual
sight. "Don't tell me you've taken up baking?"

She made a dismissive motion with her hand
that indicated my suggestion was ridiculous. "Of
course not. Myra Burns brought those over when she
heard about poor Dick's passing. She knew we were
an item. They're double chocolate. You want one?"

"I shouldn't, I just split that piece of pie with
Marge. And the only thing that will make the mint
dress worse is double chins wagging over the top of
it." That didn't stop me from eye-humping the plate
with longing.

"Oh, Jackie. When did you become the kind of
girl who counts calories? Splitting dessert and all.
Didn't I teach you to do what makes you happy?"

I scowled. "Yeah, but Celeste—"

"Mom," she interrupted with a sharp hand
motion. "If you can call Marge Parker mom, you can
damn well use it for the woman who gave you life."

It was easier to eat the brownie than to argue
with her and infinitely more enjoyable. I snagged a

couple of paper towels, and unwrapped the plate. The brownies smelled even better than I'd imagined. Celeste poured us each a tall glass of milk and we sat side by side at the counter, indulging.

This was a side of Celeste I'd forgotten about, the low key side. Though I detested her natural hedonism with a vengeance, there were plusses to having her for a mother. She never encouraged me to diet, to exercise or get my hair cut in a certain style like so many of my friends' mothers. I never had a curfew and she never gave me grief about my clothes. Instead, she insisted I live life to the fullest and enjoy every minute. Did I wish that some things had been different with her? Yes, but not that.

I took a bite of brownie and forgot everything. "Mmmm..."

She grinned at me then, her eyes fixed on a point beyond me. "You were right, I like her." Her tone sounded mildly surprised.

I was too lost in a chocolate-induced orgasm to follow her train of thought. "Huh?"

She snorted. "Told you so."

"You were right, they're worth the double chin. Who do you like?"

"Marge. She's so....." She waved her hand as though she could capture the perfect word.

"Fun? Sweet? Caring?"

"Here I'd been thinking she was some tight-assed white collar trophy wife who brainwashed you. I almost fell over dead when she invited me to meet up with the two of you at the bridal shop. "

My gaze darted around. It was too soon to joke about the dead with the dirt still fresh on Dick's grave. My mind churned up the picture of Mara Young and I almost regurgitated my brownie.

"Jackie? Are you all right? You're white as a sheet."

"Too much dessert." And too much death.

Celeste pushed the rest of her brownie aside and leaned her elbows on the table. "Will you tell me what's bothering you? Why you've been looking over your shoulder all day?"

I stared at her for a minute, shocked that I actually *wanted* to confide in her. It was the same sensation as when I'd opened up to Logan after moving Dick's body. What did it say about me that the two people I tried to push away were the two I trusted with my darkest secrets?

"Jackie?"

Nothing. It didn't mean anything other than I was free to open up to them because I didn't care what either of them thought about me. Logan's opinion was already swirling down the toilet. Nowhere to go but up. And Celeste had made so many mistakes that she had no room to judge, even if she'd had the inclination.

So, where to begin?

Thinking about Logan brought back the reason I'd left the house that morning. "Luke had his brother spying on me when he was overseas."

Celeste blinked. "You're kidding."

"Believe me, I wish I was."

"Do you know why?"

I shook my head. "I haven't confronted him about it yet."

Her thin eyebrows drew down, creating a crinkle over her nose. "Then how did you find out?"

"Logan, the brother, fessed up to it this morning."

Celeste whistled. "Wow."

I leaned back in the barstool. "I'm not sure what to say to Luke about it. I mean, I'm angry because who the hell would think asking his brother to spy on his wife is a good idea, you know?"

"But?" Celeste prompted.

I blew out a breath. "But, I know he did it out of love and concern. Can I really chew him out over that? And the three of us work together now. We've been doing well working as a team. Rehashing the past is just going to complicate our professional lives. Then again, if I just let it slide, what's to stop him from being all high handed again? It's like rewarding bad behavior. Ugh, this is giving me a migraine." I dropped my head into my hands.

A hand landed on my back and rubbed in a soothing motion. "It'll be okay."

I turned to face her. I was mired up to my neck already, might as well go all-in. "There's more. Logan and I slept together."

Celeste froze mid-rub. "You cheated on Luke?"

I shook my head violently. "*Never*. I'd never hurt someone I loved like that."

She frowned and withdrew her hand. "Then when?"

"The night after I met my father."

Silence. Celeste had seen me in the aftermath of the Bradley James debacle. A shaking, sobbing, mess. She'd witnessed firsthand how messed up I'd been over the incident. What she hadn't understood was that I'd cried over more than one man, my good for nothing sperm donor...

And my first lover.

"Will you tell me about him? About Logan, I mean."

Even Marge hadn't asked me about that. Sure, she knew but she was focused on keeping the peace between her sons. An odd thought occurred. Maybe, Celeste would actually understand my side?

"I went to a club, I told you that much. That's where we met. And it was like something fell into place, like I already knew him. Which was ridiculous, but still. We connected."

She said nothing, about the only response that could encourage me to keep going.

"And he wasn't just trying to maneuver me into bed. The way he looked at me, talked to me and, God, *listened* to me slur like a drunken idiot. If I accurately remember half the things I said to him, I'd be surprised. He was so...?" I groped for the right word.

"Perfect?" She whispered it.

I nodded miserably. "Yeah. Too perfect for where I was right then. I wanted him though, I never knew what it was to want a man that way."

"He was your first?" There was no censure in her tone.

I started shredding my paper towel into even strips, just to give my hands a chance to do something. "Yes. It was such a mistake. I knew it, like way deep down in my gut, but I wasn't thinking. At least, not until the next morning, when I walk of shamed it all the way home."

"You just left him without a word?"

Another miserable nod. "I couldn't have survived another man disappointing me, you know?"

Her hand covered mine, squeezed once. She had tears in her eyes. So did I.

I took a deep breath and admitted something I'd never copped to before, not even in the privacy of

229

my own head. "I could have loved him, Mom. I knew I would fall for him if I stuck around. Hell, I was already falling for him. It scared me to death. I might have gotten over it, over him if I'd never seen him again. That was the plan."

She gave a watery laugh. "You and your plans. You can't plan everything, Jackie."

"I know. You know the worst part? I was attracted to Luke because he reminded me of Logan. I mean, they look so much alike but I never imagined they were related. How sick is that?"

"But that was years later. Maybe that's just your type of man, physically. Did any of the other men you dated—?"

"There weren't any others. Not serious boyfriends."

Her mouth fell open.

I shifted, uncomfortable under her disbelieving stare. "I mean, I was focused on my career." That sounded lame, even to me, especially considering where I'd wound up working.

"Are you telling me you've only ever been with two men? Two *brothers*?"

I made a face. "Don't say it like that. It's not like it was at the same time or anything."

"Oh, Jackie...." She shook her head.

I blew out a sigh. It took a lot to shock Celeste. "And now we are all related and in business together. Luke doesn't know. Telling him would only hurt him, right? But keeping this secret is hurting Logan and that's not right either."

"How is it hurting him?"

"He met me first, wanted me first. I ran out on him but stayed with Luke. I see it in the way he looks at me sometimes."

"See what?"

"He knows I could have loved him, but that I didn't want to get hurt. Like he wasn't worth risking my heart on, but his brother was, you know?"

She fiddled with her necklace, a thin gold chain with a small C charm. I'd given it to her on her last birthday and every time I'd seen her since she'd been wearing it. "So your choices are to tell Luke and hurt him with the truth, or keep your secret and continue to hurt Logan. Either way someone is going to get hurt."

That summed it up. When not three sheets to the wind, Celeste was sharp as a tack. "I don't know what to do."

"What about you?"

I frowned. "What about me?"

"Well, you've had years of opportunity to tell Luke, but you haven't. There must be a reason for that. Something more than you didn't want to hurt him."

My gaze slid off to a distant corner. She was right, again. In a small voice I said, "Luke worked hard to win me. He was relentless and I guess he kind of snuck into my heart when I wasn't looking. I mean this super sexy man thinks I hung the moon. Who could resist that forever?"

Her smile was knowing.

"But then when he introduced me to his brother, I was shocked. Logan's face... I can still see the anguish. He covered it up quickly, but in that second he looked so betrayed. It hurt, the way he glared at me. I didn't want to lose Luke's good opinion of me, too."

"It's been years," Celeste pointed out.

231

"Years of us lying to him, conspiring like we covered up a crime. It's worse now, not better. Why would I risk my marriage for a man who can't stand me?"

Celeste mulled it over for a time. "Do you want to know what I think?"

"Shoot."

"Okay, well those years that Luke has lived in blissful ignorance, Logan has suffered. At the end of the day, Luke has you and Logan doesn't. He's endured twice the burden so Luke wouldn't have one. And with the three of you working together he's a ticking time bomb. Sooner or later every man reaches his breaking point. Do you really want to break him?"

I swallowed hard. "What if I already have? He hasn't been in a real relationship since I've known him."

"You can't take the blame for everything that's wrong in the man's life, Jackie. Maybe he's just a prick."

I laughed. "Okay, you've convinced me. I'll pick a time and tell Luke. Thank you, Celeste."

"Happy to help." She switched subjects. "So, Margie's re-bachelorette party is tomorrow night, right?"

Inward groan. I knew where this freight train was going to crash and the carnage would be awful. "It is."

She drummed her fake nails on the table. "She invited me to attend."

"Of course she did," I said in a dead tone. The temptation to close my eyes was strong but somehow, I managed to resist.

"You can just say you don't want me to go, Jackie."

Could I, after she'd been so helpful and understanding and listened to my big bag of crazy? But I'd worked so hard to keep my life with the Parkers separate from my life with Celeste, always worried about her getting wasted and embarrassing me in front of my new family.

I must have taken too long because she rose. "Just forget it. You should get going, your husband is probably wondering where you are." Her tone was breezy but I sensed the layer of hurt beneath it.

Damn it, why did I feel like such a heel all of a sudden? Should I throw caution to the wind and open up both of the compartments I'd relegated my life into? Trailer trash meets society hob-nobber?

Hell, I'd been rolling around in human waste yesterday. Could anything Celeste did at a re-bachelorette party be worse than that? "Promise me you won't drink."

I thought the condition would be a deal breaker but she nodded eagerly. "Of course not."

No backing out now. "Okay, you can come."

With absolutely zero pride, my mother threw her arms around me.

"I promise you won't regret it."

Too late, even if I did.

Chapter Twenty Three

I meant to talk to Luke the instant I got home but I didn't expect him and Logan to meet me in the driveway. Both were dressed in dark cargo pants and black utility shirts topped with utility vests.

"Where have you been?" Logan asked as though I'd gone out of my way to irritate him.

I ignored him and focused on Luke. "Is everything all right?"

For once, Luke looked as annoyed with me as his brother did. "I've been trying to call you."

Internal wince. "My cell phone died somewhere between the dress fitting and Celeste's house. Why do you two look all combat ready?"

"We gotta go."

Work mode, of course. My big reveal would have to wait. "Okay, give me five minutes to change and—"

Logan cut me off with a sharp, "You're staying here."

"Um....let me think about it for a second. No."

"Logan, start the truck." Luke grabbed my arm and pulled me a few steps away. "Jackie, this isn't something we need you for, understand?"

Panic made my heart pick up. "Tell me what's going on at least."

"No time. You've been out all day, go inside and put your feet up." He pressed a perfunctory kiss to my lips and then jogged to the idling vehicle.

I stood there on the walkway and watched them drive off. An uneasy feeling had taken up residence in my chest and I rubbed over the spot. Being left behind by the Parker brothers wasn't a good sign. While I'd been running around all over town, Logan had had ample time to convince Luke that they should kick me off the team. Had it worked?

I let myself into the house, which seemed eerily empty without anyone else in it. Luke had left the light on over the stove and a lamp in the living room but all the other spaces were shadowed. I shivered and wrapped my arms around myself. Out loud I asked, "So...now what?"

I plugged my dead phone into the nearest outlet and left it to charge. My mother-in-law was out with friends. Damn, if I'd known this was what I'd be coming home to, I would have stayed over at Celeste's.

How the mighty have fallen.

"You're being ridiculous," I told myself sternly. "You spent years alone while Luke was overseas. It's one night. Take advantage of the quiet. Have a bath."

No, wait, I'd have to clean the tub first. Scratch that. "Have a shower."

I took my own advice and went to the bathroom.

Ten minutes later I was clean and no longer wafted diesel fumes. Progress. When in doubt, check the fridge. There were leftovers galore, but my stomach was uneasy so I settled for a package of saltines. Restlessly, I stalked to the television and turned it on. Flipped a few channels, wondered where Luke and Logan were headed, then set the remote aside.

I left the television on for company and strode into the office. The place looked all official, clean and down to business. I sat in my desk chair and opened my laptop. There were no new messages under the Damaged Goods account. I checked my twitter profile @DamagedGoodsAce, just to be sure I hadn't missed anything. I hadn't.

So, there must have been a call from one of our preexisting clients. I ticked names off on my fingers. Aaron Tanner on the Gomez case, Joel Amony who owned the cryonics lab, Mr. Fisk whose house I exploded and Mr. Esposito with the shithole in Wynwood. M'kay, so what did I know?

The cryonics lab had been relocated, the prepper's house was toast, and the shithole...well, no one with half a functioning brain cell would be squatting in there anytime soon. The call must be about Gomez. *Had* to be.

My excitement built. Had Fester Gomez come home? Were the police dragging him downtown for questioning even now? And most importantly, would the girl with the purple nail polish finally get the justice she deserved?

I could get in the car, drive right back down there and be a part of it. I needed to see this through to the end. But there was a chance, no matter how slim, I was wrong and the last thing I wanted to do was cross Sergeant Vasquez twice in one day.

My phone had powered up to a small sliver of green. I unplugged it and called Luke. When he answered I blurted, "Hey, is this about Gomez's condo?"

A sigh. "No, Jackie." Noise filled the background. Not like cops busting down doors noise, but laughter and happy chatter.

"Where are you?"

"We're at Dad's bachelor party."

Disappointment filled me. "Didn't he already have one?"

"Yeah but it was so lame Logan and I decided to show him what he was missing."

"Why the hell were you dressed like you were going out to bust heads?"

"We had to abduct him."

In the background I heard Logan ask, "You got any more tens?"

"Are you at a strip club?"

"Depends," Luke murmured.

"On what?"

"On how mad you'll be if I say yes."

Damn it. I heaved a sigh. "Don't give the strippers anything larger than a ten."

"Yours is the only G-string I'm stuffing anything down."

Catcalls filled the background.

Luke spoke louder. "Settle down, you pervs. It's my wife." A few groans.

"Guess I'm not a crowd pleaser."

"Just the way I want you. See you soon, love."

"Call me if you need a ride home."

"You're the best," he murmured.

"Don't I know it," I hung up, plugged my phone back in and flopped on the couch.

237

I circled every channel at least twice and finally stopped on a rerun of *Bar Rescue*. Taffer would make it all better. Of course, it didn't help that he was rescuing a bikini bar while I knew for a fact that my husband was ogling strippers. Bastard.

Luke, not Taffer.

Why hadn't he just fessed up about where he was going? Last time I checked I wasn't a harridan wife that sucked all the joy out of everything by imposing unrealistic expectations. I knew he looked at other women. Healthy men in their prime did that. Women too, hence the re-bachelorette party tomorrow night. I was secure in our relationship.

Really, I was looking at this all wrong. I'd been granted a reprieve, time to consider how to broach the whole *I slept with your brother and now he hates me* discussion. Would probably go over better if I came up with a game plan.

I bit my lip and wondered exactly what Logan was doing with those tens, and imagined him hooking up with a stripper. With that forbidden fruit vibe, the dancing girls would be on him like flies on a cow pie. Would he hook up with one of them? Would he bring her to the wedding?

I went to the kitchen and poured myself a shot of tequila. No salt, no lime. Downed it and then poured another.

No, I couldn't get drunk, I'd promised to give Luke a ride if he needed it.

Maybe I could call Marcy and see if she wanted to drop by, hear the latest crazy Gertie story.

There was a dog barking outside. Not like a casual woof, but more insistent like a canine early alert. With nothing better to do, I turned to the window. A few of the streetlights had come on, but there weren't any near our driveway. I studied the shadows and a dark shape shifted, ducked down beside Bessie Mae and uncoiled a hose.

"Son of a gun," I muttered and threw open the front door. "Cooper! Back away from my car, you asshat!"

"You blew up my house, bitch," Horace Cooper grated. "You owe me."

"It wasn't your house. You were renting it. The owner hired me to get you out."

Sense didn't faze him in the least. "All the stuff in it was mine. Took me years to ready all that."

"Didn't you have renter's insurance?" I asked as he brought the hose up to his lips.

He glared at me and stuck the hose in his mouth. His cheeks hollowed out as he sucked like an industrial strength vacuum.

"I'm going to call the cops," I warned him.

Out came the hose. "I'll be long gone before they get here."

"I'll take out a restraining order."

He actually rolled his eyes at me. "I'm so scared." He deep throated the hose again, bending down low.

Freaking nutjob. I ran and grabbed my cell phone, knowing he was right about the cops not arriving before he took off. I ran toward him, not sure what I could say or do to make him stop.

My bare toe got caught on a coil of hose and I stumbled directly into him, knocking him back onto his ass. His eyes went wide as gasoline spilled from his mouth. He yanked the hose out violently and struggled to cough.

"Did you swallow some?"

He was too busy choking to answer.

239

I swore viscously as I dialed 911.

"What's your emergency?" A crisp dispatcher asked.

"This guy was siphoning gas out of my car and he swallowed some."

"Is he breathing?"

Cooper fought for breath, his eyes bulging, arms pin-wheeling frantically. "Not really."

"He might have gotten gas in his lungs. I'm dispatching an ambulance to your location."

I gave her my address as Cooper struggled for breath and gas leaked all over the ground. "He's not turning blue or anything, I think he's getting some air." At least I hoped so. Visions of doing a home tracheotomy with a Ginsu knife and a Bic pen made me retch.

"See if you can get him to drink some milk, something to coat his stomach. And keep him in the fresh air. Is there anyone else with you who can contact poison control?"

"No, it's just me and my local grudge-holding prepper nutjob." I scurried into the house, poured a glass of milk and ran with it back out into the yard. "Horace, drink this."

He batted the glass away weakly and milk slopped over both of us. His eyes glared at me in accusation as though I'd forced the gas down his gullet. Sirens blared in the distance and that damn dog would not shut up.

I wagged a finger in his face. "Don't you dare look at me like this is my fault."

Cooper retched and gasoline tainted bile spattered the ground. I shoved the glass back into his trembling hands. There was about an inch of milk in the bottom. He drank it.

240

"Is he going to be all right?" I asked the operator.

"That depends on how much he ingested. Help is on the way."

The ambulance screeched to a halt and I backed up so the professionals could see to Cooper. "They've got him. Thanks for your help," I told 911 lady.

"It's what I do." She hung up, so I figured that was her good bye.

I watched as the EMTs worked on Horace. They talked about intubating him and I drifted back toward the porch. Damn it, this wasn't my fault, I refused to take the blame for someone else's crazy. I had plenty of my own to manage.

My cell phone rang. "Jackie," It was Luke and he was slurring. "I love you, beautiful girl."

"There's no way I can give you a ride." I told him. "Call a cab if you have to."

"S'okay. Logan's gonna drive."

"Put him on the phone." I wanted to make sure he was in better shape than Luke.

There were scuffling noises and I watched as Horace walked under his own power to the ambulance, still sputtering and glaring at me over his shoulder.

"Hello?" His voice was gruff but crisp.

"Did you have anything to drink tonight?" I snapped.

"Ginger Ale."

"Get my husband home safely. I'll be at the hospital."

His voice sharpened, the Dark Prince on high alert. "What's wrong? Are you hurt?"

241

"No. It's a long story and I don't have the time. Just drive safe, okay?"

A pause. "Damn it, Jackie—"

I hung up, downed the second shot of tequila, slipped into my sneakers and ran for the ambulance.

So much for my quiet night in.

Chapter Twenty Four

"**A**re you going to stop stealing my gas?" I asked Horace Cooper.

Cooper—my personal nutjob—was intubated, but his squinty-eye death glare spoke volumes. The room's other occupant lay in the bed by the window and stared at me with a strand of drool dripping down his stubbled chin. I was fully aware of how I looked after a night spent in a hard plastic chair, clothes coated in drying milk and gasoline, so I didn't take it personally.

"Didn't think so." I sighed and rolled my stiffened shoulders. The sun had already broken over the horizon and I was running on zero sleep, bad coffee and was fresh outta patience. "You know, someone with your particular...interests should really *own* a home. If you stop siphoning gas, I'll help you find a place. I have mad connections."

Cooper's mulish expression didn't alter, so I figured he wasn't impressed. Still, I plucked a business card from my wallet and left it next to his unused bedpan. "Okay Cooper, here's the deal. I've got a real aversion to corpses and I'd already met my quota, but the next time you choke on my gasoline, I'll just watch you die. We clear?"

A subtle nod.

"Good. And no more following me around in a van like a kidnapper or I'll change my mind and press charges." The officers who'd taken my statement had left hours ago, but he didn't know that.

Another half nod.

"Then I'll leave you to it." I trusted him about as far as he'd like to throw me, but at least I'd made the effort. The one-sided conversation was getting old, so I nodded crisply and moseyed out of his semi-private room.

I made it down to the emergency room entrance, keys in hand, when I remembered I'd come to the hospital in the ambulance. Damn. Okay, next problem on Jackie's never ending to-do list, who to call for a ride?

Luke was the logical choice, but since he'd been three sheets to the wind the last time we'd spoken, he was probably sleeping off his hangover. Marge would be busy with vow renewal stuff. Celeste's car wasn't running, again. Marcy was the most logical choice. She was an early bird and lived not too far from the hospital. Plus, she owed me for the Post-it incident with Gertie. I rooted around for my cell phone and prayed the battery had sucked up enough juice last night and was still kicking. A red light blinked furiously but a quick SOS text wouldn't need too much power.

My best gal-pal pulled up promptly three minutes later in her well-kept Impala and like a champ, handed me a steaming cup of java.

"Marry me," I murmured as I took a sip.

244

"You're already married. Besides, I'm saving myself for Logan."

Some coffee went down the wrong pipe and I choked. Marcy braked for a red light and looked at me. "You dying?"

"I'm fine," I wheezed, grateful it wasn't gasoline. "You just surprised me is all."

Her keen eyes glinted with suspicion. "Does it bother you that I want to date your brother-in-law?"

"Not at all," I lied so smoothly I almost convinced myself it was true." You can have him if you want, but you'll have to beat the strippers off him first. I hear he has a fetish."

She shrugged as though unconcerned. "Boys will be boys."

I was hot and grubby and smelled of milk gone sour and way too tired to talk about Logan's love life. "You're coming to the re-bachelorette party tonight, right?"

"Wouldn't miss it. Where are we going?"

"Some club on the beach that Marge picked out. It's eighties themed."

Marcie groaned. "I don't have to break out a Madonna cone tits top, do I?"

I didn't bother to hide my grin at that mental picture. "Do you have one?"

"Best Halloween costume ever." She tuned the car onto my street as I finished my coffee. "We're all meeting up here, right?"

I nodded. "Seven o'clock. I've got a limo coming."

"Awesomesauce."

"Is that even a word?"

She shrugged. "All the cool kids are using it."

"Just say no, Marcy. Thanks for the lift." I exited the car and made for the house.

I was still fumbling with my keys when the Dark Prince threw open the door. "Where the hell were you?"

"Jeeze, Dad, sorry I missed curfew. It will totally happen again." I ducked past him and entered the house. "Where's Luke?"

"Sleeping it off." He chucked a thumb toward our closed bedroom door. "I was just about to wake him up."

"Why?"

He goggled at me like I'd sprouted a third nostril. "Um, maybe because you were missing."

Huh? "No, I wasn't. I told you I was going to the hospital."

"Yeah, but you neglected to mention why or which one. I've been calling them all to see if you were admitted."

I paused in the process of dropping my keys into the dish and looked over at him. "You did?"

He glowered and I studied him. His eyes were red-rimmed and he appeared scruffier than usual. It looked as though he'd been running his hands through his hair. He still wore the stealthy outfit from last night, but his clothes were rumpled.

"You were worried about me?" I turned to face him fully.

He looked away without answering. A muscle jumped in his jaw.

Well, damn, I guess I owed him an apology. "I'm sorry I worried you."

He blew out a breath and his ridged posture eased. "What the hell happened?"

I was tempted to tell him the whole story, but I didn't want to waste the alone time. "Later. I just wanted to let you know I'm going to tell Luke."

He frowned. "About why you were at the hospital?"

"No, about us."

His lips parted and he sucked in a sharp breath. "What changed your mind?"

"Several things. It's complicated," I hedged. "But I came to the conclusion that there's no way for the three of us to work together with this secret festering like a dead rat in the wall."

"You have such a poetic way with words."

"It's a gift."

Logan shifted his stance. "So, it's because of Damaged Goods then?"

"Partly. It's also because I don't want to lie to my husband, not even a lie of omission. He's got to wonder why we are the way we are with each other. And I'm sure he's tired of playing the middle child." I took a deep breath because the next part was tricky. "And because I realized it's not fair to you either. You're a good guy, Logan and I don't want to keep hurting you. And I recognize that asking you to hide something from your brother does hurt."

He didn't deny it.

"Well, I just thought I'd give you a heads up." I turned and had my hand on the bedroom doorknob when he murmured my name. Glancing back over my shoulder I took him in and if I lived for a thousand years I'd never forget the expression on his face. Like I'd just given him the best gift in the world while simultaneously slipping a knife between his ribs.

"I'm..." he cleared his throat and tried again. "I guess I'm glad?"

247

He said it like a question, as though trying the word on to see if it fit.

I swore mentally and pivoted, leaning back against the door. "It's the right thing to do. And I'm sorry it took me so long to see that."

His eyes conveyed a world of emotion, relief, fear, sadness, longing and a few others I couldn't name. This was dangerous ground, I needed to turn the damn knob and put a locked door between us. I'd said what needed to be said, so why was I hesitating?

Suddenly, the door behind me flew open. With no time to brace myself, I fell backwards onto my ass between two looming Parker brothers.

Luke had severe bed head, his short hair mushed flat on one side. His pallor was off too, a pasty white beneath his perpetual tan.

I gave him a finger wave. "Hi."

"Babe?" Luke asked with a raised brow. He extended a hand and helped me up. "Where've you been?" his nose wrinkled. "And why do you smell like sour milk?"

I opened my mouth to explain but he cut me off. "No, it'll have to wait. Go get cleaned up. We have another job."

****

In deference to Luke's hangover, I tabled the much needed discussion in favor of a shower and a vat of coffee. Damn it, how long had it been since I'd had a decent night's sleep? And tonight was the re-bachelorette party, so there'd be no rest for the weary in the foreseeable future.

While I zoned out under the spray of tepid water—damn hot water heater was acting up again—I briefly considered sitting out the new job in favor of some R&R. It was a warehouse out on Dodge Island,

248

near the Port of Miami. The property was zoned commercial, yet the owner had heard reports of an abundance of foot traffic, noise and suspected squatters. Squatters in a commercial area didn't need to be served with papers, so I wasn't really needed. Yet my disquiet from the night before lingered. I didn't want the Parker brothers to get in the habit of leaving me behind. Maybe we'd hit traffic on our way across Port Boulevard, the bridge to the island, and I could snag a catnap.

Reluctantly, I shut off the water and climbed out of the tub. A quick pass with a comb and I pulled my hair into a ponytail while considering what to wear. In other words, what outfit would I ruin next?

Deciding on jeans, a tank top and sneakers—items easy to replace in case of mishap—I dressed in a hurry so they couldn't accuse me of holding things up. I took another minute to locate the car charger I'd purchased but never used because Bessie Mae's cigarette lighter/ power adapter didn't work right. I could charge up in the truck though.

The guys were ready, both looking frayed around the edges. If I was a squatter I sure wouldn't want to tangle with them. I swallowed a gulp of superheated coffee and burned the top layer of skin off my tongue. Perfect, I was ready to kick some squatter butt. Or at least call in the cavalry to do it.

The Port of Miami was the eleventh largest cargo container port in the U.S. as well as the cruise capital of the world for the last two decades. Last time I checked, over four million people a year passed through the port, never mind the miscellaneous goods that were constantly imported or exported, earning it the nickname "Cargo Gateway of the Americas." All

249

that considered, squatters in that area were probably engaged in criminal activity.

"Did the client call the cops?" I asked Luke as Logan directed the truck out into morning traffic.

Both brothers wore sunglasses and stark expressions and Luke grimaced as though I'd shouted in his ear. "She says they're doing periodic drive-bys, but if anyone's there, they scurry like roaches when the lights come on."

"What about vehicles? Have they run the plates on any that are hanging around the area?"

"Nothing on that end, but they could be parked in one of the cruise line's long term lots. And could you not talk so loud? Your voice is like an ice pick stabbing into my brain."

"Oh, you silver-tonged devil," I snarked and leaned back in the seat.

Since the port was such a major employer as well as a tourist destination, morning traffic moved like cholesterol through a fat man's vein on the bridge, full of herky jerky starts and stops. No napping for me. "It'll be nice when they get the tunnel up and running." The Port of Miami Tunnel was under construction to connect Dodge Island with Watson Island and the MacArthur Causeway. Translation, more than one way on or off the island meant less traffic.

Logan shuddered noticeably. "If you say so."

"Logan's claustrophobic." Luke added. "You ever notice how he never takes an elevator without breaking into a sweat? Being trapped in an underwater tunnel will drive him nuts."

"Shut up," Logan said. The car rolled to yet another stop. Horns blared. I couldn't see Logan's gaze behind his dark sunglasses, but I had a feeling it was locked on me.

So, no tight spaces for Logan. I thought he'd looked a little peaked in the elevator the other night. I made a mental note and ignored the bevy of jokes about tight fitting pants that my brain offered up. We were starting over, or we would be after I told Luke.

The endless car ride gave me exactly what I didn't need, more time to fret. I was worried about my upcoming talk with my husband. I was sure he'd be hurt, but I wasn't sure how he'd react. Would he yell or go silent? We never really fought, we didn't have enough time together to bicker and snipe at one another. But my secret was in a whole different league than your garden variety squeezing the toothpaste from the middle instead of the bottom, type.

I gnawed on my lower lip as other possible scenarios popped into my muddled brain. Maybe he'd go out and get drunk again, or pick a bar fight. Would he fight with Logan? I had no doubt that Logan would take any hit his brother dealt and wouldn't fight back. In many ways my husband and I were still strangers, but Logan's responses were obvious to me. And what the hell did that mean?

Nothing, I told myself firmly. *Nothing except that you're sleep deprived and wigged out. It will be all right. Eventually.*

Somehow, that didn't help one little bit.

Chapter Twenty Five

The derelict warehouse looked exactly like one would envision a derelict warehouse—cracked concrete walls, broken windows, twisted metal scraps lying about haphazardly, oxidizing in the briny air. Our new client, Mrs. Gimble, could have a hell of a lawsuit on her hands if the squatters hurt themselves in this place.

I debated waiting in the car, fully charged cell phone at the ready to call in law enforcement. But neither Luke nor Logan had the patience or the people skills that I had honed and I was more likely to get a nonviolent response from the squatters than they would.

Logan opened his mouth to tell me to wait there, but I shook my head once. "I'll be careful, but I'm going in."

His expression turned dark and he worked his molars together as though he could grind the inevitable argument to paste. "Stay in sight and be careful."

Luke retrieved three Maglites from the cargo hold, along with a stun gun and pepper spray. When I eyed the items he added to various cargo pants pockets, he shrugged. "Just in case."

My husband, the Boy Scout, always prepared.

With Logan on point and Luke bringing up the rear, we made our way across the crumbling asphalt to the door. It was shut, but the padlock that had been on the roll up garage door lay on the ground, useless. Big red flag that someone who didn't belong here had wanted in to this place very badly.

Luke devised a plan of attack with Logan, something that no doubt left me lagging behind, but my gaze caught on something off to the side. A bright pink piece of paper crumpled into a ball. Gingerly, I stooped down and picked it up.

Luke noticed my movements. "Jackie?"

I pulled the opposite corner slowly until I could read what was written on it. "Uh...guys?"

"What have you got?" Logan read over my shoulder, then snorted. "An underground female wrestling ring?"

"That explains why the cops can never find anyone here," I added. "They're meeting at all different times."

Luke took the paper from me and read the message. "At least it's not criminal activity."

"We still need to put a stop to it. Not only are they trespassing, they're risking injury on Mrs. Gimble's property and she'll be liable for it."

"Wait, Jackie, did you see this?" Luke pointed at the bottom of the page. "The sponsor is listed as A. Gimble. You don't think that's our client, do you?"

Uh oh. "If it is, she's colossally stupid to be staging something like that on her own property. And why call us?"

Just then, the door rolled up and a tall, muscular woman in her fifties with a barbed wire tattoo encircling her left bicep and a shock of cropped white-blond hair peered out at us. "You here for the auditions?"

"Auditions?" Logan asked at the same time as I said, "Yes."

I could feel both of the guys staring at me but I didn't look away from the woman. She eyed me up and down, her flat black gaze assessing. "You look a little puny for the ring."

"Looks can be deceiving." Just not in my case. I had no doubt that even an amateur female wrestler could kick my ass, if given the opportunity. I had no intention of letting the ruse go so far. All we needed was information.

Normally, I wouldn't lie to a tenant, but this woman was no tenant, she was a squatter and in order to ensure that she and her cohorts vacated the premises for good, we needed leverage. And what better way to gather intel than by pretending I was there to support their little entrepreneurial venture?

"I'm Lusha." She extended her formidable meat hook.

"Jackie." I clasped it like I'd seen men do, squeezing for all I was worth, a physical warning.

Both Luke and Logan were probably mentally shouting, *What the hell, Jackie?* But since I couldn't list extrasensory perception on my resume, I ignored them.

"During trials, we'll pair you up with someone in your weight class. You get five hundred flat if we pick you and a percentage of the door if you win your round. You bring a suit?"

"Um...?"

254

"Never mind, we have some in the changing area."

Somehow I doubted she meant pantsuit, a supposition that was confirmed when she led us through the outer ring. Women of every shape and size, all clad in itty bitty bikinis faced off with one another inside kiddie pools full of different substances.

"Please, tell me there's Jell-O," Logan said. There was a brief expelling of air as Luke undoubtedly elbowed him in the ribs.

"Lime, orange and strawberry," Lusha confirmed. "Those are for the heavy weights though. "Your girl's probably a baby oil."

I got the feeling I'd been insulted somehow but wasn't about to act offended.

"Do you have any more fanboys coming?" she asked.

It took me a moment to realize what she was implying. "Um, nope, just these two fanboys here."

"Jackie," Logan growled.

"When I want your opinion, I'll give it to you," I said in my most haughty tone.

Lusha nodded at me with respect. I figured Logan was deciding if he should gag me of stuff me back in the truck.

"So, who's in charge of all this? I hadn't heard about it until recently." Very recently.

Lusha opened her mouth to answer but a woman who bore a striking resemblance to the Incredible Hulk, if he had come in albino coloring, approached. Shock white hair, pink irises and skin that probably glowed in the dark charged directly at me, eyes wild.

255

"Demon, stop!" Lusha yelled, throwing herself in the monster's path. Demon struck her and she went down like a tackling dummy. Luke and Logan moved to intercept. It took both of them to wrestle her to the floor.

"Bitch," the woman named Demon snarled at me as she writhed under four hundred plus pounds of male muscle. "You had me evicted from my house."

"Do you know her?" Luke blinked up at me.

"I think I'd remember someone named Demon."

"Her name's Beth Ann Brown," Lusha informed us. "Demon is her stage name."

Frick, now I recognized her. The white was actually body paint, it left streaks on Luke and Logan's dark clothing. Beneath it, she had the deep tan of a sunbather. "Yeah, I know her. Shyster Stan worked for the guy who owned her apartment."

Demon struggled anew. "The bastard was my ex. We broke up when I found out he was married. He had no right to toss me out!"

Though the details of the case were fuzzy, I dredged my memory to bring it back into focus. "You didn't have a rental agreement."

"I did," she shouted with all the righteous indignation of a woman scorned.

"Then why didn't you show it to me?"

"Because he took it out of my apartment while I was on tour and destroyed it!" One of her contacts popped out, so now she had one pink iris and one light gray one.

If I had a dollar for every time I heard that excuse I could retire with a cooler on the beach. Why people rented from their significant others astounded me because it *never* ended well. Still, I needed to

256

defuse Demon before she hurt someone. "Look, if that's the case I'll help you find—"

Other wrestlers had paused in their practice sessions to watch the spectacle. Some abandoned their kiddie pools. Lusha's head whipped back and forth between us. "Just who the hell are you?"

Logan sighed. "This has gone on long enough, Jackie."

Spoilsport. "Fine, we work for the owner of this building. You're trespassing."

Lusha shook her head. "No, the owner gave us permission to use this place."

I wasn't sure how the property was zoned but somehow I doubted that an underground female wrestling ring was a legal tenant. Still, it might be a scam. "Do you have any paperwork on—?"

Someone grabbed me from behind and lifted me off my feet. I just caught a glimpse of the panic in Luke and Logan's eyes before I was tossed into the nearest kiddie pool, the one filled with baby oil.

There was enough liquid to cushion my impact, plenty to gift me with a face full of slippery goo. Stunned, I relied on instinct and tried to push myself up with my hands. I managed a gulp of air before a hand yanked me up by my hair and I stared into the furious face of yet another female wrestler. This one was a redhead with freckles but in no universe would anyone dare call her cute.

"You think you're tough?" she sneered in my face.

"Hell no," I wheezed. My sneakers skidded in the oil and the only thing keeping me upright was her grip in my hair. Distantly, I heard the Parker brothers shouting, but the female wrestlers had formed a line the guys couldn't cross.

257

Big Red ignored my protest. "You wanna play with the big girls? We'll see just how tough you are." She didn't have near the difficulty I had staying upright and she maneuvered me with ease into a headlock.

I smacked impotently on her arm and struggled for breath. She flopped on her ass and we both went down in the oil, her laughing, me gasping for breath pinned to her chest. Her purple bikini was stained with underboob sweat and oil, and from the stink of her I'd wager she was a big consumer of garlic.

Suddenly, she shoved me away and I skidded on my ass until I connected with the far side of the pool. Big Red took a flying leap and landed smack on top of me. All the air rushed out of my lungs in a *whoosh*. Too stunned to struggle, I lay limply as a dead fish as she bench pressed me over her head like I weighed less than a bag of kibble. The room spun and I caught glimpses of Luke and Logan fighting their way through the endless sea of cheering female wrestlers before I was airborne once more.

I lost track of time as she flung me from one side of the pool to the other. At one point, she wrapped thighs like tree trunks around my midsection and rolled. Again I went face down into the glop, this time with her rubbing my face in it like a dog who'd messed on the carpet.

I flapped and struggled anew, but Red didn't relent.

"What the hell's going on here?" A new voice called. "Who is that in the ring with Pricilla?"

Big Red—Pricilla, I presumed—let me up. I rolled onto my back and gasped in sweet, oil free air.

"Jackie, are you okay?" Luke had climbed into the pool and was struggling to get a hold of me. It wasn't easy, I was as slippery as a freshly caught eel and moved like all my bones had turned to pudding.

"Baby, say something." I couldn't hear him so much as read his lips. My ears rang and were clogged with oil to boot. He looked anxious and murderous at the same time. "Is anything broken? Do we need to call an ambulance?"

"S'all good," I forced out, hoping saying it would make it true.

Eventually, I managed to wrap my arms around Luke's neck and he got me upright. Logan and a nervous looking woman in a one piece pink bathing suit were bickering by the edge of the pool. Compared to the colossus I'd tussled with in the ring, she looked practically petite. My hearing was gradually improving but I caught the gist.

"Mother's, not...someone...hurt...liable," Logan said to her as he grabbed a hold of my feet and pulled me out of the pool.

"What's going on?"

Logan ignored me, instead, waiting only until Luke was out too, to hand me off. "Calling..cops and...mother."

Luke led me back to the car, leaving a slimy trail in my wake.

****

"Well, that was fun." I said to Logan an hour later, still shiny with baby oil but at least I wasn't dripping it anymore. Luke had wrapped me in an old Army blanket he kept in the truck and I stood off to the side while the police cleared the warehouse of the female wrestlers. "So, A. Gimble was the property owner's daughter?"

259

Logan nodded. "Apparently, she lost her job a few months ago and decided to fund this little venture without her mother's knowledge."

Luke finished talking to the cop and jogged over to join us. "Do you want to press charges?"

I shook my head and Logan winced as droplets of oil landed on him. "No, it won't endear us to the client to have her daughter arrested. I'm not hurt and sadly, I've been covered in worse stuff this week."

Luke took that in, his face inscrutable and then turned away.

"I was thinking," Logan started and then paused. "You've had a rough week. Maybe you should wait until after the wedding to talk to Luke."

I glared up at him. "I think my ears must be clogged again. I've been going insane with guilt over this since you brought it and now you want me *to postpone*?"

He exhaled and looked skyward. "Must you argue with everything? I thought it would be better to wait until things aren't so hectic."

"That's what I've been doing for the last seven years." A new thought surfaced and I had to fight back my nausea. I had to lean back against the truck, probably leaving a human shaped greasy stain. "Do you think he's going to leave me after I tell him?"

"He'd be an idiot to leave you," Logan snapped irritably.

I noticed he didn't assure me that Luke *wouldn't* leave me, which could only mean he thought the chance existed. Shit, it had never really occurred to me that Luke and I wouldn't recover from my grand reveal. But obviously, Logan thought it was in the realm of possibility. Sickened, I bent over at the waist in case my dry heaving turned into something more.

Logan crouched beside me and tipped my chin up to meet his penetrating gaze. "It'll be okay."

"I can't lose him." The instant I said it, I wanted to call the words back. *Smooth, Jackie. Admit to Logan how badly you need his brother. Let's just twist the knife again and rub some salt on it.*

God, would I *ever* stop hurting him?

But Logan didn't flinch, didn't even blink. "I know. You won't, I promise."

I had no idea how he could slap a guarantee on something like that. He had known Luke all his life though and was in a better position to anticipate his brother's response to the news.

"Everything okay?" Luke called as he approached.

I rose and wiped my wet eyes on the oily blanket. "Yeah. We need to get going if I'm going to make the bachelorette party."

"Right. I think there might be a few more blankets in the back, let's spread them for you and Luke to sit on so we don't ruin the upholstery." Logan was up and moving before I could thank him.

Luke moved closer and tipped my chin up to meet his gaze. "You sure you're all right? You've been acting kind of weird all day."

That's because I have something potentially life changing to tell you. My stupid eyes filled again and I shut them.

Ignoring my oily topcoat, he pulled me against him. "It's okay if you're not. Mom will understand. We could stay in, pick up a few movies from Redbox and some takeout and just hang."

That sounded so epically wonderful after the crappy week I'd had. But even if I did stay home I couldn't relax, not now that my mind had been made up. Logan had granted me a reprieve but I promised myself right after the wedding, we would talk it out. "Rain check, promise me."

"I promise," Luke said.

And I planned to hold him to that.

Chapter Twenty Six

"**I** never knew Madonna had so much chest hair," Ursula Parker shouted to me from across the table.

I let my gaze wander to the raised runway where the 80's review was going strong. The latest Madonna— because every third one was Madonna— sashayed down the aisle to *Like a Virgin*. Sure enough his halter had a thick matte of black and curlies peeping out around it.

"It's not really Madonna," I called back. I wasn't sure how much of tonight's activities Granny Parker understood, but figured an explanation wouldn't go amiss. "It's a man dressed up like Madonna."

Though I didn't think it was possible, her expression soured further. "A man? So where'd he put his twig and berries?"

Beside me Marcy choked on her Appletini and Celeste threw her head back and laughed.

"You'll have to ask him," Marge slurred. She was rip-roaring drunk once more, had been since we climbed in the limo at the house.

"Call me if you need help getting her home." Luke had said. "And don't let her drink too much more. She's been self-medicating since she found out Granny invited herself along. "

Marge had patted him on the cheek. "Is it any wonder your brother's my favorite?"

"Yeah yeah, we'll see who gives you grandkids first."

I'd buried my apprehension for the future under a smile, kissed him on the cheek and climbed into the limo.

Now, I was surrounded by rip-roaring drunk middle aged women in neon hot stirrup pants who were *Vogue*-ing their rhinestone encrusted hearts out.

"Isn't this great?" Celeste, sporting bright red leg warmers and a matching sweatband that made her look like Richard Simmons, raised her glass. "I've always wanted to come here."

"We'll have to make this a regular thing," Marge slung an arm around her neck. "You and me and Jackie. And you too, Marcy, dear."

Ursula made a sound like steam escaping from one of those microwavable veggie bags.

I eyed Celeste's glass warily. Vodka or club soda? Honestly she appeared sober, but then she often did up until the moment she climbed on the tables for a grinding strip tease.

"You wanna dance?" A Cher with a baritone and five o'clock shadow asked me.

"Where do you keep your twig and berries?" Ursula snagged his arm before I could politely decline.

264

His lips twisted. "You mean my log and boulders, yeah? I'd show ya granny, but you'd never be the same." His accent was distinctly Jersey. Maybe a cross dressing snow bird? I wondered if they had a support group.

Ursula *pffted* again. "Men like you are all talk."

"The ones in the pleather skirts?" Marcy snarked low so only I could hear.

'Cher' had obviously had his fill of insults because he reached for his zipper.

"Okay, let's dance." I stood up and hauled him away before we entered the show and tell portion of the evening.

The club was crowded as any other club on South Beach on a Friday night. Cher was an excellent dancer but my attention was helter-skelter at best. Someone bumped into me from behind. A hand with purple nails landed on my shoulder and I froze.

"Sorry," the drunk woman looked nothing like the Jane Doe from Fester's apartment. She was in her mid-forties and top heavy with bleach blonde hair. As much as I wanted to forget about her, about Gomez and Mara Young and all of it, I couldn't. The police had all but given up. If I did too would anyone avenge them?

Idiot. Since when was I a member of the Justice League? My head throbbed in time to the music. I was tired and dehydrated and I just wanted to sleep for a week. I made my excuses to Cher and returned to my table and put in an order for a bottle of sparkling water.

"What's up with you?" Marcy asked. "You look like someone told you *Bar Rescue* was canceled."

"Chocolate forbid," I offered a half-hearted smile. "I'm going out for some air."

265

Marcy nodded, then followed a six-foot two-inch Cindi Lauper out onto the stage for a little bump-n-grind action. Girls weren't the only ones who wanted to have fun.

I pushed past the line to the restroom and toward the rear exit, which had been propped open. The club was several streets back from the water but a cool ocean breeze lifted my sweat slicked hair. God, the heat, the noise, everything reminded me so much of the night I met Logan, the calm night, the salty air, the lingering sense of depression and the fruitless wondering if there was a point to any of it.

Why did I keep fixating on that night? In the past, I'd been able to block out the memory for months at a time. Until Logan's blue eyes smoldered at me and brought it all rushing to the surface. But like the tides, it ebbed and flowed and I'd learned to live with the memories when they came, to bury any lingering regrets and move forward. It had to be my upcoming talk with Luke. That and the sheer chaos I passed off for a life that made me feel as though I was caught in an inescapable undertow.

To stave off real melancholy, I walked at a brisk pace to help clear my head. Though I had no real destination in mind, it didn't surprise me one bit to end up in front of the 11th Street Diner. From there it was just a hop, skip and a jump to Fester's apartment.

I looked back in the direction I'd come. It was early yet and I doubted anyone would notice I was gone. And at the bottom of my bag was the key to Fester's place that I hadn't gotten around to returning yet.

Before I could talk myself out of it, I had powerwalked the few blocks through the light pedestrian traffic to the condo complex. The crime scene tape was long gone so I only felt the smallest smidge of guilt for letting myself in.

The place smelled of fresh paint and new carpeting, obviously prepped for a new tenant. So what if there had been a grisly murder here, it was South Beach for God's sake. I was lucky Aaron hadn't rented it out already.

Slowly, I picked my way through the place, peeking in cabinets and closets. The holes on the ceiling were gone, the generic color scheme hiding the debauchery the place had seen. Had Gomez killed that girl then, taken his millions from his amateur porn site to Bermuda? Or maybe the Keys? And if he had, who had killed Mara Young? Was her death even related to the girl with the purple nail polish?

I was missing something and it itched like a collection of no-see-um bites. The harder I scratched, the more it drove me nuts. No one at the diner recognized Fester's picture, yet that mug was the only item left in the apartment. He didn't kill that girl, I felt it in my bones. So who had left the mug? Was it the murder victim's or had it belonged to her killer?

Exiting the apartment, I strode to the neighbor on the left, the one who shared a back bedroom wall with Gomez, and rapped smartly on the door. I didn't expect to learn anything new, the Parker brothers had been down this road already. A woman in her seventies with dark skin, a steel gray permanent and a tropical print muumuu opened the door with the safety chain still on. "What you want?" She asked, her voice flavored with just a touch of a Caribbean accent.

I offered my brightest smile along with a business card through the door. "Hi, I'm Jackie Parker and I work for the property owner. Do you have a

267

minute to answer a few quick questions about the complex?"

"I suppose that would be fine." She didn't take the chain off but at least she didn't slam the door in my face.

"Great. How long have you lived here?"

"About six years."

"Do you live alone?"

A nod. "My sister used to live with me but she died a few months ago."

I murmured condolences and then asked, "Do you like it here? Is it too loud or busy?"

She shrugged. "It can be in the winter and Spring Break, but the rest of the time it's quiet enough."

"How about your neighbors?" I probed. "Any difficulties?"

She shook her head. "None."

"Did you know the tenant who shared your back wall until recently, Fester Gomez?"

"Never heard of him."

Just as Luke and Logan had said. How odd. "You ever hear anything unusual from that apartment?"

Her eyes narrowed on me, suspiciously. "What you mean, unusual? Like that girl being killed? The police already asked me all these questions and I told them I didn't know him and I only saw the girl once, with that other girl."

"Other girl?"

"The one who came poking around asking questions, like you."

"Mid-forties, well-dressed, bleached blond hair?" I described Mara Young, wishing I had a picture.

But the woman shook her head. "No, she was younger, like the dead one. Like a college student."

"When was the last time you saw her?" Could this possibly be a lead? In my head I'd already speed dialed Sergeant Vasquez.

She shrugged. "A few months. She was with the other girl. They were looking for Gomez but he must have already been well away. "

My hopes plummeted. "I don't suppose you remember either of their names?"

"They never told me."

I thanked her and moved to the other side. No answer. Then the neighbors across the way. There was a middle-aged couple who never heard of Fester Gomez and they'd lived in the complex for over a decade. They hadn't seen the mysterious pair of girls, either.

The same questions rose to the surface of my brain. How could a man who lived in a place like this never encounter his neighbors even in passing? The mailboxes, the laundry room, the parking lot? Never mind that he was operating an illegal business out of his home. Yet every person I asked had never heard of him, had never seen him.

I decided to try just one more when my cell phone rang to the tune of *Baby's Got Back*. "What's up, Marcy?"

"Where the hell are you?" she bitched.

Crap. I hadn't intended to be gone this long. "Sorry, I'll be back in a jiff."

"Seriously, you left me to baby sit *Girls Gone Wild*, the premenopausal edition."

I turned away from the door I'd been about to knock on and headed to the breezeway stairs. "Sorry, is Celeste making trouble?"

269

"Celeste is fine, it's your mother-in-law and *her* mother-in-law causing all the trouble. The DJ had to hush them they were shouting so loud."

"Shouting about what?"

"Hiring strippers. Marge wanted to go to a male review and Ursula called her, quote, *a used bag of cheap goods.*"

If I hustled, I'd be back to the bar in ten minutes flat. "Okay, call the limo and tell the driver to wait by the back entrance. It's easier than navigating them through the line out front. I'll meet you there."

"I don't have their number."

"I'll text it to you."

"You so owe me Gertie detail for this." She hung up.

I moved across the breezeway and was scrolling through my recent contacts in search of the limo service's number when something struck the back of my head. My phone fell over the railing and I collapsed in a heap. Though my vision was spotty I didn't lose consciousness. I heard him when he said, "You just couldn't leave it alone."

I knew that voice but my head throbbed. A pair of men's dress shoes moved to where I could see them, black and shiny. He crouched down next to me.

Recognition hit as I stared up into his handsome face, but I didn't cry out, stunned into silence. Something sharp jabbed into the side of my neck and the world went dark.

Chapter Twenty Seven

The steady hum from an engine pierced the fog settled over my mind. I sensed movement but couldn't lift my head to see if I was really in motion or the world was just spinning around me. My tongue was stuck to the roof of my mouth, my lips dry and cracked. I tried to move, but neither my arms nor my legs responded. No words came from my parched throat, no matter how hard I tried to push them out. Not even a rudimentary croak. What the hell had happened?

It came back to me in a rush, the man who hit me, who'd injected me with some sort of drug.

Aaron freaking Tanner.

As though I'd conjured him, he appeared. It was then I realized the thrumming of the engine had died away and I felt the steady rocking that could only be a boat on the water.

"You are one of the most stubborn people I have ever met," Aaron mused.

Since the only body parts that responded to my commands were my eyelids, I blinked furiously at him. He didn't seem to notice.

"I never wanted it to come to this." His tone was filled with regret. "I wanted to help you. Luke and I have known each other for years. Hell, I was helping you build up your business, wasn't I? All you had to do was walk away. The police walked away. You know I left Mara for you to find. I could have gotten rid of her body, but I wanted to give you one last warning, so is it my fault you were too fucking stupid to get the message? What the hell is your damage anyway?" He seemed genuinely bemused and not the slightest bit manic.

That's when I understood he was going to kill me.

The knowledge must have shown on my face because he smiled. "Your death will kill Luke, you know. Both of them really. Were you doing them both? I had a bet with myself that you were. Kinky bunch of bastards. Of course, it takes one to know one."

He'd fallen into classic villain monologue with zero prompting on my part. I was literally a captive audience, ideally rendered mute by whatever he'd used to drug me. I thought my finger twitched but couldn't be sure.

"Do you know, I made more money in a quarter with the porn than five years with the South Beach property? Of course, when you rise high enough, other people just want to tear you down. Like that blackmailing bitch."

"Who...?" I managed to croak and he looked at me, startled.

"You want to know who she was? Is that why you kept at it? I'd wondered. Usually people are driven by something—greed, lust or demons. I guess you're the last type."

Give the man a cigar. I rolled my eyes to show him just what I thought of his pop psychology bullshit.

He laughed. "Damn it Jackie, I like you. And because it means so damn much to you, I'll tell you. A sort of final request. You ready?

"Fester Gomez was a senile old fool who moved out over a year ago. Alzheimer's I think, though he might just have been an incompetent kook. It was simple enough to photocopy his lease and alter the dates so it looked like he was still living there. Meanwhile, I had the perfect location and cover name for my porn business. In essence, *I* was Fester Gomez. It even sounds like a pervert's name, doesn't it? Sheer brilliance."

Brilliance was not the word I'd use for stealing a confused man's identity so it was probably just as well I couldn't answer. I was regaining some large muscle control, enough to know he hadn't bound my hands or feet. I stared at him, hoping he'd talk until whatever drug he'd used wore off.

"It was all completely under the table. Of course Mara knew Fester was gone, though. Money bought her loyalty and this yacht. It was all going so well, until Gomez's daughter showed up looking for him. Her and her meth-head roommate." He made a disgusted noise.

His *daughter*? My eyes went round in horror and Aaron laughed again.

"No, the daughter wasn't the dead one. It was the roommate who heard about Gomezgirls.com. Her drug problem and daddy issues made her the perfect cheap labor to suit my purposes. Until the little bitch got greedy and tried to blackmail me. Me!" His outrage was in no way feigned.

I had enough feeling back to start imagining a plan of escape. My shoes were gone, which was a bonus for running, but since we were on a boat God knew how far from shore, running didn't seem to be an option. I glanced around in search of a weapon, something to konk him over the head, but didn't see much. I was on a raised platform bed. There was a small galley kitchen right in front of me, but no visible pots or pans for konking. In fact the stove didn't seem to be hooked up, with the propane tank exposed. He was bigger and stronger and hadn't been drugged so I was at a serious disadvantage. I needed to pick my moment.

"I still can't get my head around the fact that that worthless skank actually knew Gomez's long lost daughter, the one obsessed with finding her sperm donor father. What the hell are the chances? If there's a God, she's a spiteful bitch. It was all unraveling because of her. So I lured her there, under the pretense of paying her off. She never saw it coming."

Just like I hadn't. His urbane façade and connection to Luke had fooled me into thinking he was a stand-up guy, not a freaking sociopathic murderer. But the shine was off that diamond because he had his crazy flag flying at full mast.

"Then it was just a matter of hiring your team to "discover" her. That, and getting rid of Mara. No sense leaving loose ends. You know I was down here that day you showed up at the marina, listening to your conversation with her? It was all I could do not to pop up and yell 'surprise'. Of course, forcing her to make up excuses and navigate out to sea so I could kill her was a good second option."

Oh, God. He'd been aboard the *Forever Young*. No wonder Mara had been so nervous. Had she tried to signal me in some way and I missed the signs? Too caught up in my own mess to see what was right in front of my face?

No, I couldn't dwell on that. Mara was past saving, but if I had a hope in hell of getting off this boat alive, I had to clear my mind and ignore the panic that flapped about inside my head screeching that I was doomed and the end had come.

Losing my shit was not an option.

Aaron Tanner was an egotistical bastard but he was right about one thing. Logan would be just as affected by my death as Luke. They'd mourn me and the truth would either come out to tear them apart, or Logan would continue to suffer in silence and it would tear them apart. No, I couldn't check out yet. I *needed* to make things right and in order to do that I had to live, to get off this boat and have a conversation that was seven years past due.

"So that's my tale. And while fate's been a bitch, once you're taken care of I'm free to start it up all over again. After all, there will always be an overabundance of perverts to bilk. Supply and demand, baby."

His cell phone rang and he turned to take it. I briefly considered shouting for help but dismissed it. Even if I could speak clearly the person on the other end wouldn't be able to help me in time. Instead, I checked the immediate area around the birth. There wasn't much. Either Aaron had gotten rid of Mara's things or the police had carted them off. I saw a small first aid kit, a stack of life jackets and a small orange flare gun. My gaze traveled from the last to the propane tank and back. Did I have the *cojones* to pull it off?

There was no other option, I had to try. My fingers felt numb as I reached for it. Arron had pivoted away, intent on his phone call. Fumbling with the small orange ammo shell, I maneuvered the barrel

275

away from the butt until the chamber for the flare was exposed and I could load it. If it had been a real weapon, I would have worried I was doing something wrong. Flare guns were meant for the average law abiding citizen to use under stress.

My situation definitely qualified.

I considered shooting him with it then and there but had a hunch it wouldn't be nearly as effective as it was in the movies. With literally one shot at this, I needed to get it right. I stuffed the gun under my waistband instead.

"Fax me the papers and I'll look them over first thing," Aaron the affable businessman said and dropped his smokescreen as he hung up and turned back to me. "As much as I've enjoyed this, I have a party to attend tonight, to secure my alibi."

He grabbed me by the hair. I tried to scream but it came out as more of a gurgle. He laughed as he dragged me toward the steep stairs, my body banging against the deck and my scalp burning as though it had been lit on fire. It took every ounce of effort not to flail about or warn him that I wasn't as bad off as he'd thought. *Wait for it, Jackie.*

It took little effort to mock stumble and land on top of the propane tank. I prayed it was full and that he wouldn't notice what I was doing as I turned the little metal knob to open the valve. How long would it take to fill the small cabin with fumes?

Aaron hefted me up by the armpits and for a second I was afraid he'd find the flare gun. But he was single minded in his determination to get me up those stairs.

Up on deck, the night was foggy, the moon obscured behind scudding clouds as two fronts collided. In the distance thunder rumbled. A storm

276

was coming. Instinct prodded me to fight or flee but I didn't struggle as he maneuvered me ever closer to the railing. Aaron produced a knife with a wicked looking serrated edge. His plan was clear, stab me and push me over the side, never to be heard from again. The blade glinted in the moonlight and I knew an instant of paralyzing fear. My heart pounded and there was a roaring in my ears. I braced my feet and tensed my muscles. This was it.

His hand sliced down. I dropped like deadweight and pushed off with my feet until I shoulder-checked him in the groin. The knife slashed through air and he gave a strangled yell. Snagging the flare gun from my waistband, I aimed for the opening to the small cabin. I saw his shocked eyes as big and round as duck eggs when he saw what I held.

Aaron fell back, probably thinking I was aiming for him. I scrambled to my feet and fired, simultaneously throwing by weight over the railing.

Kaboom.

Salt water rushed into my senses. The force of the explosion pushed me deeper under. I wasn't sure if I could swim with the drug still in my system. *Don't panic.* Overhead, orange light flickered as what remained of the *Forever Young* burned. Had the blast killed him or was he still out there with that knife, hunting me?

A more urgent worry took root. I needed air, soon. But I couldn't tell which way was up. Marge's home cooking paid off. I was buoyant in salt water and floated to the surface, expelling the exhausted breath before greedily sucking in a fresh one.

Water splashed over me as I scanned for any sign of Aaron. I couldn't see anything as the storm broke and rain pounded down. My numb limbs

277

treaded water. I dogpaddled gracelessly, trying to get away from the burning wreckage and went under a few more times. Something bobbed by and I gripped it and pulled it in. A life preserver. Slightly scorched around the edges, but still afloat. Snaking my arms through the bobbing ring, I had a feeling I was only postponing the inevitable. No one knew where I was and even if I waited for the fog to lift, I doubted Aaron would have planned to dump me ten feet from shore.

A sob escaped. I really was going to die.

****

The fire had mostly burned itself out. I'd lost all sense of time or place floating alone in the rain, occasionally opening my mouth to ingest a few drops. Fatigue replaced the drug-induced lethargy. Maybe I'd make it until sunrise and someone would come to investigate. It was a distant hope, one that faded with my strength. More likely I'd get eaten by a shark.

I thought about the people I loved and who would mourn me, their faces flashing in my mind one at a time. What wouldn't I give to say a final word to each of them? Luke. Logan. Celeste. Margie. Shonda. Marcy. Hell, I wasn't picky, I'd even take Gertie or Granny Parker. I didn't want to die but it appeared what I wanted wasn't a factor anyone else took under advisement.

"Up yours, Aaron!" I shouted, my voice hoarse. My anger was still white hot and about as useful as heels on the beach. No answer other than the distant cry of a gull and whirr of a motor.

A motor?

Jolted out of my pointless pity party I turned in the direction of the noise. It really was coming toward me.

278

"Help!" I rasped, my throat parched from thirst. With my luck they wouldn't hear me and would run right over me and then I'd be nothing more than chum.

But no, the engine slowed and sputtered, idling close enough for me to hear.

"Jackie!"

I'd know that panicked voice anywhere. "Over here. Logan, over here!"

There was a splash and then I saw him cutting through the water towards me like a shark. I tried to swim for him, but my aching limbs had all but frozen to my life preserver. The small flotation device had really lived up to its name. All I could do was hold on and wait for him to reach me, tears of relief tracking down my face.

And then he was there and had pulled me to him, floating doughnut and all. "Are you hurt?"

I had a million things to say to him, but was crying too hard to respond.

"Logan?" Another familiar voice, though not the one I longed to hear. Sargent Vasquez.

"I've got her!" Logan called out. He pulled me in close to his chest. "Are you hurt?"

"It could be worse," my voice quavered. "So, so much worse."

"We need to get you out of the water." He looped his arm through the other side of the life preserver and started swimming back toward the boat one handed, towing me like a barge. The closer we got the more I could make out the vessel's running lights.

I had to stop crying or I'd drown and this close to the finish line that wasn't an option. "How'd you find me?" I asked purely to distract myself.

279

He didn't answer as we reached the boat. I was in no position to climb the ladder but they loaded me onto an emergency gurney and hauled me up over the side.

Logan came closer, water dripping from his shaggy dark hair. He inspected me for injury and then started piling blankets.

"Logan?" I sat up."

He wrapped his arms around me, sharing his heat. "I bugged your bag. We followed the signal until it went blank. When the coast guard reported a vessel on fire in the same area I knew it was you. Who else can cause so much damage?"

"You are my favorite person right now, you big jerk." I started sobbing again.

His arms tightened as though he'd never let go. "It's okay, baby. I've got you. I'm going to take you home."

Chapter Twenty Eight

"Logan Parker, you are a lying jackass," I seethed from my hospital bed.

"How's that?" he sat beside me in a plastic chair, his posture relaxed. His smug look said he was a big damn hero and all the kvetching in the world wouldn't change that.

"Don't play dumb. You know *exactly* what I mean. You told me you were taking me home. Last time I checked the house we were fresh out of heart monitors and my wardrobe did not involve ass-exposing threadbare gowns!"

The Dark Prince hadn't brought me home, instead taking me to the closest ER. I had hit that point where sleep no longer seemed necessary and insanity loomed on the next horizon.

He gave a half-hearted shrug. "And the last time *I* checked, you weren't the boss of me."

"Is she being difficult?" Luke, who'd been conversing with my doctor, reappeared. He looked like absolute hell. He'd gotten stuck in traffic when

Logan called him and had been too late to go out with Sergeant Vasquez and the shore patrol.

"No more so than usual." Logan looked particularly evil when he steepled his fingers that way, as though he'd just brokered a deal with a coven of witches. I fervently hoped he wound up with warts for his trouble. "She doesn't believe me or the doctor when we tell her that between the alcohol, the drugs that bastard injected her with and being immersed in salt water for three hours, she's severely dehydrated. She'd cut off her own nose to spite her face."

I tried for a witty retort but was fresh out. "You suck."

He had the audacity to make a kissy face at me as he rose. "I'll leave you two to talk."

Was there extra emphasis on that last word?

Luke watched him go through bloodshot eyes before turning back to me. "I owe him everything."

"Luke...," Damn it, this was neither the time nor the place for the conversation but I'd made myself a promise while I'd been slowly brining in the sea. And I wasn't in the habit of breaking promises.

He held up a hand though as he pulled the uncomfortable looking chair Logan had vacated closer to the side of the bed. "The doctor said you need to rest. There'll be time later to talk."

"There's never time later," To my horror, my eyes filled but I furiously blinked the tears away. "I need to tell you something now and it's ridiculously past due. Something about Logan."

His chocolate gaze melted a little. "Jackie, it's okay. I already know you slept with my brother."

My jaw dropped. "*What*? Since when?"

282

"Since the first time I brought you home." He sighed and picked up the plastic cup of stale water, aiming the straw at my cracked lips.

Though I was hooked up to an IV to rehydrate, my mouth was still dry. I emptied the cup one suck at a time, my gaze locked on his, waiting for an explanation. How could he know?

Luke set the empty cup aside and took my hand. "I heard you guys talking, out on the back porch. Heard you beg him not to say anything to me, that you would tell me yourself. I'll admit it shocked the hell out of me. And I waited for you to say something, only you didn't."

I wanted to look away but forced myself to hold his gaze. "I was afraid you'd hate me."

"Hate you? Baby, I loved you even back then. It was just a freak coincidence. And then when you didn't say anything, I thought about bringing it up. But you were so skittish back then, like a wild rabbit and I was afraid you'd bolt."

This was too much for me to process—no pun intended. "So, you're not angry?"

He actually laughed at that. "Why would I be angry? You picked *me*. Why should I care if Logan and I were...what's that term for two guys who've slept with the same woman?"

"Eskimo brothers." I didn't bother to stifle a shudder of revulsion. "But how could you ask Logan to keep an eye on me while you were gone if you knew about what had happened? It seems so cruel, like you're waving me under his nose."

Luke did look away then, but only for a moment. "He's family. Who else could I trust with the person who matters most to me? What he did last night proves that he'd go to any lengths to see you safe."

Though I was on the verge of getting away clean, I had to ask, "And you weren't worried about things reigniting between me and him?"

He shook his head then cupped my face. "Jackie, I keep telling you that I trust you. And I trust Logan. Neither of you would ever hurt me that way."

I smiled then, relieved that my deepest darkest secret was finally out in the open. Hell, maybe I was even a little miffed that it had caused me so much pointless angst. As I sat forward to embrace my husband the best I could with various tubes and wires attached to my carcass, I had to wonder if he'd overestimated our loyalty.

Or underestimated Logan's and my attraction to each other.

No, he'd been right. Logan and I would never act on our spark because it would hurt the person we both loved most. Instead of relief though, an uneasy thought took root in my mind.

Could we say the same thing about Luke?

****

It was a beautiful vow renewal, as usual. Twinkle lights had been strung up in the palm trees surrounding the private beach. They glowed bright against the cloudless night sky. I was genuinely happy to see Logan and Marcy swaying on the dance floor and even more glad that my hideous dress only had another few hours to hold up before it could rest in pieces at the back of my closet.

Luke sat by my side, holding my hand. He'd been super solicitous ever since I'd been released from the hospital, fetching my favorite ice cream, wine and trashy magazines, even going so far as giving over possession of the remote. The perfect husband and Logan got his wish, it was all out in the open. Yet I was still a little bit uneasy with Luke. He'd lied to me and though his explanation made sense, the feeling of betrayal lingered like a bad smell. I told myself to get over it already and be happy, but I'd never been a good listener.

Marge, looking elegant and only a wee bit tipsy as she and Gerald cut a rug. They were so genuinely happy it was impossible not to be thrilled for the two of them.

"That's going to be us some day." Luke raised my hand to his lips.

"Oh yeah? Are you planning to take dancing lessons?"

"For you, anything." He rose and extended his hand to me. Not bothering to don my satin pumps, I padded barefoot after him.

We moved in silence though it wasn't exactly comfortable. At least he didn't step on my toes. When my bare back brushed Marcy's, it seemed only natural to swap. I heard Luke say something to my friend and heard Marcy laugh.

"Are you all right?" Logan asked, his expression concerned as he studied my face.

"Fine, just tired." I said. "It's weird not having you at the house. Quiet."

He shrugged easily. "My apartment was ready and I figured you guys would want some alone time."

"So, are we good now?"

Logan stared down at me, blue eyes intent. "I don't know, are we?"

It was a loaded question on both our parts. "I want Damaged Goods to work out, for all of us."

285

He nodded. "I think it will. Aaron Tanner did one decent thing, giving our business a leg up."

"Two, if you count dying." I shivered involuntarily as I recalled how close I'd come to joining Aaron the whacko in Davey Jones's locker. Logan pulled me in a little tighter and I let his warmth seep into me. "Thank you again for saving me."

He drew back, his expression startled. "It's what family does, right? Looks out for one another, no matter what."

I nodded, then stopped dead. "Shit, I know where he is."

Logan stared down at me like I'd lost my last marble. "Who?"

"Fester Gomez. Give me your keys." I started frisking him right there on the dance floor.

He gripped the truck keys and said, "No way, we're going with you."

He signaled to Luke and Marcy and the four of us took off for the truck.

"Want to tell me what the hell is going on?" Luke shouted as we ran.

"Jackie thinks she knows what happened to Fester Gomez. And no way are you driving without shoes." Logan hip-checked me over the bench seat and I slid into the passenger's side.

"You've been drinking. No way am I letting you drive."

"Oh, for crying out loud." Marcy said. "I'm both shod and sober. I'll drive. Where are we going, anyway?"

I tapped on the GPS, praying the coordinates were still in there. Score. "Follow that line."

Marcy did as I explained my theory to everyone.

"Aaron admitted Fester was senile. The police found no record of him in any of the local facilities though, at least according to Vasquez. So, someone had to take him in. And when shit goes down who do most people turn to? Family."

"But the daughter went looking for him." Luke said. "Who does that leave?"

"His ICE contact." Logan said as realization dawned. "But she hates him."

I shrugged. "You said it yourself, you do for family. And love or hate, they were family."

He nodded once. "You might be right."

The creepy doll lady's lights were on when we pulled up in front of her house. A silver Volkswagen bug was parked in front of the house. I was out of the truck as soon as Marcy hit the brakes, hopping over the still hot concrete.

"You lied to me," I accused when Rosie Harris opened her front door. "You've been harboring Fester this whole time."

She shrugged as if my accusation didn't mean diddly freaking squat. "I lie to everybody. What makes you special?"

I pushed past her and ignored the hollow stares from the dolls. "Where is he?" After all this hoopla I needed to see the man with my own eyes.

"Did I say you could come in?" Rosie's track outfit was lime green today yet she had the audacity to sneer at my wardrobe. "That is the most butt ugly dress I've ever seen."

"Just what I was going for, where is he?"

Marcy and the Parker brothers had made their way through the still open door and were regarding the scene.

287

"Aunt Rosie?" A pretty girl with long dark hair and light gray eyes poked her head out from the hallway. She looked to be in her mid-twenties. "Is everything all right?"

"You're his daughter, right?" I moved closer to her and looked her over. "You went looking for Fester Gomez at the South Beach address. You knew the dead girl?"

She blinked, obviously taken aback by my full frontal assault but then nodded. "Annie was my roommate at school but she ended up dropping out."

"She had a drug problem?"

"Shelly, you don't need to answer her questions. Get out before I call the police." Rosie poked at my arm,

"Meth," Shelly said, ignoring her aunt. "She said she could help me find my dad. My biological father I mean, but then she just sort of disappeared."

Onto the amateur pornography circuit and right into Aaron Tanner's soulless clutches. "Did Annie have any family at all? Anyone we can notify?"

Shelly shook her head. "No, she grew up in a bunch of different foster homes. Her mom had a drug problem too and she was in and out of jail. Annie told me she OD'ed a few years ago."

My shoulders slumped and Luke put an arm around me. "You did your best, Jackie."

It still broke my heart a little bit but I forced a smile for Shelly. "I'm glad you found your dad."

Speak of the devil. Rosie let out a startled cry when Fester Gomez shuffled in. His skin was paper thin and a shock of white hair stood out at odd angles. His eyes were a little bit vacant as he scanned the room. "Rosie?"

"Here, love. You shouldn't be out of bed." Rosie's harsh demeanor melted away. I sank my teeth into my lower lip to keep my mouth from falling open in shock. I'd truly believed from everything she'd said that she'd despised the man. But there was no mistaking the tender way she wrapped her arm around him, as though she were his badly dressed guard dog. "I trust y'all can see yourselves out."

We did, abandoning the touching scene that we had no right to witness.

"Peace be with you, Annie." I held the image of her purple nail polished hands in my mind and then let it go.

"Didn't see that one coming," Luke murmured.

"There's a very thin line between love and hate." Logan said. I glanced over at him but he wasn't looking at me, instead staring back at the house.

Marcy clapped her hands together. "Interesting job you guys have."

"Never a dull moment." I looked at Luke, then at Logan and smiled. "We wouldn't want it any other way."

~ The End ~

Coming January 2015

Lease on the Beach

Book 2 in the Damaged Goods Mystery series

About the Author

Former navy wife turned author Jennifer L. Hart loves a good mystery as well as a good laugh and a happily ever after is a must. When she's not playing with her imaginary friends or losing countless hours on social media, she spends her free time experimenting with both food and drink recipes and wishing someone else would clean up. Since she lives with three guys and a beagle, that's usually not the case. Her works include The Misadventures of the Laundry Hag series, the Damaged Goods mysteries and *Murder Al Dente*, coming soon from Gemma Halliday Publishing.

Visit her on the web at www.jenniferlhart.com or www.laundryhag.com.

CPSIA information can be obtained at www.ICGtesting.com
Printed in the USA
LVOW07s1927220415

435653LV00002B/443/P